TOM

And The SubNeptunian Circumnavigation

BY

Victor Appleton II

Made in The United States of America

©opyright 2019 by the author of this book (Victor Appleton II - pseud. of Thomas Hudson). The book author retains sole copyright to his or her contributions to this book.

This book is a work of fan fiction. It is not claimed to be part of any previously published adventures of the main characters. It has been self-published and is not intended to supplant any authored works attributed to the pseudononomous author or to claim the rights of any legitimate publishing entity.

The cover image is a composite based on a NASA/JPL photo of the surface of Neptune.

THE NEW TOM SWIFT INVENTION SERIES

Tom Swift and the SubNeptunian Circumnavigation

By Victor Appleton II

There are things considered to be impossible and things considered possible, but when Tom Swift is asked by a nine-nation consortium to find a way to not only visit the other blue planet in our solar system, Neptune, they want him to get to the surface—more a gassy thick atmosphere—and below it to the very mantle of the planet.

They want to know what is down there.

It is intriguing enough for him to not turn it down out of hand, but the physics of dealing with an ice giant planet where the surface temperatures are more than 200 degrees below zero Celsius, yet the core may still a blazing 5,400 degrees C!

With it coming into a position compatible with travel to and from, he has only five months to design and build whatever his solution will be. Whatever it is, he and his best friend, Bud Barclay, need to get there quickly, explore what they can of the planet that is nearly four times as large as Earth, and get back safely to their wives and families.

This book is dedicated to some pretty smart people who were certain the planet Neptune existed long before they could ever see it just by using mathematics. Among them were Alexis Bouvard, Johanne Galle, and Urbaine Le Verrier. If I've neglected to mention any of you who may still be around, give me a call.

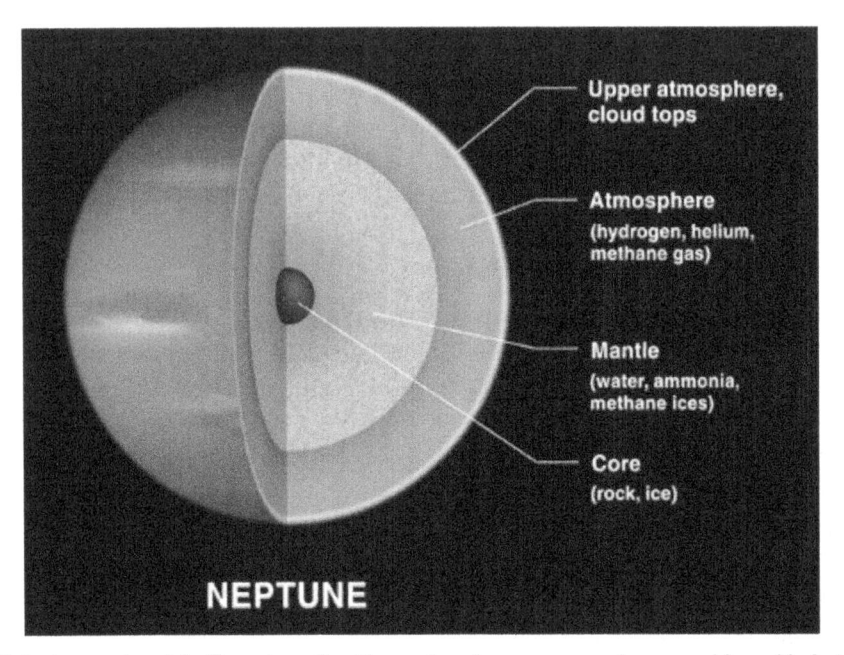

[Diagram of Neptune showing cross-section with labels: Upper atmosphere, cloud tops; Atmosphere (hydrogen, helium, methane gas); Mantle (water, ammonia, methane ices); Core (rock, ice). Labeled NEPTUNE.]

Pointing at the slide Tom described how the planet was made up, and how likely it would be they would have to get all the way down to the mantle. **CHAPTER 6**

The above image was found in several English and foreign language forms on the Internet. This version had no attribution. No copyright infringement intended.

TABLE OF CONTENTS

CHAPTER		PAGE
1	Two Vacations in Three Years?	9
2	Amanda Lends a Hand	19
3	"Could You, Sort of, Maybe…?"	29
4	DEE	39
5	A Second Attempt at Persuasion	49
6	It Becomes Official	59
7	The Design Begins in Earnest	69
8	When is a Sub not a Sub?	79
9	It's An Attack!… Sort Of	89
10	The Worldly Test	99
11	Adjustments to Cover Problems	109
12	An Homage to Japanimation	119
13	Another Big Space Build	129
14	Heading to Neptune, As You Do, on a Thursday…	139
15	An Even Bigger Blue Marble	149
16	Diving into the Atmosphere Ocean	159
17	Touchdown	169
18	The Very Odd Find	179
19	The Circumnavigation	189
20	Coming Home Never Felt This Good!	199

AUTHOR'S NOTE

As I have harped on several times, I originally wanted to write maybe six of these books and have kept myself surprised that I've managed to complete 25 before tackling this one. Now, I am setting a personal goal for myself and I hope I don't let me down. The Tom Jr series lasted 33 books (even though some people claim that final one as being not a real Tom story and more like a Hardy Boys *with* space aliens book).

I want to best that and it *will be a feat*. You probably know that all previous series have been a team effort with multiple authors taking on the Victor Appleton name. And, with the exception of the reimagined stories—plus more than a dozen new *Tom Swift Lives!* novels—no one author had written an entire Tom Swift-centric series all by themselves.

This has been mostly a one-man series with the exception that I borrowed some characters early on from the TSL! books (with that author's permission!)

And, as I have mentioned *ad nauseum*, coming up with title invention after invention is a chore, as much for me as it is for Tom. Once that is out of the way, writing the things is not difficult at all. So much so that it surprises me when people tell me they can't believe I can write so much. I guess I have all this pent up after working at writing technical stuff, training materials and product information for so many years (about 34 in all). That is not a lot of fun, but when you are forced/asked to write somewhere around 300,000 words a year to earn your salary, you knuckle down and do it.

I thank you all for making this rewarding and enjoyable. Without an audience I would still be doing this, if only for my own amusement. While I am easily amused, it is nice to know some people out there (as far away as Japan, Germany and Morocco) appreciate what I do. Here's to those next 7 books!

Copies of all of this author's works may be found at:

http://www.lulu.com/spotlight/tedwardfoxatyahoodotcom

My Tom Swift novels and collections are available on Amazon.com in paperbound and Kindle editions. BarnesAndNoble.com sells Nook ebook editions of many of these same works.

Tom Swift and the SubNeptunian Circumnavigation

FOREWORD

In a previous book, Bashalli Swift nearly left Tom when she felt he didn't take her needing him to be home seriously. As I spend an inordinate amount of time sitting at the computer hammering my fingertips against several dozen mostly unyielding keys, I sometimes feel my own spouse may feel ignored. It hurts and is something I try to not do, but there you are...

I struggled long and hard with that part of the storyline as it was taking a huge deviation from the "Tom succeeds and everyone lives happily—" and so on and so forth.

Then again I set out to make this Tom a slightly different version of Tom, one who is not perpetually eighteen and forever forgetting to clean up and go on dates. Speaking of which, other than the original Tom Swift, mine is the one who got married and actually kisses his girlfriend/wife passionately and has a couple kids. (The Tom in the Sandra Swift novels by another author also gets married, but to Phyllis Newton and only as they approach 30!)

I like to think of my Tom as more a realistic man.

I also have tried to make all the characters grow as they age. It pleases me to see people like Sandy Swift-Barclay learn how to grow up and make other people a priority over her own desires. I honestly hurt when I discovered that Damon Swift was going to be close to death with his brain tumor. And, I was constantly excited to find out what Anne Swift had been doing behind everyone's notice with her medical mysteries.

Ditto the little invention stories about Damon Swift, especially the ones taking him to Australia and his new friend, Lady Penny Schott and how her crush on him makes him so uncomfortable.

Finally, I've had a blast "helping" Chow Winkler with his cookbooks. They are serious recipes presented in his relaxed, Texas style and have been keeping both of us busy on and off.

Victor Appleton II

CHAPTER 1 /
TWO VACATIONS IN THREE YEARS?

TOM SWIFT was nothing if not a workaholic. However, unlike the traditional definition and embodiment of that sort of individual, he actually found a great level of satisfaction and personal achievement and identity in things he did outside of the "office." He considered that office to extend all over the surface and in the air of the world, to deep under the Earth's oceans, into space, and even beyond the edges of the known solar system.

During even the most stressful situations, he found ways to relax and had never approached complete exhaustion. But, he also had been remiss in recognizing that his family needed a change of pace and a vacation more than the two he'd taken in three years. One of them had been only three days long while the other one had led to a lengthy project creating underwater growing domes for a Caribbean nation that needed more food farming space.

At dinner about a week after returning home from his final tour and flight on the HoverCity, and its subsequent official launch, just before it settled into position three thousand feet over the coastline north of New York City for a planned week's stay before floating off on a cross-country voyage, he sat at the dinner table with his wife, Bashalli, and their two children, Bart and Mary, talking about what might come next.

He surprised and nearly made Bashalli spit out a mouthful of salad when he said, "I was thinking we ought to take a nice family vacation. Maybe all fly out to California or even Hawaii."

Bart wanted to know what a vacation was and once Tom explained about a fun trip and trying new things, he smiled and declared, "I want a vacation, Daddy!"

Bashalli tried to catch her breath. "I also want one and really want us to go somewhere new and as a family. Bart is old enough to remember what we do for the rest of his life even if Mary might be a little young. Oh, Tom! When can we go?"

"Well, Bash," he said using her shortened, more affectionate name, "first we need to agree where to go. As for timing I checked with Trent today and he tells me I have a gap of some three weeks coming up in about two weeks. We might not want to be gone all that time, but a week to ten days seems to sound about right to me. What do you think?"

"Well, it is spring and I hear that California is jam packed with pollen and I don't think my hay fever would like that, and I have never been to Hawaii, but I hear that the big city of Honolulu is just about like going to New York City and not really relaxing." She looked a little sad at the thought both places might be no-gos.

"Then, how about one of the other islands? Like the Big Island of Hawaii or even Maui?" He reached around to his back pocket and pulled out a couple folded travel brochures. "Take a look at these and we can talk more about it in the coming few days."

After dinner and getting the children to bed, she sat on the sofa leaning against Tom's shoulder engrossed in the travel guides.

She spent another hour in bed before turning off the lights re-reading a lot of the information.

The next day she packed the kids up and headed for the local bookstore where she bought a "definitive Guide" to the entire set of islands.

When Tom got home a few minutes before five that afternoon she jumped into his arms, hugged and kissed him and whispered in his right ear, "Big Island, Kona side, at a resort!" She released herself and stood back checking his face to see if he agreed. He smiled so she added, "And, I know which resort area but not which resort, and I think it should just be you and me. Besides, Bart still has his school."

It turned out she had spotted a lot of intriguing information about an area up the western coast from the Kona airport called Waikoloa.

"There is a small town up the hill called Waikoloa Village and that is *not* where I want to go. It is the resort area on the actual ocean. It is also called Waikoloa, but I believe it is the Waikoloa Resort we want and not the Village." She smiled at her husband and leaned forward to whisper what she wanted to do with him once they arrived.

His eyes went wide but he smiled and nodded a few seconds later. Secretly, he wondered if swimming in the ocean when she was about two months pregnant with their third child was going to be too strenuous, then he found the website of the hotel she wanted to go to and saw they had a private, safe lagoon.

The trip was planned for ten days later. Their recently acquired nanny, Amanda Strong, would watch the children and take care of the house while they were gone. She had been told to expect the two grandmothers—Tom's mom Anne and Bashalli's mother Lalisha—would be coming over with some frequency and probably with the excuse of "just looking in to see if you need anything," or some other transparent reason to see the grandkids.

"It is not a worry," the young woman told them. "I am used to grandmothers, aunts, sisters and most other female relatives coming in to check on the children, and also to assure themselves I am not torturing the kids or getting them ready to be sold for medical experiments."

When she smiled, Tom laughed but Bashalli looked horror stricken for a second before she realized it was only a joke.

"Happen often?" the inventor inquired.

Amanda nodded and rolled her eyes. "All the time. And, some of them are not satisfied with just a single visit; they come every day. I will ask that you set limits with them before you depart to make things easier for the children and for me. Perhaps they can each have a full day to take the kids to their homes? But, the rest of the time they should call before coming over to see if I have plans to take Bart and Mary out. Well," she said with a shrug, "Bart *after* his summer school classes. At least those only go until noon."

It was true. In preparation for starting grade school, Shopton Elementary had been worrying about having another Swift child they could not keep ahead of, so they had suggested Bart come to three hours of summer school each weekday for eight weeks to see just where he really should start.

In the three weeks so far they told Tom and Bashalli the boy probably should just skip first grade and go right into second.

"I would say he is educationally ready for the third grade, but he really needs the socialization of first or second and his peers. I hope you can impress on him the need for him to just play when recesses come along and not to tease of correct the other students when they get things wrong in classes."

"Of course," Bashalli and Tom chorused.

Now, the boy was excelling at his studies, which he actually enjoyed as long as it wasn't something he already knew. He was slightly lagging behind in his social skills, but was catching up quickly.

When they went to the senior Swifts' home that evening for dinner, Tom outlined what and what not to do with the nanny. Anne feigned innocence until Damon gave her "a look" that said more than mere words might. She promised to be a good and only an occasional grandma.

"So," she said changing the subject, "doesn't this make more than two honest-to-gosh vacations in less than three years for you? Could it be my son is learning to relax?"

Bashalli gave her a very enthusiastic smile, nod and a, "Yes!"

Tom chuckled. He'd come home from the first one with a massive headache and the second one with a project to build his underwater growing domes to help feed a trio of islands in the southern Caribbean. But, he'd also come home more relaxed from that one than he had been in at least five years and that left a lasting impression in his mind.

He was, in other words, darned good and ready for this one!

A couple days later Tom received an automated message from the HoverCity—the mile-wide floating city in the sky he had finished and launched a few weeks earlier. It wasn't anything dire, but the main computer system was letting him know that at least once every day someone in the control room was attempting to either fly the ring-shaped town faster than he knew it ought to go or making turns that were on the edge of being too sharp or sudden.

He TeleVoc'd his best friend and brother-in-law, Bud Barclay, asking if the pilot wanted to take a flight toward Chicago, the current area in which the HoverCity was heading.

Bud snorted. "Well, as Sandy—you *do* remember your sister, my wife?—anyway, as she says, duhhh! What a stupid question to ask a pilot. 'Do you want to go flying?' I think you can guess what the answer is."

Tom was smiling as he silently intoned, "Duhhh, Bud. Get over to hangar two and I'll be there in fifteen minutes. Have the ground staff pull a Model Three Atomicar out and make certain it is charged up and ready to go."

He tapped the collar-mounted pin shutting off the channel. In a minute he got up from his desk in the large office he and his father shared, went out to tell their secretary, Munford Trent, where he would be for at least the rest of the day, and headed down the long hallway of the Administration building.

Downstairs and outside he located one of the electric runabouts kept at Enterprises so people could scoot around the four-mile-square grounds without using their own cars or having to walk. When he closed the door a voice he recognized as his wife's—she was the official voice of all Swift products that spoke—saying:

"Tom Swift in vehicle. Do you wish to check this car out?"

"Yes."

"Car number one-two is checked out to Tom Swift."

It energized and he drove it away from the automatic charging pad over which it had been parked.

The flight toward Chicago, and more correctly to Akron, Ohio, where the city currently was approaching, took just two hours. The Atomicar was fast in flight, could be driven on the road and even taken to depths of a few dozen yards in water.

"I see it," Bud announced as he was looking through a pair of Tom's Digital BigEyes special binoculars. "She's got to be about thirty miles out on a heading of..." and he checked the automatic compass readout, "...two-five-nine. Altitude looks to be around three thousand. Are we just landing unannounced?"

Tom shook his head and reached for the microphone button of his headset.

"HoverCity One, this is Tom Swift requesting permission to set down near your control room entrance."

A few seconds went by before they both heard, "*Uhh, yeah. This is the HoverCity... umm, number one. I guess you can land up there. I'll send Candy up to clear a spot. Are you a helicopter?*"

"Negative. A small VTOL craft with no propellers. We only need a fifteen by fifteen spot to land. We will be over you in three minutes. Thanks."

There was a gathered crowd of people who had been nearby when a woman—named Candy, Tom guessed—had popped up and out of the semi-disguised door and told them to move away.

Not actually understanding what she was being asked to do, and hearing the fifteen-by-fifteen comment, she gathered as many of the residents as she could find and had them make a square of that size.

Tom brought the Atomicar down inside the people and was shaking his head as Bud opened the front canopy.

"I actually wanted people a bit farther away and only said anything about the size spot we needed to ensure that much was clear."

A woman looking a little bit like refuge from the 1960s stepped forward, tears coming down from her eyes.

"I'm sorry. Bobby only asked me to stand in for his regular, uhh, pilot helper thing because Richard didn't set his alarm. I didn't understand."

Tom assured her he wasn't angry about it but did need to get to the control room quickly. This alarmed the woman even more and she nearly wailed as she stated that she didn't mean to break anything.

Without explaining further, Tom and Bud headed for what looked like a small garden shed of about three-feet by four-feet and headed down the stairs inside.

Tom knocked on the door at the bottom before opening it.

A man Tom and Bud believed had been one of the several residents they had trained in the piloting duties stood at attention.

Knowing that Bud was smirking, Tom told the man to relax and take a seat.

"We received a computer call and came out to see what's going on."

Unable to do many things remotely, Tom accessed the computer logs and searched for more than one instance of improper piloting.

In under five minutes he found what he needed. He turned to Bobby.

"So, what can you tell me about the times Richard is in here piloting the city?"

"Uhhh, well, he and I trade off flying the thing. It's pretty automatic, but we do try to give people a bit of a ride and new things to see."

"It is that 'bit of a ride' that might be the issue. And, are you always here together, except for today, that is?"

Bobby looked miserable but he took a deep breath and told them, "Sometimes Richard wants to be alone with Candy, so I sort of step out for an hour or so." From behind Tom came a gasp and a sob. It was Candy.

Tom sighed. "Get Richard here as quickly as possible while I call the City Manager, Mr. Smith."

Within ten minutes the other pilot and the man they all knew as Bill Smith—but was the man behind the finances to build this incredible structure, William Boyd, grandson of the actor who'd portrayed famous cowboy movie star Hopalong Cassidy—were in the room.

Tom wasted no words explaining that the sloppy piloting that the computers logged as coming from Richard Longleaf was endangering the HoverCity.

"It has to stop right now," he said with a hint of anger coming through.

"I'll say it does, Longleaf," Boyd/Smith told him. "What the heck is going on?"

In the end of the explanation, it seemed that when Richard and Candy were left alone, she was given the opportunity to try flying the ring. She was not good at it and frequently forgot about the limits on maneuvers.

Boyd/Smith told Richard the situation was to change immediately and promised Tom he would get another resident trained to fly.

Tom shook his head. "I think Richard here is a very good pilot, but he cannot be allowed a distraction." He looked straight at Candy. "You are banned from this control room and from any further attempts to fly it.

By the time Tom and Bud left Candy had run home to have a good cry and Richard was being chastised as was Bobby who had left the room and that led to the problems.

The two pilots were to be split up and assigned to work with others.

To ensure Tom did not bring work with them, Bashalli insisted on First Class seats from Boston to the Kona International airport on the Big Island of Hawaii.

He was also only allowed his smallest tablet computer for reading purposes. Novels and not journals if she had any say.

Their rental car was waiting and the drive north was pleasant if a bit stark.

Bashalli laughed when they came across road signs stating this area was a "Donkey Crossing." Even Tom had to grin at that. About forty minutes after leaving the airport they turned in and followed a road around until their resort hotel sign could be seen coming up.

Tom pulled up to the main doors and a valet came to take his keys and hand him a receipt card.

"Just dial one-seven-seven and give your name and room number when you want it to be here. It generally takes six minutes but most guest find it takes as least that long to get from their rooms back to here. Aloha and Mahalo." With that the man hopped into their car and drove it away.

After checking in and finding they were in a deluxe suite in the middle of the three main buildings, Bashalli nearly squeaked with joy at seeing they could either ride a sort of tram/monorail or take one of the many boats plying the canal system. At Tom's insistence she picked what she wanted to ride first and it was the tram.

If she felt like she was in seventh heaven at the ride, their accommodations—a two-bedroom suite with a living room, three bathrooms, dining room, den and a kitchen—coming with a view of the lagoon and the Pacific Ocean made her giddy.

While Tom took a shower to wash away the Hawaiian heat, she sat reading the resort brochure and when he came out she told him there were places in the lagoon a person could get a nasty bite from an eel.

"Remember when we go swimming tomorrow, we do not go within ten feet of the waterfall... wherever that is!"

Tom solemnly held up his right hand in what he believed to be the Boy Scout salute and told her, "I promise!"

They had dinner that night at a nearby and very popular restaurant, somehow getting a great table without even mentioning who Tom was, and fell into bed at nine Hawaii time which was five hours later back home!

They spent three hours just floating and paddling around the lagoon the next morning spotting everything from small, blue fish you might want in a saltwater aquarium up to the one thing that made Bashalli scream through her snorkel. A giant sea turtle passed within inches of her left shoulder and when it came into view in her goggles, it was such a surprise Tom had to support her for a minute until she could breath normally. But, she wanted to swim after it and see it again.

"Just on my seeing him before he sees me, sort of thing," she explained.

Tom suggested they had eight more days so she could see her turtle friend tomorrow.

The rest of the vacation was wonderful for them both and when the final day came they had trouble getting up early enough to catch their flight back to the mainland. But, they made it with time to spare, which was good because Bashalli's purse became the subject of a hand search when the x-ray machine detected something in a jar that looked "suspicious."

Tom believed it was because of either boredom on the part of the security people or because of her dark skin.

In either case, a jar of local honey she'd forgotten was in there was confiscated and they boarded the jet with her very sad about the experience.

Their flight took off ten minutes late and had barely crossed the halfway mark over the ocean when one of the flight attendants came to speak with Tom. As she leaned over, the plane took a little dip and a bump.

In a whisper she told him, "We have a very ill second pilot and for once in about ten weeks we are not flying with any other airlines' pilot aboard. I know this is strange and awkward, but the Captain would appreciate it if we didn't need to make any announcement about this and could continue the flight. If the airlines provided you and your companion with another pair of First Class tickets for anywhere we fly, could you step up to the cockpit and possibly help with the piloting duties, Mr. Swift?"

Bashalli grabbed his forearm and squeezed it. "You must go, Tom. We may need you and you are the best pilot in the world!"

Tom smiled at her and patted her hand, also giving her a brief kiss.

He rose and followed the woman three rows forward and through a drawn curtain. In the small kitchen area the copilot was sitting on the floor looking decidedly pale. He glanced up, nodded and then wretched into a bag he was holding.

"Food poisoning, I'm afraid," the head attendant told him as she gave a special knock on the cockpit door. A moment later it opened a fraction and she pulled it the rest of the way as the pilot eased back into his seat.

"Man, I'm hoping you're the man the flight attendant thinks you are because we're in a bit of trouble. You see, I don't think I'm feeling all that well right now!"

CHAPTER 2 /
AMANDA LENDS A HAND

TOM SLID into the second seat with a grin to the pilot. "Sorry about the copilot, but I'm well versed in flying jets," he stated as he buckled his harness.

"You *are* Tom Swift... correct? I hope to heck your answer is yes." The man winced and let out a groan as another stomach pain hit.

Tom grinned despite the situation. "Yes. I am Tom Swift. So, do you want me to take the controls and you try to come to grips with whatever is bothering you?"

The pilot nodded. "That would be great. I believe the safety of the passengers might depend on you and your world-famous skills."

Tom put the plane into autopilot, something that had become disengaged either in getting the copilot out of his seat of by the Captain as he struggled with his own illness.

The inventor asked if air control had been notified.

Wincing in stomach pain, the pilot said, "No. Too far away from mainland and too far away from Hawaii. Dead zone for another fifty minutes."

Tom nodded and pulled out his special cell phone, one that could contact the network of satellites around the globe and relay word to the Outpost in Space and from there down to Enterprises. He was connected with George Dilling in Communications and explained what was happening.

"Get on the phone to LA Control and ask them if they want us at LAX or an alternate field. We are in a long range 737. We have a Captain and copilot out of the cockpit vomiting and they may be getting worse. I'll head wherever they say but they need to have ambulances at the field."

Dilling agreed and asked Tom to hang on.

"Sure, but before you put me on hold, have someone give my house a call and talk to our nanny. She's expecting us by eight tonight and I doubt we'll make that."

When George came back five minutes later it was to tell Tom to head for San Diego because it was closer and would mean an almost direct landing and not a big circle as with the LA airport.

"Oh, and Amanda says to tell you and Bashalli she's having a ball and if she needs to stay tonight, even though it was supposed to be the first of two nights off, she'll lend a hand and keep the kids safe."

Tom thanked him and got a heading to fly.

Twenty minutes later the Captain had started filling a bag of his own and Tom found the intercom button. He spoke with the head flight attendant.

She started to argue but he assured her that the person he requested was qualified on four-engine jet aircraft and had nearly five hundred hours.

"Okay, but this is very, very against regulations," she told him.

A little bothered by her attitude he asked, "So, are you saying that you have that many hours and can sit up here and fly? Or, land?"

"No, sir," she answered meekly. "Sorry."

A minute later Tom had to rise to open the door and there stood his confused wife.

"Why did you have them ask me to come, Tom? Surely you are too busy to spend any time with me."

"It is the *pilot* Bashalli I need and want right now. Come on in and take the right seat while I slip over to pull the Captain out and take that seat. Come on, sir. Let's get you into the galley and you and the copilot can lean on each other. We'll be in San Diego with ambulances and all in just two hours."

Bashalli was a very good and careful pilot but she was unsure of herself. It took her ten minutes to scan the instruments and figure out where the important gauges and buttons and handles were.

"Okay. I'm ready, Tom," she announced. "What do you want me to do?"

"While I'm flying I need to have you switch the radio to a new frequency; I'll give that to you in a minute. Then, declare a soft mayday and explain the Captain and First Officer are incapacitated with food poisoning. It shouldn't come as a surprise. Both George Dilling and the FAA ought to have called them. Oh, and ask for San Diego Control."

Five minutes later she was in contact and sounded as professional as possible given the circumstances. They quickly had a slightly altered heading that would take them over the northern tip of Mexico and from there a single turn to the north and straight into San Diego's international airport.

Tom heard the knock on the door and asked Bashalli if she could peek through the spy hole and tell him who was out there.

"It is the chief waitress and she has two mugs of, uhh, maybe coffee."

When the chief flight attendant came in and handed them their cups she assured them it was nothing the Captain or First Officer had drunk.

"They both are sleeping in the galley. If it weren't so bad it would almost look cute. The passengers have asked what is going on, and the couple across the aisle has asked where you two have gone. I've told anyone who asks who you are and that the airline is treating you like a VIP."

Tom shrugged. "Well, in a few minutes I am going to need to tell them we are stopping in San Diego for a small emergency. But, do you have a better word for emergency?"

"We usually call such things a mechanical warning light that must, by FAA regulations, be checked at the closest airport."

Tom picked up the jet's microphone and the attendant showed him which channel to use. "I think telling them the truth will be best," he told her.

"If I may have all passengers' attention, please. All passengers attention. This is Tom Swift. You may have heard of me or my father. Regrettably, the Captain and First Officer seem to have eaten something this morning that is making them ill and unable to fly the aircraft to airline standards. They have requested that I step in to fly. I want you all to know I am a very seasoned pilot in jet aircraft as is my wife who is now sitting in the copilot's seat. Nobody in this aircraft is in the slightest danger. We will, however, be landing in San Diego to offload the two pilots and likely to take on a new crew for our continued journey to Boston.

"Please do not worry about this. Most co-pilots have more that three or four thousand hours of flying time; I have more than six thousand. We will all land, safely, in San Diego in one hour and twenty-two minutes, give or take a minute. I will let you know our status about every fifteen minutes, Or, possibly my copilot whose voice is much more pleasant. Thank you for being calm and remaining in your seats unless, well, you have to use the facilities."

The flight attendant asked for the mic.

"Ladies and gentlemen, and all passengers over the age of eighteen. The airline is now offering a free adult beverage of your choice, unless we run out of something. Eighteen to twenty-year-olds may have a complimentary beer and twenty-one and older a hard drink. We will be coming down the aisle in a few minutes. Thank you."

She handed him back the microphone. "That generally gets the worriers to concentrate on something else." She left the cockpit a few seconds later.

When he let Bashalli make the next announcement about their progress toward the mainland, the head attendant got on the intercom to the cockpit.

"A lot of people are asking if that woman is the voice of some of their electronic products and their Swift cars."

Tom laughed and Bashalli blushed slightly. She was the official voice for anything the Swift companies made that spoke.

"Yes. Tell them it is her and she will be coming out to acknowledge them in three minutes." He turned to her and nodded. "You have an audience awaiting your appearance. I suggest you walk through First Class and to the front of the main cabin smiling and waving a little. Try to come back in a couple minutes."

She pushed herself up from the seat, leaned over to kiss him and then checked that nobody was standing just outside the door.

When she opened it, the attendant smiled at her and let her get past, then stood guard with one of the food carts between her and the passengers.

Bashalli came back, smiling broadly and giggled a little when she said, "They actually applauded me, Tom. Can you imagine?"

He nodded. "Just wait until we get them safely on the ground!"

San Diego Approach had them make a sweeping turn and a flight over Balboa Park at an altitude that made Bashalli nervous. But it was when she looked out the window to Tom's left and could see they were flying even with more than one building's upper floors that she just shook her head in amazement.

As they touched down the lead attendant clicked on the microphone and both of them could hear the cheers and applause erupting in the back.

"*Uh, Mr. Swift,*" came the call from the control tower, "*If you can manage to taxi that seven-three-seven off the runway and over to near the terminal, umm, gate forty or forty one at the end of the westernmost terminal would be great. Don't pull all the way in. The grounds people will stop you so they can roll a lift truck over and get your stranded pilots off.*"

"Roger, turning off main runway and heading to the terminal. I am able, if you can agree, to bring it all the way in."

"*Negative, The ambulances are on the tarmac there waiting. New pilots will be available in thirty minutes for the continued journey. Uhh, and thank you to you and your fill-in copilot, sir!"*

"Roger. Not what we expected but happy to have been here."

The announcement had gone out to the passengers to remain in their seats so the medical people could do their work, but Tom wanted to stretch his legs and opened the cockpit door. Several passengers saw him and started shouting their thanks.

He smiled and waved but had to step back as the left-side door was opened and two paramedics charged inside.

Four minutes later the First Officer, the worst off of the two, was placed on a gurney a third man brought part way inside and was taken out followed by the Captain a minute later. The second man had the paramedics pause a moment while he thanked Tom for being the hero of the day.

"Glad to help, sir. You go and get better now."

Ten minutes later two new pilots came onboard and taxied the jet to the gate. They allowed Tom to stand at the back of the cockpit while Bashalli said she'd rather go out and be a passenger again.

"Come sit with me as soon as you can," she told the inventor.

All passengers were allowed off for fifteen minutes while the plane was being refueled, something that normally would have taken place in Las Vegas during a planned hour layover. All that time would go toward trying to get them to Boston within thirty minutes of their original scheduled landing time.

When they did take off, it was without five passengers who had decided they'd had enough adventure in the skies and were taking a train home.

The small jet they'd left at the civilian terminal in Boston, one of Tom's Toads, was there waiting for them to head for Shopton. They landed at Enterprises thirty-five minutes behind schedule and drove home.

Amanda was sitting in Tom's favorite easy chair—it was hers as well—napping when they came through the front door.

She opened her eyes. "They're asleep and dreaming of getting up in the morning to have breakfast with mommy and daddy," she told them. "You two have had too much fun today, so if it is okay, I'll stay on all of tomorrow to give you the chance to recover. I don't mind it at all because I had no plans other than to sleep a little longer than usual."

"You would do that for us?" Bashalli asked.

"I gladly will lend a hand, Mrs. Swift. You guys are so great I will gladly do it!"

When he finally got in to work two days after coming home, Tom was rested and full of excitement.

Bud dropped by before noon and said Sandy was itching to hear all about the vacation and suggested they all go to dinner that evening.

"The Italian place was her suggestion. You willing?"

"We'll have to call in a grandmother or two because the nanny is on a two-day day off after everything she did during the vacation. But, let me call Bash..." He looked at the flyer and nodded. "Right. Sandy and Bash have already conferred on this, correct?" Bud nodded. "Then, what can I say but yes?"

"Very little, skipper."

The couples met at Bud and Sandy's house as it was closer to the restaurant than Tom and Bashalli's before they drove into town in the Barclay's sedan.

Dinner was a slow and pleasant affair at this restaurant and they used the leisurely-paced mealtime to talk all about the vacation. Sandy was particularly proud of Bashalli for her stepping in to be the copilot. She knew how her sister-in-law was—very proficient but not totally convinced she was up to the task.

"I'm so proud of you, Bashi," she stated, and not for the first time that evening, as she took another bite of the tortellini dish she had ordered.

Sandy looked up from her dinner and her brows furled. "I believe it is time for an LGR visit," she told the other three.

Tom noticed Bashalli got a sudden startled look on her face before she nodded. "Me, too."

They both excused themselves and headed to the side of the dining room and the restrooms.

Bud joked, "I've been reliably told that women have psychic bladders."

Tom looked across the table and grimaced. "Do I want to know this?" he asked.

"Yes. It seems that once one woman in a group decides she needs to go to the restroom, her bladder sends out a signal to every other woman near her and their bladders suddenly tell them it is time to go. That's why they move as a herd." He smiled and nodded.

Tom looked around them at the sixty or so other diners.

"So, tell me why all those other women haven't jumped up and ran after Bash and Sandy?"

Bud shook his head. "Doesn't work that way. The women have to either know each other fairly well, or at least be within transmission range. Those ladies are just too far away."

Just then, and almost making the young men break out in loud laughter, a woman at a nearby table rose and the two others at that table also got up and they headed as a group to the restrooms.

Their wives returned a minute later.

"And, what are you two grinning about?" Sandy demanded as she sat back down.

"Bud as just making an observation," Tom responded, "about a trio of women at one table that had to all get up and head for the ladies room in a group."

Sandy laughed. "Yeah. I've noticed that before as well. Pretty funny."

As she took another bite Bashalli looked at Tom and blushed. She'd realized she and Sandy had done just that moments before.

The rest of the meal was spent in quiet conversation followed by a walk in the downtown Shopton park the Swift family had build more than a century earlier as a gift to the people of Shopton. Today, it was a favorite of strolling couples at night and of families and skateboarding teens by day.

As they walked hand-in-hand and four abreast, the conversation turned to what Tom and Bud might be getting into in the future.

"Not sure, to tell you the truth. Flyboy here has a new version of a new version of an old favorite, the *Pigeon Commander II* coming up. I might want to spend some time on one of my inventions. You all recall the Deep Peek? Well, we found we could have used greater depth of penetration when we went after that ground water and the shale oil, so I want to see how much farther I can get it to go."

Sandy had smirked at something Tom said but never mentioned what it was to them.

By the time they got home both Swifts had nearly forgotten the bathroom event, but Bashalli told him she understood the little inside joke even if Sandy didn't.

They climbed into bed and both read for about an hour before falling asleep in each other's arms.

Morning sunshine got Tom up but not before Bashalli. She was in the shower when he checked, so he pulled on his robe and headed downstairs to cook breakfast.

Amanda had been faster.

"Good morning, Mr. Swift," she greeted him, her smile saying she was truly happy to see him.

"A beautiful Saturday morning to you, Amanda. Did you have a couple of nice days off? We both feel we owe you more time off for covering with the kids for what turned out to be eleven days."

She shook her head. "Nope. This is about the easiest job I've had. Bart is more mature than any young boy I've encountered and lends a hand with keeping Mary occupied. So, it was really a breeze. Besides, I don't have a boyfriend right now so I don't really have a need for more time off. My one day and night a week off is fine. Really, it is."

Bashalli came in with her hair up under a towel and smelled the aromas coming from the frying pans. One had sausages she knew were made from tofu but tasted great—Chow Winkler, the Swift's personal chef at Enterprises had introduced her to them a few years earlier—along with some frying eggs, while the other contained what she recognized as being a Dutch Baby, or fluffy pancake filled with thin apple slices and dusted with powdered sugar.

"I thought I'd make this for you and then something a bit simpler for the kids once I go get them up," the nanny explained. "Sit down and dig in," she told them as she filled two plates.

When the girl left to see about the children, Bashalli leaned over and gave Tom a kiss before saying, "That girl is spoiling us, you know?"

Tom grinned and nodded. "Yes I do. But the kids love her and I think having her around here has let you relax for the first time in more than five years. Other than the new baby," and he glanced at her tummy that had not yet decided to even slightly show her condition, "that I know you will want to be fully in charge of for a year or so, I can't see any reason why you can't go back to work at some point, Providing, you want to."

She took a deep breath in through her nose while keeping her lips clamped together. But, in a few seconds she nodded.

"I've really missed being around adults all day long. Does that make me a bad mother?" Now, her eyes glistened with possible tears.

"Not in the slightest," he assured her. "It makes you an adult and a human and a wonderful woman who does not want to stagnate sitting in the house all day long for the next dozen years. I think we agree we trust Amanda with the kids. There's no reason she can't take on the third one. She knew you were pregnant when we offered her the job."

Bashalli nodded and smiled. "Yes. I know that and agree and might even feel like looking into part time work now if that is okay with you." She looked a bit nervous as if Tom might tell he, "No!" he did not. In fact he told her to, "...go for it."

"Then, come Monday I might make a call and see if anyone at the advertising agency remembers me."

Now, Tom laughed. "Remember you? Heck, Bash, they have kept a candle burning in the window hoping you'd come back. When I'm downtown and run into any of them they always, and I meant *always* ask if you are going to be back. And, soon."

"Then, perhaps I'll just show up and see if anyone has time to go have lunch."

"Or, you could call them first thing and arrange a lunch with as many as possible. They might be with clients at noon. Just a thought."

"And, a good one. That's what I'll do!"

CHAPTER 3 /
"COULD YOU, SORT OF, MAYBE...?"

SEVERAL MONTHS earlier, Tom and Bud, and at Tom's father's request, took a prototype of the newest version of the *Pigeon Commander*, the Model II, for a test flight. The *Commander* line was based on Tom's own SE-11 Commuter Jet, known informally as the Toad, and featured two piston-driven engines and two propellers. It was a six-seat plane capable of flying at more than three hundred-fifty knots.

The flight had not been a huge success.

An old enemy, a bitter woman named Octavia Whitcomb, had tried to knock them from the sky. She had partly succeeded and the young men parachuted to safety. In turn, her efforts nearly destroyed her own small jet and she barely escaped from a crash landing before disappearing from sight.

That had been while Tom was building his HoverCity, a floating city in the sky.

Now, in the latter part of summer, the twenty-eight-year-olds had been requested to take the replacement up for a flight.

"Just as long as Harlan guarantees he ferreted out the person in the FAA tower who was passing info about when I am in the air to others, like good old Octavia!"

Damon Swift smiled at his son. "He says so and that there are no new personnel up there to investigate, and I say we believe him."

Soon after that conversation, the two men were running up the engines for the flight. However, Tom had stood outside for a full five minutes looking at the wings and the engines and propellers before completing his walk-around checks.

Much to his surprise, the propellers on this new version were now at the back of the wings, so they would be pushing the plane through the air and not pulling it as the first model had been set up. Also, the wings that previously had only been swept back a few degrees were now a full fifteen degrees.

The young inventor knew this would mean the plane was built for speed and had the thrust to match the design. Now he understood why his father had smiled when Tom had asked what things needed to be checked.

"I'm assuming the engines are still the W-series ones, just that the props are set to shove us into the sky," Bud said as Tom strapped in.

"That's what dad, Jake and Hank all tell me. We are going to fly her with the three-blade props, four blade ones and they even would like a multipeller test."

Tom's multipeller had been first created for a small airplane built mostly for Australia and Mongolia to be used as a rescue vehicle that could be parachuted to downed military personnel. It had to pack a lot of thrust in a small diameter package and so the original nine small blades, with their acute twist to give maximum thrust, had evolved into as many as fifteen blades in the largest aircraft to use them, and likely to be thirteen in the *Pigeon*.

"Hank believes the four-blade set will work best, but that's why we have test pilots like you, Bud," the inventor told his friend and brother-in-law.

After the traditional warm-up and check in with the tower, they taxied to the end of the shorter, diagonal runway pointing to the southeast and the nearby Lake Carlopa. The plane scooted forward when Bud released the brakes and was rotating the nose wheel off the runway before they hit the nineteen hundred foot mark.

Tom was taking the notes for the first part of their flight and he noted that distance and also their altitude as they passed over the east walls of Enterprises.

"Not bad. Six hundred-thirty feet at the wall, Bud."

Bud whistled. "Beats the front prop version by a hundred feet!"

They soared up and over the lake and across the hills on the other side before heading for the standard test route northeast over a sort of valley then to the north before crossing over the small town of Paradox—close to, not surprisingly, Paradox Lake—and on to the north until they crossed over Interstate 87. From there it was a wide left turn and flight back to Shopton.

However, it was along the way they would perform multiple maneuvers meant to test the airframe and power plants.

In this case, the plane performed very well, but both young men found themselves scanning the sky around and above them rather frequently.

"Looking for Octavia out there?" Bud queried. "I am even though I know she is in the insane locker at some unnamed Federal prison in the Midwest. I know that and still I am a little skittish about getting knocked from the sky."

Tom gave him a rueful grin. "Yeah. I know the feelings. But, at least this version of the *Commander* is performing at a very high level. Want to go for altitude?"

"You bet!"

They were thirty miles north of Shopton but this was near a flight lane for commercial aircraft coming down from or heading up to Canada usually at about fifteen to eighteen thousand feet, so Tom radioed the FAA tower on the hill above Enterprises to see if they could go for maximum climb.

"Roger, Swift Test Plane A. Remain at current altitude for two minutes before coming to new heading of two-seven-zero. You then have clearance for a climb up to no greater that twenty-seven thousand."

"Roger and we understand." At slightly less than the two-minute mark the control came back with permission for their turn, climb and maneuvers.

Bud pushed the throttle lever all the way forward and as they picked up speed from the current two-eighty he pulled the nose up about ten degrees. Very soon they were traveling at three hundred-fifty knots and had passed fifteen thousand feet.

"She is still climbing like she means it," Bud commented as Tom took more notes.

By the time they surpassed twenty-two thousand feet the rate of climb had dropped, but not significantly.

They made it to twenty-five thousand with the oxygen condensers working hard to keep up with their demand, but it was enough to keep both men fully aware of what they were doing.

At twenty-six thousand feet, Tom called a halt. "Let's do the standard maneuvers up here and head home."

When they landed fifty minutes later Tom had three pages of notes, all of them good. And, since the basic airframe was tied and true, most concerned the speed, climb and noise—practically none—of this combination of engines and propellers.

Bud taxied them to the completion building where all Swift aircraft coming from the older Construction Company were finished. This is where the other props would be installed and more flights taken beginning the following day.

When the time came to test the four-blade prop Bud told Tom to take the controls and he would provide what he called "the secretarial services."

In a repeat of the previous day and flight they took off and climbed to their ten thousand foot altitude.

"She crossed the wall at an even seven hundred," Bud said.

"Pretty good... and the climb rate is about a hundred feet a minute better."

Tom grinned noting their airspeed for the same three-quarters setting was at least ten knots higher than before. He pointed to that readout.

"Jetz! Now I'm looking forward to seeing what top speed we can make."

"And flying it yourself, no doubt."

With a little laugh Bud concurred. "Yeah, no doubt about that!"

The four blades exceeded the flight characteristics of the three-blade props by as much as 15%, although Tom noted their fuel gauge, accurate to the half gallon, was dropping at a slightly faster rate indicating the additional speed was coming at a potential loss of range of more than three hundred miles.

By the time they returned to Enterprises, he'd calculated in his head that at top speed, the lost distance would nearly be made up by the faster flight speeds. At least to within about twenty miles. It was something to note to his father and Jake at the Construction Company, but it was not a deal breaker.

"Could it be offered in two versions, Tom?" the flyer asked seeing the lower fuel level.

Tom explained his calculations.

"Oh, so not a big deal then. Well, all things considered equal I'd go for this set of props, at least until we test out the multipellers tomorrow.

By the time Tom got to the plane the following morning, Bud had it running and was ready to go.

"A little eager are we?" Tom asked with a smile.

"Eager and ready to fly, skipper. I hear this set of blades numbers thirteen and Jake has a nine-blade version to also try. Good thing tomorrow is Friday because I could not wait for an entire weekend to fly this plane again." Knowing that Tom's Toad jet was the inventor's absolute favorite small aircraft, Bud hastened to add, "Not a jet like the Toad, but about as close as ninety percent of our customers will get to that level of fun!"

One of the first things Tom noted was the increased noise from the multipellers. So much more he pulled out a decibel meter and found it was a full fifteen decibels noisier inside the closed canopy than the previous versions.

"I hope that noise goes away as we get to speed," he told his companion.

"At under half-Mach I sort of doubt it. Can they add noise-canceling like the Toad has?"

"Already has that. Go back to idle and I'm going to climb out and see what it is outside."

When he came back and strapped in again, Tom was shaking his head. "It's noisier than I thought. As noisy at idle as the Toad with its turbines."

"Oh. Maybe they can fine tune the blades?"

"Perhaps," Tom stated noncommittally.

Their test flight went off without any problems and they did achieve another advance over every flight characteristic, including an even more noticeable fuel consumption.

Tom did the figures, this time using his tablet computer, and found the faster flight would not compensate for the 20% higher fuel burn by as much as three hundred and eighteen miles.

It did provide better acrobatic maneuvering, but that was not a primary or, to Tom's mind even a secondary, flight mission for what was seen as a commuter plane.

"But, tomorrow, as someone says, is another day and the smaller blade load of the other multipeller might be a good middle ground. We might want to schedule a flight over a different path, though," Tom suggested. "Perhaps out to the coast and back? There is some unrestricted airspace out over the northern tip of Maine and Grand Manan Island."

"Count me in, but it has to happen after eleven. I have a demo flight of a Swift MachJet One at nine."

That jet was a two-seater that was capable of nearly eight hundred-sixty miles per hour or over the Mach point. Due to its advanced design and a wasp-waist narrowing just behind the cockpit, it made no noticeable sonic boom so was cleared for top speed flight over land.

"Well, I'll take care of some office work until eleven and meet you at the Barn?"

"Works for me, skipper!"

The following day Tom had to beg off going back up with Bud and with the lower blade count multipeller props. He had received a phone call and a request to meet with a senior political official regarding a new request of his and Swift Enterprises' time and knowledge.

The man flew in on an Air Force business jet and Tom decided to meet him at the civilian terminal and not to drive all the way over to the offices should this prove to be a short meeting or what he and his father termed, "A fishing expedition," where someone was only sounding them out over something unrelated to what the Swifts actually did.

"Hello, I'm Joey Binghamton, and I've heard all the *McHale's Navy* jokes and references before." The man looked at Tom and could see the inventor wasn't going to make any comments about his name.

"Sorry," he said and explained about being teased unmercifully since he had been about sixteen and the old situation comedy had been restaged for four recent and popular seasons. "It gets even worse if you take the time to watch the original series."

"Well, as you probably know I'm Tom Swift, and I am curious about this meting you've requested. Come inside and we'll use the smaller of the two meeting rooms."

He headed inside the terminal as did his guest, but the man stopped suddenly, looking up. There, ten feet over their heads was a satellite. It was obviously a real one that had been retrieved, cleaned up and now was covered in gold Mylar.

It had been one of the second generation GPS satellites until it failed and was replace by Tom. NASA and the U.S. Government had suggested letting it burn up on re-entry, but Tom brought it back and had it, cosmetically, brought to new condition.

The inventor chuckled. It had the same impression of nearly every visitor coming into the terminal.

"Tha-tha-that can't be real?" Binghamton stated, very unsure. "Is it?"

Tom nodded. "As real as they come if only a little better for the twelve years of wear and tear in space."

He explained the replacement and retrieval as if it were something happening every day at Swift Enterprises. The man was stunned but found his voice as they sat down in the meeting room.

"Well, it is mostly because of your track record with doing the seemingly impossible that has me here today. You see, NASA has passed on a special mission we want to see happening. It is as close to seemingly impossible as you can get, and yet it might not be all that far off what you can do."

Tom liked people who got to the point. This man was not getting there so he prompted him.

"Not to try to cut something that is important to you short, but you need to tell me what this mission impossible is and make it important to me or else I may ask you to get back in that jet. So?"

The man was startled. "Well, I thought you would have read about it in the letter I sent you."

Tom shook his head. "First thing I heard about this was your call first thing this morning. No letter unless it arrived today and is in our Security department. Hang on and I'll check." He tapped his TeleVoc pin on his collar and asked for Security. Gary Bradley answered.

"*Yes, Tom?*"

The inventor asked about any letter coming from Washington that morning.

"*Nope. Nothing has shown up. I'll keep an eye out.*"

"Thanks," and Tom cut the connection. He turned to his guest. "No. No letter. So, again I shall ask you to tell me what this is or I will leave."

Binghamton looked sadly at the Inventor. "Okay," and he sighed as if he was not prepared to tell Tom everything. "As I said, NASA is passing on a very important, to our President and Vice President, project and mission. They want a manned probe to head to Neptune and to dive into the atmosphere, which is ocean-like and made from hydrogen—"

Tom held up a hand. "I am aware of the gaseous nature of the atmosphere and the great pressure that makes it more a liquid than a gas. Go on."

"So, could you, sort of, I mean maybe, well, mount a mission to do that? Go to Neptune and find where the solid crust starts and get some coring samples?"

"And, samples of that atmosphere to ascertain the actual makeup?"

"Well, yes, that as well. Can you do that?"

"I can, or at least I cannot think of a serious impediment other than the lengthy trip out there, coming up with something to take along that can survive pressures twice that of the deepest point on Earth's oceans, and do all the science stuff you seem to want but are not able to articulate. Can I ask something and not have you take it as an insult?"

Joey Binghamton nodded.

"Okay, then it is this. Why did they send you to talk to me about this if it is so important? If it is, why didn't the President call? He has our private number?"

Binghamton looked down and muttered, "Because I'm the Vice President's nephew and he wants me to be more of a political player. Sorry."

This had a double affect on Tom, neither of them positive. Firstly, it was because both he and his father had had run-ins with the Vice President of the United States in the past. The man was not very well educated in technology, and he believed he wielded far more power than he did. On a few occasions the President had to take him aside and tell him to, "Cool it!" when the man tried to bully the Swifts.

The other affect the statement had was to make Tom pity the man before him for being put in this position. He, like his uncle, had no idea what was possible and had been primed to come in to insist the Swifts jump and make it all happen.

"Listen, Joey, I'll tell you what is going to happen. I am going to ask if you have any details of what this planned expedition is and you are likely to tell me there are none. Then I will ask that you leave our grounds and fly back to Washington. During that time I will be on the phone with the President who is not well disposed of your uncle and will probably make that man's life miserable. Besides, there are only a couple months until the election and your uncle did not garner the party's nomination for President, so he is all but gone from the political scene.

"I have to tell you the Swifts to not react kindly to bullying or to being told we need to get on any stick and make something happen.." He looked at the very miserable man. "We also do not like politicians or their nephews just dropping in. If no letter arrives then this is doubly exasperating to me. I don't hold you responsible for this failure, but I do want to suggest that your uncle is not a nice man and maybe you should not get involved in his dirty work. Good bye, Mr. Binghamton."

With that, Tom stood and left the meeting room. He tapped his TeleVoc pin and called Harlan's office to ask that at least one Security person be sent to the terminal to ensure the departure.

Before he got into his car Tom also called Munford Trent on his cell phone and asked to be forwarded to the number of the President's Executive Assistant at the White House.

After identifying himself and telling the woman he was fine these days and would pass along her "hello" to his father, Tom asked if she could either take a message or send the call to voicemail.

She laughed. "He would never get out from behind his desk if he had to listen to all the voicemails people want to leave, Tom. I'm ready to take your message down."

"Okay, and thanks." He dictated a moderately short message regarding the unexpected and undocumented visit and the Vice President's supposed connection to his visitor. He ended with, "So, sir, if this is something *you* ask us to become involved in, that is fine and we will expect more information to be forthcoming. But, if this is the V.P. going rogue again, please understand we do not wish to have any dealings with that man between now and the time he leaves office. Oh, and we will certainly miss you when you leave, sir."

The next morning Harlan was waiting in the big office when Tom and Bud, first, and then Damon, a minute later, arrived.

"Got bad news that turned out sort of okay in the end," he said before either one could get a word out of him.

"Last night, or rather at three a.m. this early morning, a pair of intruders were detected inside construction shed number one at the Construction Company. They were very careful or so they believed, in hiding their faces from our cameras. They didn't anticipate the multi-spectrum cameras that can get a good face shot through a knitted balaclava." He gave them an encouraging smile.

"What did they do or take?" Damon asked.

"They looked around for five minutes and had that leisure because shed one is not occupied after midnight. Anyway, to your question, they found a terminal and inserted a memory stick. Before you ask I've had computer forensics do a check and they did not insert a virus or any worm; all they wanted were some files. They took the plans for the latest version of the *Pigeon Commander II* and the multipeller Tom and Bud proved is not the best match."

Tom moaned. "Then, they can sell that to anyone and our plane might get undersold!"

The Security man looked at his two bosses, shaking his head.

CHAPTER 4 /

DEE

HARLAN WAS absolutely certain the intruders were employed at, or had been employed at, DeCorsay Engineering and Electronics, or DEE as it was known in the industry, at some time in the recent past.

He begged off any explanation by saying he had to go to Shopton Police Department for an identity line-up.

"In case that hint escapes you, the police apprehended two men who got sort of hung up on our razor-wire fence this morning. I need to take a printout of their faces from our security cameras. Back in less than an hour."

"I saw those two men we have on our video when Angela DeCorsay invited me to lunch last year and tried to buy me away from Enterprises," he finally explained once he returned. It was an episode he had reported to Tom and Damon after the interview and offers more than eight months earlier. They had laughed at her attempts at offering him more money, then an executive title, and finally had hinted at being interested in "personally sweetening the pot."

Tom didn't like this latest event, or the possible connection with a rival company, and said so. "But, what can we do? My guess is Angela DeCorsay is far too smart to let them be traced back to her company. It's likely she dismissed them months ago, keeping them on an invisible payroll in the meantime, until now so she can claim they were working on their own."

Harlan nodded. "I agree, but from what I heard down at the P.D. I think they are going to turn on her unless she comes through with a lot of cash for their, uhh, *suffering*?"

Damon agreed. "The sort who do this dirty work for their boss generally are money motivated."

They talked about what anyone could do now the men were in the hands of the police.

"I think I might pay her a social visit," the younger inventor declared. "Interested in a little trip and perhaps a bit of wandering through the brush around their compound, flyboy?"

Bud grinned. "Count me in!"

"Be careful. You'll be in her territory, remember!" Damon told them.

The next morning the two young men flew down to Linden, New Jersey, and their small airport in Tom's favorite aircraft, his Toad.

DEE was situated across some railroad tracks from the parking apron of the airport so they decided to just hike over.

"Hold it right there, cowboys!" a menacing voice called out from inside the razor-wire perimeter fence. As they watched, a group of six men, all husky and carrying what appeared to be machine guns, jogged out from around the corner of the closest building.

Tom and Bud stood still waiting for them to get close to the fence.

"We're here to see Angela DeCorsay," Tom stated. "We have an appointment for one o'clock. Sorry but we thought you might have a back gate."

One of the men came right up to the fence, his gun clutched so tightly his fingers were turning white.

"You're not supposed to be here. This is a high-security area. Now, go away!"

Tom smiled innocently at him. "Just out of curiosity as we get ready to walk around the perimeter of this property so we can keep our appointment with the boss woman, if you six are all right here, what happens if someone else tries to get over the fence, say, over along that tree-lined road?" He pointed to his left.

The man blanched, said a very dirty word and shouted at the other five, "Come on! We have to get sectors seven through nine covered!" With that the team, all wearing what the boys could see were bright red sweatshirts with DEE SECURITY stenciled in bright white on their chests turned as one and ran in the direction Tom had pointed.

"And that is why Harlan not only has smarter men and women working for him, he doesn't outfit them in those 'Hey, shoot at me!' bright clothing," Bud said as they turned the other direction and continued their walk.

They located a side gate another two hundred feet along the tracks and identified themselves to the man in a small booth.

The gate guard, an older man in an outfit that screamed, "Rent-a-Guard," made a phone call, nodded twice before hanging up and issued them temporary paper badges.

After pointing to another building Tom and Bud headed that direction.

"Men with nasty guns and then old Gus who just gives us a badge any twelve-year-old could duplicate and lets us in? That's not at all strange, is it?" Bud asked.

At the front door of the building stood a woman, about fifty and quite attractive. She was slowly applauding as they came forward.

"Bravo, young Tom," she called out still clapping.

Tom grinned at her. "Hello, Mrs. D," he said. "Long time no see. I guess you've given up teaching, huh?"

She held the door for them replying, "Yes. After I had you for Advanced Placement Physics at Shopton High my husband decided to pour all our money and all his time into this company. We moved that next year, then he died a year later leaving me to try to pick up where he left things. But, that isn't any of your concern. I've managed and with a few contracts your father decided to not go after, but we did, I've actually made a good deal of growth in the company. Come on down the hall to my office and we can talk."

She ushered them into a medium-sized and austere office with a mahogany desk and three plush visitor chairs.

"Take any two," she offered pointing.

After asking her secretary, a mousy woman who looked anything but happy at having visitors, for three coffees, she turned on her smile again and sat back.

"So, what brings one of my favorite ex-pupils and the man I believe I've seen in the newspapers, Bud Barclay, with you down here?"

Tom got to the point.

"We arrested two men inside our grounds both of whom had neglected to take out their wallets or ID before coming over our fence and both carrying some pretty sophisticated data collection equipment they were in the process of trying to get back out of the facility when our people caught them." He paused, looking at her, but either it was news to her or she was a good actress.

He continued, taking a wild stab to see if she would react. "They both had ID badges from your company. Not evidence at all as they could have manufactured it to throw us off the scent, but one of them did say, while in police custody, that 'Mrs. D will get us out of this.' I just wanted to ask if they might be working for you or if they used to and have gone rogue? Any ideas?"

The coffee arrived and she said nothing until the secretary left.

"Were their names McDaniels and Wilbur?"

"I actually don't have that information," Tom lied. "Why?"

She sighed. "Because, Tom, we had two former Security guards who were fired for cause about two months ago. Peter McDaniels and Edward Wilbur. We caught them a few too many times inside buildings where they were not supposed to be. Never found them to be stealing, but always with flimsy excuses like, 'We heard someone inside so we came in to check it out,' and, 'We got a phone call telling us there was a break in.' After four instances we dismissed them."

It *sounded* plausible, but Harlan had warned Tom that Angela DeCorsay had been caught lying to Congress twice and had a reputation for being underhanded in her dealings.

Tom fixed the smile back on his face. "I thought it was something like that. Uhhh, did they ever get any secret information or plans from you?"

Angela DeCorsay's face clouded. "Maybe. Perhaps. Ummm, we don't exactly know. I think they got some plans for a new military vehicle we're working on but nothing has shown up anywhere so far." She shrugged. "Let's keep our fingers crossed that it is just a feeling and not a fact."

Tom noted that she had stopped looking directly into his eyes and also that she did not mention the attempt to lure Harlan away from his company.

When they left the company grounds twenty minutes later neither man was any closer to making up his mind as to her involvement in the Construction company's break in.

"I'd hate to think she's gone bad," Tom mused as they climbed into the Toad and prepared to fly back to Shopton. "I actually did like her as a teacher, but power can corrupt people, and if she feels a thrill at the power she possibly wields, she might just have ordered the break-in. Good thing they were such foul-ups."

By the time Tom and Bud got back to Enterprises, Harlan had gone back to the Police Department. Evidently, the two men wanted to make a deal.

"So much for employee loyalty," Bud grinned.

"Yeah," his friend agreed. "Let's see what Harlan has to say about what they might have said before we celebrate."

When the Security man came into the big office, Damon had already headed to the Construction Company to check on a new project saying he'd be back within two hours.

"Well, you two can give him the overview and he can call me for the deep details."

"Sure," Tom told him.

"Okay. The bottom line is those two idiots swear they were working on their own. The problem is they kept looking eat each other for reassurance until we separated them, then they started asking what the other had told us. Both went all wide-eyed and suddenly silent when the names DEE and DeCorsay were mentioned. I think one of them had a small leak accident."

Tom and Bud grinned.

"Anyway, we didn't break them this time around, but good old Judge Cadwalather happened to walk into the station, heard what they were accused of, and declared them to both be bound over for trial with no chance of bail. The police can hold them for five days, over the weekend, and then the good Judge will preside over their plea hearing."

"Will he allow bail then?" Bud asked.

"No. What he will do is investigate, with my assistance, whoever hired a pair of non-local attorneys for them who started hanging around before eight. And, the FBI is interested as this involves industrial espionage so it is a Federal crime. Even if the Judge is presented with overwhelming evidence, he can simply refer the case to the Feds and down to Manhattan our break and enter men go. All things considered, if they don't rat out DeCorsay, they won't have a lot of free time to enjoy anything they have been or are supposed to be paid. Not for a couple decades that is."

The Security man had a broad smile on his face as he told them he had to get back to his office, and left.

Bud turned to Tom.

"Think he'll break them?"

Tom shrugged. "If not Harlan himself, I'm sure he'll have a hand in it. Maybe if and when he does, I'll have to change my opinion of my old teacher."

"Old, yet still kind of pretty."

Tom nodded. "The worst combination, flyboy. As in avoid at all costs."

They agreed to stay clear of the former teacher and to let Harlan handle any criminal actions and Jackson Rimmer and his Legal team for anything needing those services.

Their discussion turned to Bud's final flight test with the multipeller set of fewer blades in the *Pigeon Commander II*.

"Even though the smaller set of blades takes less horse power, the four-blade props are the best for speed, distance and handling. If you want to take a spin I believe they won't change the props back before Tuesday morning."

Tom thought about it and decided his one flight as pilot had been enough.

"Yeah. If I didn't have to give it about fifteen more hours of testing I might pass as well. But, Jake Aturian wants me to give three more multipeller combinations a try. One will be about a full foot less wide. More narrow? I don't know what the proper grammar is but instead of a total width of five-feet, two inches the smallest set will be nine bladed and just four-feet, four inches. I hear he wants to wring the best overall performance from the airframe and thinks there will be a just right solution."

"Well, Goldilocks, I wish you *bona ventura*," Tom quipped.

Late on Monday morning Tom had two visitors. First came Harlan with a report on the two captured intruders.

He'd barely sat down when Bud breezed in. Seeing that Tom already had someone there he was about to back out when the Security man told him this had something to do with him as well.

"Have a seat, and I'll begin."

Tom and Bud sat next to Harlan and turned their full attention to him.

"Okay. This is going to be short and I hope sweet. First, the pair of prisoners have kind of turned on each other and on DeCorsay and her company. The finger pointing started just after midnight when the younger of the pair, Peter McDaniels, started pacing in his cell and broke down in tears. When the guards saw him on CCTV they came in and he pleaded with them to be allowed to make a statement. "Anything to get me out of here," he told them. They offered to get him some time out of the cell if he could wait until morning and he agreed. Then, at nine they contacted a Public Prosecutor and she came in, talked with him and he agreed to swear he was hired by the DeCorsay company and the other man had all but forced him to come along on the fouled up invasion attempt."

"What about the other guy?" came a question from Bud.

"Well, that would be Wilbur and he's a bit tougher than his young accomplice, but after he heard McDaniels rolled over on him he was willing to give up all on DeCorsay in return for a lighter sentence. The Public Prosecutor told him he was too late and McDaniels was getting the deal and he was going to a federal prison for at least twenty years!"

Tom took a deep breath preparing himself for his question.

"Does Mrs. DeCorsay also go to jail?"

Harlan shrugged. "Angela DeCorsay is being taken into custody as we speak. There is overwhelming circumstantial evidence but nothing to solidly connect her unless both Wilbur and McDaniels testify. Then, she'll likely go down for the crime. We, however and pending everything that will happen in the coming days or weeks, shall see."

He rose and with a nod to them both, left Tom and Bud alone.

"I know how much you liked her years ago, skipper, but for my money, anyone who either steals from this company or tries to kill anyone in it, and that goes double for you or me, I want tossed head first into a deep and dark cell."

Tom had to agree. He was just about completely tired of having this sort of thing happening over and over. And the worst part was even when Harlan and his organization stomped out one, some other person or company popped up with a new way to do bad things.

"Take my mind off this, Bud. Tell me about the latest *Pigeon Commander II* flight."

Bud smiled and settled into his seat.

"Okay. This was a test of a more traditional prop set, only this time it was a five-blade prop they put on while they build the next multipellers. Same basic diameter as the two-, three-, and four-blade sets." His eyes began to shine and Tom leaned over an inch expecting great news.

"Jetz! That plane flew. It reached four hundred knots in slightly nose-down flight and three-eighty at absolutely level. And, the really good news is we have a slightly better range even at a cruise of three-fifty. It could fly non-stop between here and Boise, Idaho, assuming anyone wanted to get from Shopton to Boise, that is."

"Is it still flight ready or have the finishers taken those props off?"

Now, Bud's smile broadened. "I told them you would likely want a test flight of your own and to leave things as is. It is waiting for us if you have an hour or two." He raised one eyebrow. "Interested?"

Tom smiled and nodded. "You bet! Give me an hour to finish something here and I'll meet you... uhh, where?"

"Well, last time our intrepid young flyer saw it, it was parked out by Hangar eight just sort of waiting for someone to come along and take it. Or, give it some love, or something. I'll taxi it over to the Barn and we can meet there. See ya!" With that, Bud turned and stalked from the room.

What Tom needed to get done was a bit of paperwork the FAA had sent regarding the near accident/attack by Octavia Whitcomb, and an investigation into her death.

Tom was dumbstruck about the term "death" so he picked up the phone and called the local FBI office.

"Agent Narz, please," he asked the receptionist.

When the man answered, it sounded terse. "Quimby Narz. What do you need?"

Once Tom identified himself, the man's attitude and tone changed.

"Oh, sorry, Tom. Thought you were another reporter. I guess you heard your favorite kamikaze pilot, Octavia Whitcomb, tried to escape today. Unfortunately, I need to call her father to tell him of his daughter's death. She'd fashioned a makeshift knife and stabbed two guards on her way out. One will live and the other is minute-to minute for now, but when she got cornered she lunged and a guard pulled his gun and... well, I suppose you don't need or want the details."

"Right. The reason I called is not specifically about that, but the FAA has sent me something to answer about my part in her death from crashing her jet. Other than to let my Legal folks answer with, 'He was not responsible for her actions,' I am stumped. Is it possible for the agency to notify them of the *real* cause of her death?"

Narz promised to get to someone in Washington who would bring in someone high enough in the chain to tell the FAA to back off.

"Thanks."

"Sure. Say, how's your mom these days? We haven't been able to entice her to come in for a project for going on a half year. Usually that is as long as one of her retirements lasts."

"I think she's enjoying being a grandmother of two and a coming baby and that is taking her mind off of anything to do with microbes and bacterium and such. But, I'll tell her you were asking about her."

Tom TeleVoc'd Bud telling him the hour of work was finished twenty minutes early so they would meet about ten minutes earlier than thought.

When he let the nose wheel come off the runway and the rest of the plane just followed, Tom had the feeling he was about to pilot the closest thing to his favored Toad jet possible given propellers and multi-cylinder engines.

The plane did not disappoint him. It was not just fast, it was responsive and one of the quietest planes he'd flown, almost as much as the Toad.

"They tell me they've worked with Electronics to come up with an even better noise cancellation circuit, with not one, not two, but nine microphones hidden all around the cockpit and a specialty computer to process all the inputs. Not bad, huh?"

"Not bad by a mile, flyboy. And, as long as we don't get—" Tom stopped realizing Bud did not know about Octavia's death. He told the pilot about her attempt to escape, about the critically injured guard and how she had done the most idiotic of things, tried to stab at one of the people she'd just attacked.

"Think it was suicide by cop?" Bud asked, very seriously.

Tom had to think about that and did not give his answer until they were on the ground fifty minutes later.

"Yes. I'm inclined to believe she knew she wasn't going to come out of the escape alive."

CHAPTER 5 /
A SECOND ATTEMPT AT PERSUASION

IT WAS just eleven weeks until the national election when Tom received a call from the current Vice President.

"I want it understood that you are not to hang up on me. Is that perfectly clear?" The man started out in about the worst possible way by almost threatening the inventor.

"As clear as you can be, and I shall call you sir in deference to your position, one that will be gone soon. In all honesty, I do not like you and it is because of your attitude toward me. I shall also remind you that the President, your superior, does not like the way you try to bully me, my father, and this organization. He also did not like your predecessor and that is why you are where you are now and he is long gone. So, what is it you called to rant and rail about... *sir*?"

There was silence at the other end and Tom could imagine the politician was getting ready to unleash his anger. Perhaps he had gone too far?

"Then, I can only ask, no, request that you give me several minutes to plead my case." The man sounded nearly civil. "A while ago a young man came to your company to suggest a project involving a flight to and investigation of Neptune. He was unceremoniously turned away. By you. Now, I understand that he might have taken a wrong tact with you, but his mission was to get you interested in a project the President believes is vital to our party."

Tom nearly sputtered as he sought to find words. "You are saying that this Neptune project is not for, oh, let's say the good of the nation. Or, for the sake of human understanding? That it is a politically-motivated project *your party wants*? Is that correct?"

There was a sharp intake of breath before the V.P. responded to that. "I may have misspoken. Or, perhaps I should not have mentioned that, but I feel I must put the cards on the table. Yes, our political party is in deep trouble and we will loose terribly at the election in a few short weeks. Too many of our sitting politicians have angered their constituents far too much and far too many times. We have made promises we had no way of keeping and it is now coming back to bite us. Chomp on our very lives.

"The President and our party wish to announce something big and that will actually get done before the changeover in January.

Something by your company because it is widely known that you succeed at substantially lower costs than other companies and I do mean succeed."

"Please give me a moment to digest what you are telling me. I will be right back." Tom placed the call on hold and sat back thinking very hard for about a minute. He came to a conclusion, picked the phone back up, and said, "Sir? I will listen to you but ask that you keep to the actual subject and do not give me platitudes or anything but the facts."

"Then, I will endeavor to do just that. So, the Neptune project is internationally backed and it is only because this administration has not been certain we could support it with the actual work that we had not previously signed on the line, so to speak. Nine of the more industrialized countries around the globe want some answers about that distant planet. We want that as well, but their schedule to take the proverbial slow boat out, with only a robotic probe to be dropped from orbit, has been deemed by our President as to unambitious and far too slow. It would have required about four years just to get things built and another five to travel that distance. And for what? Just about nothing we cannot discern using telephotographic spectography."

"Yes. I can imagine how that is not to the President's liking. I'd say personally I would not sign up to support that either. Now, let me take a guess at what is coming."

"Go ahead."

"Fine. Because Swift Enterprises has proven to be able to get to the outer edge of the solar system quickly, and also because we tend to build to our specific needs and that shortens development and production time significantly, you—the President—want us to… hmmmm. What? Take this over and just leave the consortium of nations in the dust?"

"No. To the contrary, we want you to spearhead this, direct all of the nations involved, and take this on as a fully-funded project. To be completed at your speed and convenience. All I—and the President—ask is that we be allowed to let it be known that he was the one, and our political party the ones, behind this change of direction and most likely great success."

Tom hated the way this was sounding like a political expediency rather than a serious scientific mission and he told the V.P. that.

"Well, then I am sorry to say that many good men and women are likely to be put out of office within our party and some across the aisle like your pet senator!"

"And, that sounds like another threat from you. Have the

President call if this is serious and if he can manage to keep any political agenda out of this. Good day." With that, Tom disconnected the call.

While he regretted his rash action his level of anger at the man on the phone had risen and it was all he could do to not shout. But, he reviewed the recording of the call before he called his father on his TeleVoc.

After explaining the call and his hang-up, he asked if he had done the wrong thing.

"You said he threatened Peter Quintana? How?"

"By suggesting that as his party went down to defeat he might do something to drag Senator Quintana down with them even though they are in opposing parties."

"Okay. I need to get to a phone and make a call to Pete to warn him of what is going on. Please give me the recording stamp so I can play that call to him."

Tom did and disconnected the call.

A half hour later Trent announced an incoming call from the President.

"Hello, sir, and I believe I might know what this is about. Would I be correct to conclude it has to do with the call I recently hung up on?"

The man laughed. "Yes, it is about that call and that... *person* whom I will not name. It is also about the project he and the first idiot who spoke with you both bungled. So, I don't have much time but the fact is all the other nations in this group are playing it safe, slow, and stupidly. I want this to succeed and it does not have to do with my forthcoming departure. Nor, I will add, does it concern my party and their idea to hang us all on this one small thing. The party leaders have made many foolish choices in what they promote and who they attack and I am sick to the teeth of it all. Happy to be going, even. But, I would like to get things going while we still have funding approval and can make this happen. Mostly because I fear the other team will seize on this as one of their, 'We just cut a lot of costs,' type measures. Peter Quintana being the exception, of course."

"If there is an official plan of action I might get and also some assurance that all those other nations are not going to want to look over our shoulders and tell us what they want for their money, then I can put my ill feelings for your running mate aside and see what we can do."

There was a pause at the other end. Then, "A rather guarded yes to the first one and a heavy sigh to the second. There is no consensus between these nations about what they want. They obviously all want this to be cheap, but all want it done over time and employing as many of their citizens as possible in the project and that means triple or greater the expense. Even the couple nations who have had disastrous results in not adhering to the measurement standards of everyone else, no mention of who they are, resulting in destruction or loss of spacecraft in the past… where was I going with that? Oh, right! Even those nations cannot agree to setting down standards beforehand. So, have I got you interested yet?"

"Realistically or sarcastically, sir?"

"Yes. Thought so. So, please look for a delivery, tomorrow, of the specs we believe are closest to giving everyone what they want as final results, and not what they want to build and fly this thing."

When the paperwork came through the next day, complete with at least one page of warnings and one page of non-disclosure from each country, Tom was not feeling a great deal of enthusiasm for what we had about to get into. But, he signed each page, made tick marks and initialed the variations of:

❏ I understand on penalty of money (most)/public shame (Japan)/ denial of future work (two others) that I shall not, in any way, disseminate/copy/share/circulate/distribute/propagate/disburse/ publicize (and all other words to that effect) the information I am about to open and read.

He sighed before picking everything up and taking it upstairs to see the Legal folks. Jackson Rimmer who normally handled direct contact and requests from Tom and Damon was out, his number two individual, Patrick Peck, was on vacation, and the next person in line, Lisa Ann Ekerston, was in a meeting, so Tom sat down in the reception area and read through the various pages he needed to discuss.

When the main doors opened and Jackson walked in, he stopped, looked at Tom sitting there in such concentration he had not noticed the lawyer's arrival, and went to stand next to the inventor.

In a soft falsetto voice, he said, "Tom. Time to wake up and head for school."

"Huh?" Tom startled from his study looked around and then up into Jackson's face and smiled. "Sorry, Mother, but today is not a school day. Or," and he looked back at the pages in his hand, "perhaps it is. Got five minutes?"

They went to the back and into Rimmer's office and sat. Tom handed the pages over and explained, in brief, what was possibly going on.

"Let me take care of these for you. I'll be sure to impress that the Legal department is the one taking responsibility. Generally, it is low level politicians who generate this sort of paperwork and just knowing an actual lawyer is looking over their work is enough to make them back down and go silent. We shall see. If I may, I'm going to hand these off to Lisa Ann and let her get back to you. It'll all be over my signature, but she is the go-to person for this type of paper."

Tom thanked him then asked if he could go ahead and read the real papers.

"Yes. Just do not disseminate, give out copies to the press, share, or otherwise allow distribution... et cetera!"

The lawyer grinned at him.

Tom called Trent from the lawyer's phone to tell him he was "heading upstairs."

By that, Tom meant the old control tower atop the Administration building. Empty now for more than eleven years, it had been replaced by the concrete and steel structure sitting at the exact center of Enterprises. All the old equipment had been removed—some of which was still in use at the Shopton Regional Airport where they had been thrilled to be receiving the more advanced technology—and it now featured a comfortable couch, a plush easy chair, a small desk with a telephone... and nothing else but quiet and space.

It was the inventor's favorite retreat because it not only allowed him a peaceful environment, it provided an exceptional view to the south, west and north. East of him was a taller building that blocked that view or else he would be able to see the older Construction Company. He could, to the south, see the Swift MotorCar Company.

As he read through the often contradictory information, he firmly believed he gleaned a sense of what most of the nations wanted to accomplish. In the main, that meant a visit not just to the planet but a dive into the atmosphere that quickly turned from gas to a semi-liquid and then to an absolutely icy slush before the actual mantle could be reached.

That core was believed to be greater than twice the diameter of the Earth.

At possibly 1/2% hydrogen and 1/4% helium, the rest of the liquid atmosphere was believed to be methane, and some of that was believed to form into diamond crystals under enough pressure and cold.

That same methane was a large component of the gaseous atmosphere.

The biggest abnormality was that this dense liquid pseudo-atmosphere was very cold while the core of the planet was a scotching 9,260°F.

The density of the mantle/core combination was only about that of the Earth, but here is where opinion was divided. Some believed the liquid atmosphere likely at great depths was also a solid, while others stated their studies showed it to remain a liquid all the way down to the solid center.

This project was designed to see who was correct, or if either was right.

Tom chuckled when he read a report by a Belgian scientist and planetary physics expert.

"I believe, with the minority, there must be liquid water (H2O) held either in suspension pockets or mixed throughout inside the other liquidity of the planet. I do not believe the reports/guesswork stating that the surface temperature must be below minus 55° Kelvin as that would not explain why the surface can be seen to move about."

Some of his reasoning was built around the detectable temperatures of the planet. Something that large and that far from the sun *should* be much colder. That also pointed to a hot core keeping things warmer that expected. This led to a belief that the hot core would not allow even the deepest of the liquid gases to actually freeze and that the deeper you went, the warmer and therefore thinner they actually became.

Two of the objectives set forth by more than five countries, each, regarded a study of the very thin and dark ring around the planet with an eye toward determining if this was once a moon. And, the other was the retrieval of some of the possible diamond crystals.

China wanted at least a ton of them returned to: "help defray our enormous fiscal burden in supporting this adventure."

Tom did a quick calculation that told him they expected to get back nearly five times the value in such diamonds as they intended to put out.

"I figured it was something like that," he told his father as they sat having a late afternoon cup of coffee. "Do we know much about what the first probe sent back?"

"Voyager 2? Only the basics and those are all available on the Internet. The photographs were assembled from low-resolution data blips, but it did show four thin rings rather than the single one earthbound telescopes detect. And, it gave a reality check regarding the large moon of Triton and how it circles retrograde to the planet's rotation. Other than that, not a lot, but nothing that was totally off track."

"So, what do you believe is needed to do this little adventure?" It was a serious question from his father and Tom wanted to give it a well-thought and serious answer.

"Can I get back to you on that? I've only just finished the papers."

Damon's smile told him that was expected. "When you are ready I will make time to listen, Son. On a slightly different but connected issue, when do you need to get back to whomever with our agreement or refusal?"

Tom sighed. "The President said he'd appreciate an answer by Friday, the day after tomorrow. Do you think we should do this?"

Damon laughed. "Will Bashalli let you out of the house long enough to go to Neptune?"

"She told me as long as I am home before the baby arrives, I am allowed to go on at least one adventure."

"It is going to be a heck of an undertaking and I believe you do not have the time what with all the transit it is going to take."

"I'd sort of planned, in my mind, to use the *TranSpace Dart* to get out there towing whatever we decide to take. We can get to Neptune fairly fast as it is going to be close to straight out from us in another three months. As little as two weeks or less travel time. Stay there a little—maybe a week or two—and come back. I'd use the word *easy*, but I think you might take exception to that."

"However you are going to travel—make certain we have the funding in place—finalize your the design, and make sure Jake has the ability to build something as fast as you seem to need to, or else put this off until after Bashalli has the baby. You haven't missed the first two and she will likely be very hurt if you miss this one."

By that late afternoon Tom had been at his drafting board for an hour and at the CAD computer terminal another two hours. What had come to his mind was not one large craft dropping off another one to plunge down and explore, it was a single ship capable of transiting the distance at great speed, easing into the atmosphere to the surface, and then submerging into the dense, liquid atmosphere.

It was going to mean recreating some of the drive systems of the *TranSpace Dart* as it became fairly obvious the one ship might not have the ability to both hold onto and use the small black hole that drove/yanked her forward all the while keeping the trailing ship firmly under control.

One thing was clenched firmly in his mind and that had to do with the control cockpit. In the *Dart*, and because the ship was pointed like an arrowhead, there was little space at the nose for much more than two close seats and the instruments. For some, it was a little claustrophobic.

This one will have a proper, big control room, he thought. *Maybe not as large as the Challenger*, he told himself, *but big enough for crew, air space and that swinging cat we all talk about!*

The dynamics of a submersible hull were vastly different than for a spaceship. For one, outer pressures wanted to crush a sub's hull where the vacuum of space wanted to pull anything inside to the outside.

Neither scenario was good, and Tom knew he had to accommodate them both in one vessel.

He called and apologized to Bashalli for needing to remain at work. When he described the project and his deadline of less that thirty-nine hours to respond, she understood.

"It's okay, Tom. Amanda is making grilled tuna sandwiches for the kids and she and I will have grilled, pulled chicken. She turned the leftovers from night before last into something I think even Chow would approve. Call me before you come home, or if you are going to be later than ten, just let yourself in and kiss me when you get into bed."

He worked on the design, and in his mind he only came up with just a single main one, until after eight in the evening before looking at his watch, counting the time he knew he still needed to come up with something to either tell him is was possible or not, and found he was going to make it.

He headed home, but not before he stopped at an ice cream store and purchased Bashalli's absolute favorite, butter pecan with dark chocolate drizzle.

The front door was unlocked and he opened it to find Amanda sitting on the footstool from his easy chair massaging Bashalli's feet.

"She was walking like she had egg shells in her socks," the nanny explained. "My mother had that with my youngest brother, so I told her I'd do what I did for mom."

"Can we keep her?" Bashalli asked in a soft purr, not opening her eyes as she was enjoying the special treatment.

Tom rattled the paper bag holding the ice cream.

"Yes, and now my question to you is do you want any of what I have in here, or are you in too much personal heaven right now?"

Bashalli's left eye opened and she focused on her husband and his bag of potential treasure.

"Whatcha got, mister?" she asked in a little girl voice.

"Something cold and creamy and sweet and, well, that is enough description. You want some? You as well, Amanda," he said as he opened the bag showing her what he had.

The nanny smiled. "I'll consider that both my reward for the foot massage as well as my once-a-week cheat. One scoop, please."

Bashalli giggled. "If I asked for two, would that mean you don't get any, Tom?"

"Nope. Got the big bucket so there's enough for tonight and even a scoop or two for you tomorrow. Maybe for the kids."

"Fat chance of that," his wife stated with a snort.

Tom chuckled as he went to the kitchen. Four minutes later the three sat on the sofa enjoying their ice cream, although Bashalli was trying to decide what was better between that and the massage.

CHAPTER 6 /
IT BECOMES OFFICIAL

TOM'S CALL to the President on Friday morning caught the man in an unexpected lull in his day. That fact even surprised his secretary. "I don't know what is going on, Mr. Swift. He actually has time to speak with you; hold, please."

Following a pair of double clicks, the current occupant of the Oval Office came on. "I am happy to hear from you although it has interrupted the seventeen minutes I find are not packed with wall-to-wall meetings and conferences and one of the oh-so-fun press conferences I have each Friday afternoon. But, I digress, Tom. Have you got anything good for me?"

"Yes, I believe I do. Swift Enterprises will take on this project and believe we can have it completed in under six months, and that includes actually going out there. Now, before you tell me that sounds impossible, there are stipulations. First and foremost is that we will not speak to any representative of any nation other than you or Senator Quintana. Nobody from China, nobody from Japan, England, Germany, France or any of the others.

"We will give weekly status updates to them all but believe direct contact will interfere with our ability to complete this mission. In the past we have had dealings with them all other than Russia on other projects and they all like to poke and prod and, 'We now want you to do this,' sort of things. None of that will work. I feel the need to repeat that. None of it will be acceptable. If that is not the way this is going to work for all of them, and if the US does not want to foot the entire bill, then we wish whoever takes it on the best of luck."

There was a second or two of silence so Tom added, "And we respectfully will not act as a subcontractor to anyone, sir."

"I fully understand. Uhh, I'll take a stab and say you spotted the Chinese money making scheme attached, right?"

"We did."

"Okay. If you do find diamonds, can you at least bring back a few pounds of them and share them equally?"

"I plan on bringing back a number of samples from the outer atmosphere to the liquid one and even a try at some of the solid materials under that. If we encounter any diamonds or other small crystals, those will also come back."

By Monday, Peter Quintana was detailed to come to Enterprises as the President's proxy for a meeting with Tom.

"Glad to see you, Tom," he said as they shook hands. "The top man sends his regards and tells me to assure you he wanted to be here, or have you down there, but said something about an anomaly that is not going to be repeated for weeks. Said you'd understand." He looked curious so Tom explained about the Friday call and the uncharacteristically un-busy president.

"Ahhh. That does sound like an oddball thing. Anyway, here I am with a good idea of what is going on but zero idea what you might be able to do. Fill me in, please."

"Best thing to do is to show you a few selected slides and then my preliminary design. Of course, and as the President understands, this all depends on funding coming in pretty darned soon." He detailed the demand that no country be allowed to try to exert force or make changes.

"Got it, and I'm going to be in charge of that. In the mean time, let's discuss what you might or might not be able to do," suggested the senator.

"Right," Tom began, motioning to the conference area. "I've put together this slideshow with some things and views of Neptune just so we are on the same page when discussing things. So," and he reached over to pick up the 3-D telejector control which, as it energized, lowered the room lights and made the windows a dark opaque for better viewing. "So far I have only a very sketchy idea of what sort of craft is required, but while that is under discussion, design and development, I have everyone I know, including the experts up at the Swift observatory, putting together as much data and views as we can about the planet.

"We know one thing almost for certain, and that is one reason, as I have been told, for this little trip. That, primarily is the makeup of the liquid portion of what many call the atmosphere, although I have another theory."

Pointing at the slide currently floating in the air in front of them Tom described how the planet was made up, and how likely it would be they would have to get all the way down to the mantle to know the truth.

"There is a detectable vaporous atmosphere above that liquid, and I am of the belief the liquid is more a planet-wide ocean. The fact it is not made of water does not mean it is not an ocean."

Peter Quintana held up a hand.

"The student in the front row?" Tom asked jokingly. "You have a question?"

"Yes, sir, I do. How is it possible for all that liquid to be a... wait. I get it. It is the very liquid nature of what covers the planet's solid part that makes it an ocean. Right?"

Tom shrugged. "That's my thinking, Peter. It is dad's as well. That is why I believe we need to treat it as any other ocean, although incredibly colder and deeper, and go visit Neptune with a submarine."

Peter's eyes grew wide in surprise. "But, how the heck will you drag or shove a giant submarine all the way out there?"

Tom's answer was a surprise to him.

"In one possible scenario, we won't drag anything out there. We will travel there in a submarine that also will be a fully functional spacecraft capable of incredible speeds. At least, that is my hope. Now, whether or not I can make that happen is possibly another thing."

They looked at the various other slides and the combined fly-by images of Voyager 2 from decades earlier. In the end Peter Quintana had a single question.

"Do I go back to the President and report you are officially on board with this project?"

Tom stared at him a moment. "As long as our stipulations for non-interference by any other nation, all the time guaranteeing full funding up front, are met. Then, it is now official. Swift Enterprises is on board with this project and will do our utmost to see it happen as quickly as possible."

He told Peter about his promise to Bashalli and how the project, if it did not look as if it were going to be successfully completed and the crew and craft returned to Earth before the birth, then he would put the trip off until at least a month following that point in time.

"Not certain I'd couch it like that to the other big guys, but if you provide an earliest possible departure date given everything going better than to plan and then a later, more reasonable departure time without telling anyone other than me the real reason, I think that will be acceptable to most."

"Sound good to me."

Five days later Tom received a call from Harlan.

"I just got a heads-up from the city courthouse. You are about to be subpoenaed to appear at the trial of Angela DeCorsay. She has been arrested and charged with industrial espionage, or at least causing it, and her attorney wants to head you off and call you as one of their witnesses. Their process server is on his way out here now as I am telling you this. Now, before you say anything, I am getting ready to run over and hand you a different subpoena from the Attorney General for the State of New York who wants you on his side."

Tom thought for a split second.

"Which one do I take, or do I go into hiding?"

Harlan let out a great sigh. "I want to stop off at Jackson's office first and ask him, but if you could sort of slip out of the building and get ready to fly away at a moment's TeleVoc notice, that might be best until we get this sorted out."

"Okay. I'm heading for my car and out to the finalization building where I might just be taking a test hop up in a new plane."

"Great! I'll ping you in less than ten minutes. Perhaps you ought to have that plane revved up and ready to taxi."

But, even before Tom got over to the assembly buildings he received a *"Come back"* message from the lawyer.

"Also, your summons appears to be for the Prosecution, so please come up to my office to receive this nice piece of yellow paper I hold in my hands."

"Okay, on my way!"

When he walked into the office on the third floor of the Administration building, the chief legal counsel for Enterprises and the chief Security man were sitting, sipping what appeared to be some sort of liquor.

Tom looked pointedly at the bottle that was sitting upright in the open drawer and said, "Brought out the good stuff for me?"

"Well, you are certainly welcome to a small glass of celebration, because it turns out you are not going to be going to any trial after all. Ah, how things have changed in the last four minutes. Mrs. Angela DeCorsay, nee Constance Arlene Chaney—formerly of Tuscaloosa, Alabama—has just made a deal with the Federal prosecutors who were about to charge her with enough bad deeds, past, present and possibly future, to send her to prison for the rest of her life. She plea bargained down to eighteen years of straight time, no parole possible, in a maximum security prison located in North Dakota." This all came from the Lawyer who was ill disguising a grin.

Harlan added, "What she does not know is that the prison has only minimal heating and she will be in an area of this broad nation of ours where the temperatures generally hit 0 degrees Fahrenheit for about fifty days in the winter. Not much above five for another fifty or so. She was hoping for the women's minimum security facility out in Nevada just a stone's throw from Las Vegas."

Jackson added more information. "It isn't very large at about a thousand inmates, but it is rated high because they allow slot machines and card tables. The Vegas one, I mean. The North Dakota one is about as low rated by the inmates as you can find and still be a humane facility. It has a lower repeat offender rate!"

Tom shook his head. "You know, I do believe I'll take that little celebratory glass. I'm really sorry that Mrs. DeCorsay turned out to be a bad person because she was such a wonderful teacher." He took the small glass of single malt whiskey, sniffed and nodded appreciatively before taking it down in one large sip.

His eyes watered and he felt fire running all down his throat, but it was a good fire and it smoothed out in a second and was just a warm glow.

Rimmer jiggled the bottle but Tom shook his head.

"Fine. So, the kicker is she has been wanted all this time for beating a neighbor in Arkansas nearly to death, but he survived and testified against her in court. She escaped leaving the courthouse in an unknown vehicle and disappeared. Turns out she changed her name—not in the legal sense—to Angela Ellen Fernwood, met and married her Mister DeCorsay after a whirlwind three week romance, and they moved here a couple years before you were in her class, but she left less than two years later and joined him in his company. He died of sudden heart failure a week after passing an insurance physical and the policy paid her three million dollars."

Tom whistled. "Nothing suspicious there," he commented.

"Certainly not," Jackson agreed, rolling his eyes.

During the following week, Peter Quintana had to call and warn Tom of three possible intrusions from a few over-eager countries wanting to be assured their voices were being listened to and their money was being spent on the things *they* found important. It was a video call Tom viewed in the office via the telejector.

"As we agreed, have your switchboard, or Trent, tell them this is not a matter for discussion directly with anyone at Enterprises, that they must contact either their U.S. Government liaison or me. End of sentence."

"We received the first of them this morning. France, and with an insistence they absolutely must speak *at* me, their word, or they would shut down all funding. When the switchboard operator forwarded them to Jackson Rimmer's office, he was in conference with his chief assistant, Lisa Ann Ekerston, and she took the call since she speaks fluent French."

Cautiously, Peter asked how that had gone.

"Well, according to them both, the woman at the other end represented herself as the Vice Premiere of the French Republic. When Lisa Ann informed her there is no such office or position, the woman tried blustering and swearing at her. Then, she suddenly hung up. They have everything recorded."

"Imagine my surprise or total lack of it," the senator told the inventor in a flat tone. "Well, here is the official wording to use on any future calls. Ready?"

"Sure. Got pencil and paper in front of me. This is all being recorded anyway."

"Okay. I quote, 'By decree of the President of the United States of America, and as agreed and demanded by multi-national agreement, this call is hereby deemed to be outside of anything this company or any individual in it has any reason to answer. Kindly forward your specific reasons to the Vice President of The United States.' That ends the quote, by the way."

Tom chuckled and said he had it, and he would be sending it to the switchboard as soon as Legal had a quick look.

"I do like the part where they are to contact the V.P.," Tom stated. "I hope he is prepared for the various languages so nobody tries to slip anything past him by using a foreign term or phrase."

"Well, if they do it is on him. The other reason for the call is to check how you are doing on a plan. Not expecting a design or prototype yet, although I know you folks can do those miracles at times. So, how are things coming?"

"I have narrowed things down to a one or two ship solution. Either I use the existing *TranSpace Dart* and its ability to travel at up to light speed, towing our second ship, the submersible, behind— as you and I discussed briefly—or I will create that all-in-one spaceship and sub I mentioned. The first is much quicker to realize, and less expensive, but could ultimately prove to be a failure."

"Oh. And, the second one?"

Tom took a deep breath. "It is difficult to say, but it is my real choice for this mission. I just have to crack the problems with both the outward sucking of the vacuum of space and the inward crushing of the deepest part of the oceanic atmosphere."

"Oceanic? New word?"

"Maybe not a common word, but an acceptable one for anything having to do with an ocean."

They discussed several of Tom's ideas with Peter Quintana especially excited about the combined vessel one that could be built at Enterprises or on Fearing Island in four to six sections, assembled in low Earth orbit in just a matter of days after being carried into that position atop *Goliath*, Tom's giant repelatron-powered lifting ship, and then flown out to the position of the small black hole that normally powered the *TranSpace Dart* where it would be "attached" and used to get them out and back on the trip to Neptune.

"If I were to place a bet on that solution, what odds should I be looking for, Tom?"

The inventor grinned. Not a wagering man, he nonetheless understood the "odds" reference.

"Oh, I'd go for nothing less than two-to-one odds or perhaps even odds. Unless, that is, somebody attaches a timeframe to the bet. The real issue is the work necessary, the time to get there, explore and come back, and still have me home in time for the birth so Bash doesn't stab me in my sleep!"

His smile told the politician he wasn't serious, but Peter knew how wives could be when they are expecting and the husband has what he believes to be rational other commitments. Nothing to an about-to-give-birth woman is more important than having her mate with her.

Nothing! Except the health of the child.

"Well, if I recall what you told me weeks ago, that might mean a delay of only a couple months, so I would not, personally and off the record, be busting a gut over getting out there and back before the birth event."

"Point taken," Tom told him. It was something his own father had said just a week earlier

More importantly, it was something he believed in *100%!*

After the senator signed off and Tom and Bud had a little lunch in the cafeteria, he sat down at his CAD station in the lab next door to the big office and started in on the preliminary design for his combination vessel. But, after adding about two-dozen lines indicating the probable length of the craft he stopped.

All that spaceships need to do is hold air. They can be any shape as witnessed by my Challenger, he thought. *Submarines, on the*

other hand, need to slice or press their way through liquids and for this one that means liquids from very thin and almost gassy to very thick and almost sludgy. Hmmm?

But, the more he though about the thick ocean part the more he felt he was missing or forgetting something. So, he stopped and put his chin in his hands and leaned on the desk to have a good think.

Ten minutes later he was on the phone calling the Swift Observatory in the hills outside of Shopton.

"This is Doctor Slake," the man answering said.

"Doctor, this is Tom Swift. Do you have five or even ten minutes for a discussion on one of the planets in our system?"

"I have a very important experiment to set up for this evening, but that does not need to happen for another two hours plus a few minutes. So, tell me, what planet might we be discussing?"

When the inventor told him it was Neptune, there was a sharp intake of breath.

"Oh, goodness, Tom. That is my pet planet. Please, ask anything!"

After reminding the man of the need for secrecy, Tom told him about the forthcoming mission to the planet. He also suggested it was to be a manned mission that he hoped would include entering the atmosphere and the liquid part of the planet.

"Well, my dear planet eight is an enigma, as you no doubt realize. It is huge by Earth standards but it is a core of something we know zero about surrounded by many kilometers of liquid we know a little about, or at least what is close to the surface of that large body. It is what lies underneath that we have no specific or tangible understanding about."

"That is why this call, sir. You see, my plans are for an expedition that will pierce that liquid surface and go as deep as we can. The sponsoring nations hope we might reach the mantle and bring back samples of what we find, but my fear is that we could get in too deep, as it were. Into too thick a medium to maneuver or to rise from. What thoughts might you offer?"

There was a pause for about a half a minute and Tom thought they might have become disconnected. "Sorry. Just looking at something here in a book on Neptune. Ah, there it is. Okay, let me read this passage to you:

"Neptune is certainly mostly a liquid planet but just as certainly it has a solid core with sufficient gravity to hold the liquid around it in a sphere and not an amorphous blob floating in space. That, in turn indicates a dense core providing sufficient gravity. This liquid state also guarantees us that the core is hot and far more hot than might be indicated otherwise. At its distance from our star, without a hot core that liquid layer would be frozen totally. That says the liquid may not be very thick, deep under the surface, as it would be the transfer medium for the core's heat to keep the surface fluid.'

"That, Tom, is what I think you might find the most useful. Am I correct?"

Tom laughed. "That was exactly what I was wondering about, Doctor. And, I do not know who wrote that piece, but it makes a lot of sense to me. Who, by the way, wrote that and how long ago?"

"That was written by one Johanne Gottfried Galle in nineteen-ott-seven as part of one of his final major papers. He was, if you were not aware of it, the first person to actually view Neptune by telescope and to realize what a momentous occasion it was and what he was viewing... and that was back in the late eighteen-forties!

"He was, by the way, ninety-five at the time he wrote that."

"Gosh!" was all Tom could think to say.

CHAPTER 7 /
THE DESIGN BEGINS IN EARNEST

WITH A MUCH clearer idea of what he might find—but going there *was* the reason to find out who was correct, who was wrong and who was neither one nor the other... right?—on the distant planet, Tom had several new directions he needed to investigate before really getting down to designing a combo-craft.

"You do know," his father cautioned him, "that once you figure out what you want to build, the likelihood of building it in one giant piece here on the ground will become remote. Right?"

Tom grinned. He'd figured that out as soon as his initial idea for a spaceship and submarine hybrid first came to mind. In fact, he had a lot of experience in building things in space or in parts on the ground and assembling them in orbit, so the prospect did not worry him. Quite the opposite; it freed him to build big and not worry about how to get it off the ground and into space.

He had an ace up his sleeve in the giant lifting ship, the *Goliath*.

"So, is it going to be more like a spaceship, or a lot like a submarine?" the older man asked.

"I believe that the need for stability inside both the gaseous atmosphere and the liquid one is pointing me toward a long, narrow and tall shape of a sub, Dad. In space it doesn't matter a lot, but we have no idea about any under surface currents we might come up against. One of the last things I want is for the ship to begin to roll so the knife shape ought to help keep us upright and heading straight."

Damon looked a little amused as he asked, "And what will drive this space sub through the uncharted, umm, waters of Neptune? Propellers? Worm drive? Giant oars and a team of strong men to pull them?"

Tom had to think. He honestly had not gotten to that point in his considerations, but now realized he did need to understand what that was to be before getting too far into the design.

He admitted as much to his father.

"Well, for my money propellers may be too unreliable as your primary propulsion source. They require some sort of seal that could disintegrate under the pressure and frigid cold you'll encounter. Then, too, they need to be lubricated and the same sub-zero conditions work against that."

The enigmatic grin on his son's face told the older inventor there was something he had not considered that Tom had.

"What?" was his single word question.

"The truth?"

"Always."

"Okay then, I have absolutely no idea. But, I had considered and almost immediately tossed out the prop idea. Perhaps even the worm drive as I am not certain what it might do to the gas mixture. It certainly can't be used in the upper atmosphere, but then again, what might work in both? Repelatrons? I kind of doubt it because unless I want this thing to weigh the proverbial ton, so it sinks, there would be nothing to press against!"

Their discussion had to end as Tom had an appointment with Doc Simpson for his semiannual cranial exam. Given that the young man had suffered no fewer than fifteen concussions since turning fifteen, and several had been severe enough to require hospitalization, Doc felt a good exam and test of Tom's comprehension and memory would help show up any potentially long-lasting problems before they became major.

As he walked out the doors on the ground floor of the Administration building, Tom ran into George Dilling, Director of Communications for all the Swift companies.

"Morning, Tom. If you have about two minutes I need to ask you something. More along the lines of a favor."

Tom stopped. "George, you've always had time for me, so sure. What can I do?"

George nodded his acknowledgement that Tom would grant him his favor.

"We, or rather I, made a rather large goof in that last satellite we spec'd out for the worldwide network. The one you took up to replace the westernmost of the three satellites that mad man in southern China shot down. You see," and he paused to take a look around, "when I did the power consumption figures I transposed two numbers. Kind of significant as the available power is about to start to drop and I fear my making point-nine-two into point-two-nine is going to start to impact its mission and perhaps controllability."

He had expected Tom to either be a little miffed or at least philosophical, but George did not expect outright laughter.

"Can I inquire why the mirth at what might be a very costly mistake on my part?"

Tom nodded. "You may. You see, I spotted that mistake when I was doing a last run through of the programming and believed it was my oversight, so I fixed it before we ever took the satellites up and dropped them off from the *Challenger*."

George let out a sigh of relief. "You can't begin to understand how much better that makes me feel, and also how much a fool I feel for the mistake in the first place."

"Ah, but I can, George. I can. You see, I've lost track of all the times I've transposed numbers or written the wrong word down on a spec when I've been working myself too hard. I know we all went into double overtime mode when we had to get the sats up ASAP so the whole of Southeast Asia could have a good connection to the world. Don't sweat it, and if it happens again, just come to me or dad. We both share our goofs freely with each other and then just get on with the job of fixing things."

They parted with a firm handshake, and Tom headed for the back of the next building over where Doc had his Dispensary.

"Ah, there you are and only five minutes late," Doc greeted him on looking up from some paperwork when Tom breezed into the lobby.

"Had a short chat with one of our senior execs, but I'm only..." and Tom looked at his watch, turning a shade of red, "oh... I see that I'm actually a half hour late. Sorry, Doc. I guess I got out of the office later than I thought."

The medico shrugged. "Not an issue as it turns out. I'll just have the nurse bring in the syringe with the large *square* needle for any shots I need to give you."

Tom gulped. "Yeah... nope!"

Doc smiled. "Okay then, come on and let's get you into the exam cubicle." Together, they walked down the hall about fifty feet and into a curtained-off small room where Tom took a seat on the foot of the table.

"You've been through most of this before, but I have a new picture scenario. You've gotten far too good at remembering what the old one has in it. So, let's start with the basic finger maneuvers."

Tom held up both hands, fingers spread, and in turn touched his thumbs to his little fingers, the ring finders, middle and finally the index fingers before reversing the order. He did this five times never missing a finger touch.

Doc smiled and noted his success.

Next he had Tom grab onto his index and middle fingers and

squeeze followed by Doc holding around the inventor's fingers and Tom trying to spread them open.

Another success and another positive notation.

He asked Tom to watch as he moved his index fingers slowly around and then told him to match his movements and then touch fingertips. Every touch was perfect.

There were stand and balance tasks and a page with about a dozen line drawings of different, every day objects Tom had to identify. To mess with the physician, he identified the final object, a feather, as a, "bright red convertible Mercedes Benz automobile."

"Smart guy!" Doc declared and noted another complete success. When he pulled out the final describe-the-picture page, Tom laughed.

"Okay, I'm seeing a small boy, probably eight or nine standing on a kitchen stool that is falling over. His little sister is standing there looking horrified and also holding out her hand to take a cookie he was obviously trying to get from the jar on the top shelf all the while his mother is oblivious to the fact he is about to crack his skull on the counter as she dries dishes from a sink that is overflowing because she didn't shut the water off. And, I think the sister might have kicked at the stool to knock her brother over. She looks like that sort of brat. How did I do?"

With a shake of his head, Doc made a big tick mark on his papers and looked at Tom. "You did fine. I am happy to report, other than your next scheduled MRI at Shopton General next year that you seem none the worse for all the cracks your own skull has taken, kitchen counters notwithstanding."

"Great. So, I'm good to go?"

"Good to go, Tom. And, I am also pleased to tell you it has been more than twenty-three months since your last cranial encounter with a solid object. Keep it up for the rest of your life and I don't see you suffering anything, or at least in the foreseeable future. Just try to avoid those sort of things, please?"

Tom smiled. "Sure. Whenever I can, Doc."

As the inventor left, Greg Simpson took a look at the picture and laughed. "By golly, I've never spotted that the boy is going to hit his head on that counter!"

"How did the check go?" Trent asked as Tom passed his desk on the way into the office.

Stopping, he answered, "Doc says I'm fine as long as I duck the next few times someone takes a swing at my head with a brick! Thanks for asking."

As Tom was reaching for the door he stopped, did an about faceand headed down the hall to the large lab.

Maybe Doc missed something, because I knew I needed to get back to the design, so why did I head for the office, he asked himself as he unlocked the door and stepped inside.

He sat down, looked at what he had and picked up three of the pages prepared to wad them up, but instead he set them to the side.

For the rest of the day, other than to join Bud for lunch brought into the lab by Chow, he sat and drew design after design sketch. None of them were very detailed, but they each showed some shape or dimensional aspect he believed might end up in the final craft.

Most kept with the theme of a more traditional, 1940's or 1950's style diesel-powered boat. Something meant to run on the surface at top speed and then to dive when necessary. None were like the more torpedo-shaped nuclear subs from recent decades. Still and all, Tom's were futuristic and not historical.

Before heading home he sat back and looked at the eighteen pages on his drafting table. As he did the thought hit him that it might be nice, and helpful, to have them all in the computer where he could electronically overlay them, or parts of them, until he could come up with a more concrete design.

He made a note to call Hank about that the next day, and went home.

When he did make that call it was to hear Hank laugh so hard he started to cough.

"Oh, skipper, if you only knew! Two days ago I received a new CAD application that pretty much does that. I've been trying to practice, but it means I have to draw some things that might work together first and that is really slowing me down. Come on over when you get a chance and bring your pages."

"I'm free right now if you have the time."

"Then, come on over. I'll start a fresh pot of coffee."

Tom breezed into the large workspace that was Hank's main room. Surrounding it were six offices where he and his five assistants had their desks, but most days three to five of them were at the various work surfaces in the big room.

"Those show much detail?" the engineer asked before Tom handed them over.

"Some do and some don't. I've hit the point where I need to start combining some aspects into something I can then use to move on, but haven't been able to get up the gumption to do that. Of course, I only started this yesterday, strictly in my defense you understand."

Hank smiled and nodded. "Of course. So, let's spread these out and take a look."

He did on a worktable topped with a solid surface material made from chips of granite and epoxy. It had been wiped absolutely clean before Tom arrived. On one side sat two mugs of steaming coffee.

"I see you are revisiting the submarines of the Second World War," he commented.

Tom told him about the forthcoming trip to Neptune and his reasons for the shape.

"I can see that now. Thanks for the added info. Well, I believe we may need to darken in a few details on these before scanning them in, but I see no reason you and I can't get that done in the next half hour. Grab a stool while I get my pencils."

In practically no time at all they had the pages ready and were feeding them into the scanner attached directly to the CAD computer. One by one they appeared on screen in full and then became miniatures forming a grid from which they could be selected.

Hank showed him how to select a full drawing to be the base for adding to and changing around and how to then switch out for a different base while maintaining the current additions, and several other functions. Tom was a quick study and was working his designs within the hour.

"Did you want me to head back to my own space to do this or can I stay here?" he asked his host.

"I think wherever you feel the most comfortable and most productive. I have to go set up something in one of the 3D printers, but will be happy so sit and help the rest of the day."

By the time he'd returned, Tom had his chosen basic design enhanced with elements from eleven of the others and was starting to become enthusiastic about what he was seeing.

"You know," he said once Hank was sitting next to him again, "I almost believe I could print this off, take my own set of colored pencils back out and use it as my springboard to move along with some greater ideas that are banging around in my head. Thoughts?"

"One of the things I didn't tell you about, yet, is the sketchpad capabilities. Here," he said bringing out a flat drawing tablet about fifteen inches diagonally along with an electronic pen. "This lets you draw over your design in any of sixteen hundred different colors and shades, identify specific colors as being things like external features, internal items, et cetera. You can move forward and backward through your work and it only gets added to the original once you tell it to dedicate what you've done. Even then, you can still peel away any of the new stuff you want. It's a pretty flexible program and seems to work the way we all like to around here."

"It really looks easier than I thought once you told me about it," Tom replied, smiling at the big engineer.

"So, did you want to do more work on this here, or at your desk?"

Tom decided to continue where he was for an hour or so before he would pack things up, make the file transfer, and head back to the large lab.

As he added more drawing elements and removed some of the older stuff he did a few spot checks to see that the entire history was there. He even jumped back about seventeen minutes to check how accurate the saved interim files were, but grinned on realizing this was foolish. *Of course* they would be exactly what he had done and that was saved automatically every minute.

About ninety minutes later he finally sat back, sighed and hit the **SAVE** button. The file name came on screen and he wrote it down.

"Do I need anything else to run with this?" he asked.

Hank came over and shook his head. "Nope! Just the password I put in the system and that is Rumplestiltskin with a capital R and the two i letters are the number one. That will be active through tomorrow but I'll be changing it on Thursday morning. I'll get the new password to you before then."

When he got back to his CAD computer in the lab, Tom called up the file and was pleased to see that along with the master image all of the interim images were still there to be checked and recalled if needed, even from a remote location.

He spent the rest of the day before Bud came in at five to remind him the Swifts were having dinner at the Barclays that evening. "You and Bash are expected at 6:30, so skedaddle in a few and get yourself all pretty. I'm almost certain Bash is already pretty, smells a lot nicer than you or me, and is tapping her toe waiting for her faithful Tom to come home to her. So, go!"

"Before I do, want to see what I'm working on?"

Bud hesitated. His natural curiosity was thumping him of one shoulder while his hopes to not get on his or Tom's wives bad side by them being late was smacking him hard on the other.

"How about tomorrow?" he suggested also telling Tom of his desire to not be late.

Tom grinned and nodded.

"I bow to your impeccable logic, flyboy!"

At dinner Sandy casually asked about the Neptune trip. "Daddy says you are going out there to see what is all the way under those thousands of miles of... Oh!" She had seen the clouding of Bashalli's face at the mention of one of the dangers of such a trip. "Oops! Sorry for the big mouth, Bashi. I'm certain, as is daddy, that Tom has everything well thought out and it will be a slam-dunk. Right, Bud?" she asked looking to her husband for support.

What she found was a red face and no eye contact. Finally, he took a steady breath and said, "What my ill-informed wife is getting at, Bash, is that the trip is going to be no worse than a dive in the Pacific Ocean, just a lot colder." Having not actually talked over all of the inventor's intensions, Bud was shooting in the dark, so to speak when he mentioned the unusual heat in the planet's core.

"Well, yes," Tom said. "Any planet that far away from the sun ought to be frozen solid after these millions and billions of years. But, the ocean-like surface of Neptune is still a liquid. Made from icy gases to be sure, but it is liquid. And, as Bud said, the core is believed to be blistering hot, enough to keep all that liquid above it from freezing solid. So, I suppose the idea of this being no more than a submarine dive into the deep part of the Pacific is mostly accurate."

Everyone looked at Bashalli. She was siting there, arms crossed over her chest, staring straight ahead, but she shrugged and turned to face Tom.

"If you promise to be back in time for the baby, then I need to believe you. Right?" She looked at Bud and Sandy. They nodded. "Okay then, it is settled. Bashalli will not worry unduly about this because it is just like a little dip in the ocean. Except, the ocean is how many gazillion miles away from me?" Now, tears threatened to form in her eyes.

Tom patted her hand. "Hardly even two-point-eight billion. And the trip Bud and I took out to Eris to put that planet back together a couple years ago was twice that. Don't worry, Bash. Nothing is going to keep me from being with you when the baby comes. Even if the trip needs to be put off until after that, I'll be there holding your hand like before, and having you squeeze the life out of my fingers, just like both times before!"

She looked a little sad before that changed to mischief.

"Tom. Do you not understand that a good squeeze of her husband's fingers is a woman's way of telling him how much she loves him and is happy they are sharing the moment together?"

"And, it isn't to punish him for the pain, temporary as it is, she is feeling and wants him to also suffer?"

"Of course not. How silly of you to suggest that." She blushed slightly at her little white lie.

Yeah, Tom thought. *Silly old me!*

CHAPTER 8 /
WHEN IS A SUB NOT A SUB?

THE CONVERSATION did not return to anything approaching free and easy and so once dessert had been eaten, Tom and Bashalli said their goodnights and departed.

"Sometimes, Bud, I swear you ought to just reach over and punch me in the mouth and shut me up. I'm sure I made Bashi miserable and that is about the last thing she needs right now." She looked helplessly at her husband. "So, what do I do to atone?"

"San, I will never punch you except in jest and only in the upper arm, and you know that. As for Bash and how she feels, yes, your words were not well thought out, but they weren't malicious, so give it until tomorrow afternoon then give her a call. Take her to The Glass Cat for a decaf coffee and one of her brother's incredible pastries. Then, beg forgiveness like crazy and promise her you are her very best friend and will stand by her. Only," and he appeared to be thinking over his recent statement, "don't put emphasis on standing by her when Tom and I are away. Okay?"

"Yep! And, I'll be honest with her about asking you to give me a good slug. I think that will bring her pretty smile out 'cause that might be how she feels about me right now."

Bud kissed her and nodded. "That's my girl!"

When Sandy called the next late morning, Bashalli was taking the two kids for a walk and the nanny, Amanda, answered.

"I don't know what to say, Mrs. Swift-Barclay. Bashalli was in a good mood this morning when we had breakfast with Bart and Mary, and she seemed to be happy when they left a half hour ago. Want me to have her call you when they get back?"

"Yes, please. Tell her one of Moshan's pastries with her name on it is waiting for her. Thanks!"

Twenty-three minutes later her smart watch pinged and the message, "Yes, please!" scrolled across the face. With a smile, she texted back, "When?" and received the almost immediate answer, "10 minutes!"

When she parked about five spaces down from the shop, Bashalli was already standing there, waiting for her. As Sandy approached, Tom's wife ran into her arms and begged to be forgiven.

"I was such a spoiled brat last night and feeling sorry for myself. I should not have reacted to your statements. I am so sorry!"

Giving her sister-in-law a good, firm hug Sandy stepped back.

"No, Bashi. It's me who needs to apologize. I spoke without thinking which seems about par for this course." Then, as they turned to walk into The Glass Cat she had to explain what "par for this course" meant.

They stood in line behind a woman who seemed to be having great difficulty selecting the final pastry for the box of one dozen she was purchasing. Sandy leaned forward and said in the woman's right ear, "I'd get another of the chocolate smothered cream filled if I were you. I don't know anyone who can say no to one of those."

The woman, about forty, turned to face Sandy. As she did she patted her rather ample hips. "That, my dear, is the trouble. I can't resist them myself. But, to try to live up to the latest diet I am embarking on this week, how about if I buy you that one and let your friend—Oh! Hello, Bashalli. I haven't seen you in here for absolutely ages. I hear from your brother you've had a little boy."

"Yes, Mrs. Douglas, and a little girl and another one on the way," she answered looking down at her barely larger tummy.

In the end Bashalli agreed to let the woman give Sandy the discussed pastry while she opted for a cherry Danish.

"I have missed you around here," a rather large, dark man announced as he came out from the kitchen. Bashalli rushed around the counter to give her brother a hug and a kiss on his cheek—as soon as he remembered to lean down to be within range. "And, how are you today, Sandra?" he asked.

"Kind of craving some of your incredible pastries, Moshan. You're looking good. How is Angela working out?" she asked tilting her head to the young woman helping the next customer in line.

He grinned. "Excellent both here and in my life."

This was an amazing proclamation as he had been very against his little sister even dating Tom—a non-Pakistani—all those years ago, and here he was with an Irish woman for a girlfriend. He soon had to get back to his latest puff pastries and said his good-byes before the two women headed for a small table at the window.

There, they discussed the forthcoming baby and the trip. Even Bashalli had to admit it did not sound very dangerous as there was nothing to tell either of them that Neptune was anything but a distant planet.

* * * *

"Okay, flyboy. You said yesterday we could talk about this new project today. Still up for it?"

Bud nodded knowing that if he did not, Tom would bug him about it because Tom loved sharing his designs. "Sure."

"Great. So, riddle me this... When is a submarine not exactly a submarine, Bud?" The two young men were sitting in the big office in the conference area enjoying a late morning cup of coffee.

The flyer raised his left hand. "I know this one. When it is a door — no, wait. That's not right. It's when is a door not a *door*... when it's a jar." He looked at Tom. "Does a jar have anything to do with your question?"

Tom's eyes rolled and he gave an exasperated huff. "Not the jar thing, Bud. Concentrate and think. If I am going to build a submarine that goes up, or out, to Neptune, when is it not exactly a submarine?"

The flyer's face scrunched up in thought and then he smiled. "Do you mean when it is a spaceship?"

"Bingo! You got it, Bud. Well done."

He was finishing that as Chow wheeled his lunch cart into the office.

"Well done, huh? Wahl, I'm afeared I don't go anythin' today that can be made well done, 'cept if ya tell me ta take away these meatloaf burgers on freshly baked buns an' bring ya some steaks." He looked expectantly at them and then laughed. "Just kiddin'. Yer gonna eat what I brung ya or ya can go to see that mad Russian in the main dining hall."

He set out the two covered plates. "Come 'n get it! And, don't you say nuthin' about my meatloaf, Bud. You know... heck, we *all* know, that it is one o' your favorites!"

Bud, who had had a habit of teasing the old chuck wagon cook had lightened up his attacks in the past couple of years. With Chow now in his sixties, the flyer felt he deserved a little more respect.

As he scooped up the savory burger Bud nodded. "You know something, Chow? You are absolutely correct. I love your meatloaf. I only wish that you giving the recipe to Sandy might have translated into her being able to make it this good." He took a huge bite and smiled around it as a little juice leaked out the corners of his mouth and ran down his chin.

Chow took off his ball cap and scratched his head. "I cain't figger out why your filly has such a time with my recipes."

Tom swallowed and responded, "Sandy has never paid attention to much of anything except for her flying studies and procedures. Mom tried to teach her how to crochet... no go. Knitting? Nope!

Sewing? Let us all laugh at that idea. Cooking? Not so you'd notice it which is why Bud here is getting a little larger around the middle from all the take out food they have at home."

Once they finished and Chow had taken away the dishes, the flyer turned to Tom. "So, I assume this submarine riddle has to do with the Neptune trip, and then does that mean you have decided definitely to make this a one-ship thing?"

"Yes, it does. One ship once it is constructed in space, that is. It will also mean a few trips up with *Goliath*."

Bud looked puzzled. He had not been in on any of the discussion about building the ship in pieces, so he asked about it.

"Well," came Tom's explanation, "I haven't made up my mind about the close in maneuvering, but I am going to try to use our friendly, neighborhood micro black hole to yank us out there. That means we have to find a way off this planet and Neptune that might or might not be repelatrons, but one thing is clear to me. We need to do final construction in orbit like we did with the *Sutter* and our space stations. I can see a submarine soaring up through the liquid and very thin gas atmosphere of Neptune but not through our thick air. Too much friction."

"But," Bud asked, curious, "not out there?"

Now, Tom looked as if he were not certain. "I'm not sure, Bud, but for ease of build and speed of the entire project, we make the sub/spacecraft in something like five sections, lift them filled with breathable atmosphere in most areas on the *Goliath*, assemble and bring one final ship up with the extra air we will need. My best estimates show we can start with the basic stuff within a few weeks."

"After, of course, a test model?"

Tom nodded. "Yes. After that." He lifted his right index finger telling Bud to hold on. After that he tapped his TeleVoc pin and silently stated, "Arvid Hanson."

Within seconds his pin *pinged* inside his head.

"Yeah, skipper? What can I do for you?"

"I have the germination of a new project in Hanks' new CAD program. Familiar with it?"

"Sure am. So?"

Tom told him it was in regards the Neptune trip and his idea for the combination craft.

"Do you have something complete enough for me to look at yet? I can get a start on a few things like what goes inside, just as long as you can tell me what needs to be tested. Should I come over?"

"Yes. I'll be ready for you in the big lab."

When Tom disconnected his call, Bud said he was about to need to leave. "Unless, you can give me a quick peek at what Arv is going to see."

When the inventor showed his friend the basic shape and all indications of systems, Bud nearly choked.

"Jetz! No." he changed his mind, "Make that double Jetz!! with a couple exclamation marks to boot. That… well, that's beautiful. And that is going to be both space-worthy as well as submersible in all that deep pressure?"

"I hope so, but I'm going to build a one-man mini version of it and take that down into the Mariana Trench to test its pressure resistance. And, sorry but this can't be a two-man job or else it'll take far too long to produce and transportation would be a bugger."

Bud looked at his friend and knew there would be an argument at some point when Tom's own father put his foot down and insisted one of the test pilots or aquanauts would be the one to test the sub and possibly risk their lives, not Tom's.

The model maker arrived right as Bud was just leaving. "I'll let you two hammer out the door thing. Bye."

Arv looked at his young boss who shrugged.

"It started out as a riddle that flyboy is evidently not letting go of. So, come take a look."

Tom had his multilayer design on the screen that was turned away from the doorway. Arv sat down in a chair Tom pulled over and was staring at the intricate line art. He kept turning his head to one side then the other until Tom cleared his throat.

"So, I see that as a fifteen or sixteen foot model complete with whatever you plan to power it in the liquid medium on Neptune. My guess is you have the space travel bit covered. I have to ask, what is going to make this slide through what I believe I've read as being very sub-zero icy slush of methane and other nasty stuff?"

A notion had come to the inventor only ten minutes earlier.

"You know how the Jetmarine drive works?"

Arv nodded but scowled. "Sure. Take in a little water, superheat it as you use it to cool the reactor and shoot it out the tubes like a… well, an underwater jet."

The engineer looked back at the screen. "Well, okay. I have all the design notes from the first use of that particular technology, but how the heck do you expect to test it here on Earth?"

"I really don't. What I want to test is the hull strength of something that can head down to the bottom of the Mariana Trench, go partial vacuum inside all except where the single pilot will be, and withstand all that pressure taking readings of about every square inch inside."

Arv let out an amazed whistle.

"Okay, then the question becomes how do you get the frozen slush into the tubes to heat and expel it?"

Tom grinned. "That one has not yet come to me. I have a notion I want to explore, but it will require building a pressure tank filled with liquid methane to test. That's where one of our other departments will need to be brought in. For now, just use the smaller Jetmarine drive to shove the model along."

When Arv left Tom called the manager of the Testing Group. They were responsible for the upkeep and operation of the trio of water test tanks—including one that could be pressurized down to more than a thousand foot depth—the two wind tunnels and several other test facilities around Enterprises. He told the man about the Neptune voyage and what they expected to be able to find under the surface of the liquid gases.

"Sure, skipper. I think we can build a tank that will hold your model and give you liquid methane at enough pressure to make it slushy. Say, about negative three hundred? Oh, and you do understand that as it nears crystallization, methane tends to form hard crystals that some think might be diamonds?"

"I've heard rumors to that effect regarding this trip we are going to take out to Neptune. By any chance do you have any idea if those diamond crystals remain in solid form after coming back up to room temperature?"

"Nobody is certain over here. I have a friend over at MIT who I might check with, although he's pretty smart and might try adding two and two and coming up with someone I work with is going to try going to Neptune or possibly one of Jupiter's moons. Want to test that theory?"

"Not really, Gill. But as a side project, could you perhaps build a small pressure tank and take the methane down another fifty degrees, see if the right crystals build, and then raise the temperature and lower the pressure watching things carefully?"

"Will do. Give me a week and I'll get back with a progress report on the larger pressure tank."

When Gill did call Tom six days later it was to report their small tank experiment had been completed with mixed results.

"We managed to get about ten percent of the crystals that formed somewhere in the one-tenth carat size that stayed when we put things back to normal. However, they only lasted a few hours before either dissolving or vaporizing."

"Meaning they turned back into gaseous methane?" Tom guessed.

"Right. But it was different than when you turn ice into water into steam. These free crystals went straight from room temperature diamonds of near-pure quality, into clear vapor. In seconds I might add. This was no slow over time thing. One minute they were diamonds, five seconds later the chamber we kept them in had a higher level of methane inside."

Tom considered this after the got a brief report on the larger test tank for Arv's model. It might point at the futility of bringing back any of the potential Neptune diamonds, or at least showing a need for a real-time video of the state of them.

"China would love to try to pin something on the western world saying we plotted against them to hide and abscond with the diamonds," Damon stated when Tom reported the experiment results to him that afternoon.

"That is," the older inventor added, "if whatever you find and bring back does not vaporize. Perhaps you just do not tell the world about the diamonds—if they exist—until you have them inside a cryogenic chamber with live video feed."

The younger Swift agreed and said he would make certain they had that ability in the craft.

"Well then, tell me about this test sub Arv is making over in his shop."

"It is going to be nearly fifteen feet long and will use a version of the Jetmarine drive. For now I will be satisfied to test it to the deepest part of the ocean, plus a special test using a partial vacuum inside. Bud is worried about me wanting to take it down with me inside, but what he doesn't know is I've decided we will be going down as a chaperone ship in a full-size Jetmarine."

"Partial vacuum? Tell me more."

Tom explained that by using vacuum to the pressure found in the Earth's atmosphere at sixty thousand feet elevation, he could simulate just about the same pressures the real ship might encounter in the depths of Neptune's ocean.

"At least, from everything I've found about the planet, it looks like we will have a good test. I might like, if we had the time and extra budget, to run out there and drop a probe down to see what the real conditions are, but," he sighed a little sadly, "that is not in the cards."

Not for the first time the inventor was asked why not send a quick probe to the surface and then under and down to at least half the anticipated depth.

Tom smiled, although he looked sad. "We just don't have the time or the money. A probe might cost us a million dollars and then transporting it out there at least two times that. We barely have the funding from the consortium of nations to mount the manned mission."

"Oh. Hmmmm? Well, if Arv is making the model for use in our oceans why can't that do double duty? Then, can't a small crew take the *TranSpace Dart* out there really fast while the real ship is being made?"

Tom had to take this concept in for a moment before answering.

"I honestly have zero idea why we are not doing that, Dad. I'd hoped to get the full-size ship heading out in about two months, but in the meantime that should give us time to get the model out there. I can't go but I can put together a good small crew who can and get back in time to hand off the black hole."

He thought a moment more, then added, "You do know I now have to go and plan for this, right? I mean, I actually have the time to do this without a big hurry and not try to take off with the big ship until after my wife has our third baby. I sort of—"

Damon held up a hand to stop the inventor. "Been there, done that and never even had the opportunity to buy a shirt to commemorate it. I did get the honor and privilege, according to my wife, to be the first one to change you after we got home. She declared a three-day mommy moratorium spending the first day sleeping, the second one at that day spa downtown, and day three she sort of hung around the corners until I fell into an exhausted sleep when she took the baby and spent another day just holding you." He grinned and nodded.

Tom nodded back. Even though Bashalli never wanted to hand off responsibility, those first days of baby one had been hectic and sleepless for mother and father.

They lucked out when Bart decided on day five to get into a rhythm and sleep almost through the night as long as Bashalli gave him a good feed just before he was set down and then rose to change and feed him at around 6:00 am, about half an hour before she would have normally awakened.

Tom excused himself and went back to the big office. There,

Damon was just finishing a phone call. When he hung up he looked up at Tom and smiled.

"You might have been a good one to have for that, but Pete Quintana called to say the U.S.A. is kicking in an additional fifteen million dollars. He suggested it might be prudent, and the President agrees, to send an unmanned probe first to sort of dip a toe into the icy ocean and see what you will encounter. Thoughts?"

Tom smiled. "You know, a little bird suggested the model Arv is building should be transported out there and allowed to race around collecting data on the ocean conditions. I'm inclined to agree and this new money makes it all possible!"

They were about to discuss the logistics when the company wide announcement system blared:

"Warning! Incoming missile on track to impact in southern area of grounds. All personnel, regardless of location, take cover!"

CHAPTER 9 /
IT'S AN ATTACK!... SORT OF

AN EXPLOSION rocked the building almost sending Tom to the floor. He managed to catch a hold on his father's desk and rode out what felt like a 7.0 earthquake lasting just a second.

Within a minute, the tightly defined procedures for reporting when anything such as this was—obvious to Tom—attack occurred and calls began flooding into the system. Rather than make managers wait, the computerized system took their input from their phone's numeric keypad. Press "1" and you were reporting no significant damages to either personnel or your facility. Press "2" and you had notable damage to property. "3" said you had personnel injured and the computer would dispatch company medical personnel.

This went all the way to "0" which indicated your building had either collapsed or suffered nearly catastrophic damage.

All reports came in—with the exception of the runway inspectors—rated at either 1, 2 or 3.

When everything had been tallied, only seven people had injuries ranging from a broken elbow from a fall down several stairs to a few sprained fingers or wrists.

Property damage was mostly of the "something fell off a shelf" variety other than the closest runway to the building cluster, which had taken the hit. And, although not a direct hit, about 70% of the way from west to the east side of Enterprises, there was an impact crater some fifty feet across and twenty feet deep that had taken a crescent chunk out of the runway.

There were no other incoming objects and no indication exactly where this one originated other than to say it had come from the east and possibly as far as the coast.

"Could it have been a missile launched from a submarine?" Tom wondered out loud as he and his father sat talking to Harlan in the big office twenty minutes later.

The other two men turned to face him, their faces masks of seriousness.

Finally, Harlan spoke. "We are waiting to get the FAA computer files for the period starting about one hour before the explosion along with a Coast Guard report on any contacts their **RADAR** stations may have picked up, even if briefly."

"Okay. We're heading up to the old control room to take a look. If you need us out there, TeleVoc either of us."

Tom and his father raced from the office, down the hall and up the stairs to the third floor. From there they retraced their steps down this upper hallway until Tom stopped in front of a locked door, keyed in a 6-digit code and the two men headed up the first flight of straight stairs before taking the next set of spiral ones to the nearly empty room.

Sitting on the lone table were a pair of Tom's Digital BigEyes, a vastly superior way of looking at things over any pair of binoculars.

Tom handed them to his father. Enterprises was, after all, *his* dream installation.

Taking a look at the close view of the crater, Damon sighed. "Well, at least there is only a small level of damage to the actual runway. Take a look," he suggested handing the BigEyes to Tom.

"Yep. Looks like after a good brush down most aircraft could land there in an emergency. Good thing you thought to build so many alternates including the longer parallel one farther out. Now, I wonder who launched that missile!"

Neither had to wait or think too much longer before both their TeleVoc pins *pinged* them with an automated message from Trent telling them they were needed in the office.

When they approached his desk, the secretary nodded to the door. "You both have an emergency call from Admiral Hopkins."

They entered and sat in the conference area before pressing the phone button.

"Admiral. It's Damon and Tom here."

The man audibly sighed. "Oh. Good. Only not so good. Did you take a hit from a missile or something a little bit ago?"

Damon explained they had and asked why the interest.

"Okay. I owe you both so many times over that I am going to break secrecy protocols and tell you that it was one of ours that went wild."

"I see... only I do not. What about safety measures and self-destructs?"

"That was the first of a new breed of rockets launched from our submarines carrying something meant to go into orbit. I take it the thing exploded on contact? And, by all the gods, real and imagined, tell me nobody was hurt." He almost sounded as if he were pleading with the last part.

"We have significant damage to a runway but all personnel are reported to be safe. A few broken and sprained parts, but nothing they will not recover from. Other than the emotional damage this may have caused some."

"I see. Well, the Navy is good for repairs and any medical. Now, what I am about to tell you is for your ears only. Well, maybe your Harlan Ames needs to also know. Anyway, that was a monopropellant rocket with a payload of a satellite I cannot talk about, featuring another five gallons of monopropellant... hydrazine. Once launched it was supposed to head due east and reach orbit five minutes later with the main rocket releasing the payload and self-destructing as it re-entered the atmosphere."

"Which it obviously did *none* of," Tom stated, audibly annoyed.

"Right. It headed up then doubled back and our self-destruct sequence failed. We lost track of it but had enough tracking info to tell it was going to come down in the upper part of your state. I'm so sorry it hit your place. Damn it! The explosion you got was likely the last of the rocket's propellant and the hydrazine from the satellite."

"Do we have anything like nuclear batteries to worry about?"

"None. Totally solar powered if it had deployed properly. I'm coming up later today to inspect the damage and to file a report stating this was a failure that cannot be repeated or even chanced ever again."

They spoke another minute before the Admiral said he needed to arrange transportation up and would likely be there in four hours.

It took the Navy man and his pilot—he arrived not in a transport jet but a sleek fighter jet with only room for the two of them—a little over three hours to get there and when Tom and Damon met him at the civilian terminal it was not because they wanted to make him endure a longer ride to their office; it was because it was strategically slightly less than one mile from the impact crater.

"Uhh, yeah," Hopkins replied wearily when told they would be driving straight to the impact point. "We saw the damage coming in on the parallel runway. This is not one of either the Navy's or my finest hours, Damon and Tom. Commander," he said turning to his pilot, "go ahead and find a comfortable seat in the terminal. I think once I get the ground-level tour we'll be back here for our meeting."

"Yes, sir!" the man responded snapping a crisp salute to his commanding officer.

"And, while we are on Swift soil, please dispense with the military rigmarole. Thank you." He turned back to his hosts and they walked to the sedan Damon had driven out in.

Standing next to the closest debris to the actual hole, the Admiral let out a mighty sigh, removing his cap and running his right hand over his damp head.

"I know apologies are insufficient where lives might have been lost, and so let me tell you what I need to do. First," and he fished his smart phone from his jacket pocket, "I need to get a series of all-around shots of the hole."

Tom reached over. "I can do that pretty fast, sir, and then we can get onto your second item."

With a nod, the phone exchanged hands and Tom was asked to get shots from about every 10-degrees around the entire perimeter, including the blast debris. He was back with his father and Admiral Hopkins in three minutes.

"That was fast. So, I need to get right at the edge and see if I can spot any remaining materials from that rocket or payload." The three men carefully walked over the strewn rocks and dirt and asphalt chunks to get a good look down into the hole.

"There!" he said pointing at the twisted wreckage of something metal near the center of the hole.

As the two Swifts looked, they spotted something that might have been the protective cowling around the satellite, except this was so far from being able to protect anything it looked ridiculous. Showing both some of the original white paint as well as a lot of scorching, what had likely been about three feet across the bottom and a few inches at the top was now nearly torn in two pieces, neither of which would ever be able to be hammered out into any recognizable shape.

"It looks a little like a bomb crater," Tom commented causing the other two men to nod.

"Fortunately, the damage can be repaired," Damon started before looking pointedly at the Admiral. For his part, Admiral Hopkins nodded. "And, if this is a demonstration of the destructive power of hydrazine, then it isn't as bad as the manufacturer would like us to believe. It also, Admiral, is nowhere as powerful as the safer monopropellant Tom developed a couple years ago. But, enough about that. Let's go talk about what happened."

Once they were seated in the terminal building and had been joined by the Navy Commander/Pilot who was also part of the Admiral's staff, Damon got down to business demanding to know everything about the rocket so he might help figure out why it failed so spectacularly.

From what he and Tom could be told, it seemed the Navy brass had played fast and loose with safety.

"Just how can anyone agree to allow a missile or rocket—an unproven one at that!—go up with a self-destruct that would only activate once the rocket was either above fifty thousand feet or below two hundred if it were crashing?" Tom demanded to know. It was obvious by his face and harsh tone he was now angry.

In a more subdued tone than either of the Swifts had ever heard the man speak, the Admiral answered, "Our people believed that was the only way to safeguard the satellite falling into the wrong hands if the launch were not totally successful. It assumed, wrongly as it turns out, that the rocket would keep on the planned trajectory and not turn nearly one hundred and eighty degrees as it faltered and ultimately failed.

"It was, by the way, that lower altitude destruct setting that kept it from doing more damage. My guess, if anyone had a camera on that spot a second before impact, they would see the payload destructing and burning off a lot of that monopropellant above the ground. I can only assume from the lack of much debris down there the top of the rocket separated from the lower part at some earlier point and that means we have to go find those remains."

Father and son looked at one another and both rolled their eyes. It was an expression the Admiral missed but his pilot did not. He knew they were in for some slow flying reconnaissance in the next hour or two before they could head back to DC.

As his look of concern registered with Damon, he offered, "We can, of course, refuel your jet so you can take the more scenic route going back."

While he had not meant it to be dismissive, the Admiral took it as an opportunity to close with a repeat of his promise to pay for all damages and repairs.

"Just send me an estimate and I'll get an appropriation's check signed and sent."

A fuel truck was called and eighteen minutes later, now fully topped up, the jet restarted and headed for the far runway. It was in the air two minutes later turning to the direct east for the start of the search.

Back in the office Damon called the Facilities manager and asked her for an estimate on repairs and clean up.

"If you need until tomorrow to get things together, that's fine," he told her.

She laughed. "Oh, Damon. When do things like this take days instead of minutes or even an hour? I ask you. So, the truth is that once I saw you and the Navy brass leave the site I hightailed it out there and did a survey. Laser range finders are wonderful. Anyway, I can have a crew out there to remove the stuff blown out and, unless you say differently, shove it into the hole and compact the heck out of it before calling in for more gravel and rebar, and the welders and the concrete folks."

"That's great, Margie, but do you have a cost for me. I promised to get that to our Navy brass soon so he can get a check coming up to us."

She named the cost and he wrote it down.

"Can you give me a list of what that covers, please?"

She promised to have that in his email in box within the hour.

When he hung up, Tom looked over. "How much, of does she not know yet?"

"One hundred-nineteen thousand dollars and we'll forgive the Government the three hundred dollars and a few cents."

Tom nodded. He wanted to ask about the schedule, but his father beat him to it.

"Eleven days until we get that portion of the runway re-certified."

"Gosh, Dad. What a coincidence. That is the day Arv and everyone else involved tell me we can take the model space sub out for a deep sea trial."

Damon chuckled. "So, it is officially a space sub?" He raised one eyebrow.

Tom shrugged. "Best I could come up with until I find a good name for it. For *her*." He knew of the long-standing tradition of naming ships after women in the civilian world, and after famous persons or locations in the military side of things. And, this was going to be anything *but* a military operation!

"In fact, now I think about it I should go look in on them and see what the status really is. If I know Arv, his schedule was padded out and he might now tell me it will be ready tomorrow. I'll let you know."

With that the younger inventor left the office.

"How about tomorrow?" the model maker asked with a straight face when Tom wondered out loud if the schedule had not been a little slack.

Now, Tom was stunned. "Uhhh... *what?*"

Arv laughed. "Your dad called while you were on the way over and suggested I tease you with that. But, honestly, we are way ahead and should have things ready for the pressure tank here at Enterprises in three days. That includes the Jetmarine drives, all three of them."

"Three?"

"Sure. One on each side and one underneath to give a bit more shove to get everything thorough the slush out there."

"Okay. Sure," Tom told him. "I still have to figure out how to avoid having the slush, as you call it, seize up under the additional pressure of the drive pumps. Or, to freeze solid inside the pumps."

"You aren't going to believe it, but Bud had a suggestion that I honestly could not dismiss. He asked me if there was going to be room for a heated mesh or something at the opening to sort of melt the slush and make things run through smoothly." Arv looked at Tom who was now grinning. "Anything in that?"

"Oh, absolutely, Arv. In fact," he said looking upward as if imagining such a system, "I can see just how that is going to work. We'll use tubes at the intakes that are also cooling vanes for the reactor. Whether in space or in the slush—and I like that term all of a sudden—they will keep things cool inside the reactor while warming up what we want to ingest and shove back out once we get there. Actually, and don't tell the flyboy I said this, but it's a brilliant solution!"

"Are you going to tell him or is this to be a big surprise?"

"I haven't made up my mind. I just don't want him to take this as a sign he can start pumping out the pun names for our final space sub."

Arv smiled. "I like that... space sub. TSSS? Tom Swift's Space Submarine?"

The inventor shook his head. "Probably not that, Arv." He told the man about some of his other suspicions the flyer might try out. "I'm going to be looking into something either historical or just plain clever. Maybe both."

Arv rubbed the back of his neck. "You could always honor your darling wife and call it the TSS Bashalli." He smiled to show he was only a little serious.

The inventor shook his head a second time. "As soon as I announced that Sandy would be all over our father to name something after her. Like the *Pigeon Sandra*, or perhaps the Sandy

Coupe 1000 from the MotorCar Company!"

They both chuckled about it but also both men knew that Sandy could be both a very supportive woman as well as a somewhat jealous one.

After Tom left him, Arv walked to the office of Linda Ming, Enterprises' expert at miniaturizing electronics.

"Got a minute?" he asked the Chinese woman.

She looked up and smiled. "For something fun and exciting or another mundane, 'Now can we make the repelatrons the size of a playing card running for a year on a small watch battery?'"

The model maker was a little stunned. "Uhh, can we?"

Her smile said nothing, but she replied, "I might be keeping that one in my pocket for now, so let's just say the answer is no. What is this new thing?"

He told her as much as he knew about the Neptune trip.

"Bud, of all people, may have hit a nail right on the head with a suggestion for a pre-heating system to make the slush of the methane ocean thin enough to run through a heat exchanger inside and use that like the Jetmarines use sea water. I'm building that small sub to test out a few things, but would like to see if you can rig up such a system to use in a pressurized methane tank."

"Well, sure. But isn't methane kind of explosive?"

He nodded. "It is, but it needs a lot of oxygen and there is so darned little of that in the ocean up there, combustion is likely to be all but impossible. Same thing goes for the hydrogen in that mix. No O_2 and no *boom!*"

She asked for the size of the system and even though it fell outside of her miniaturized electronics realm, she understood enough to know it was going to take some rather tricky computer system to check and adjust the heat and therefore the flow on the fly, and possibly as often as eight or ten times a second to avoid any pressure buildup or loss of it.

Also, she knew the capability of the deep chill pressure tank, but not the size inside, so she relied on his expertise in the matter. When she learned the interior was about two feet wide and four feet long, she had a very good idea of what was going to be needed.

"Did you want me to build a small pump, or do we have something in stock?"

"I believe we have just the one test pump from the original Jetmarine build and I'm using that in the model, but I need three so

I have the Mechanical Engineering folks making another pair. I'll ask for three in total. Should be ready in three days, so let me know if I can do anything else to help."

She shook her head. "No. I think if I can pull up the schematics to see what I'm feeding into, so I ought to be good to go."

Unsaid were her thoughts of, *And, if I can't figure that on my own, then I really need that vacation Arv keeps telling me to take to get my head sorted out!*

The following morning Admiral Hopkins was on the phone with Damon when Tom arrived.

"...so as long as we understand each other, Damon, and keep this under our collective hats—and I realize that just about everyone at your company and probably three-quarters of the town heard or saw the explosion—if you can explain it as an unexpected underground gas pocket that ruptured and exploded, I can make certain no more attempts at firing rockets with satellites from subs are made. Ever."

"We only have one problem with that, Admiral. It turns out one of our secretaries spoke to the editor of our local paper and he latched onto the 'Mysterious explosions at the Swift place; can death be far behind?' aspect of the story. Unless some Governmental agency can get him silenced, I hear tomorrow's paper is going to be full of his supposed exposé!"

CHAPTER 10 /

THE WORLDLY TEST

IT WAS surprisingly easy to quash the *Shopton Bulletin's* article and get editor, Dan Perkins, to agree to keep his mouth shut according to local FBI agent, Quimby Narz.

This was in part due to an outstanding court order requiring him to clear any articles concerning either the Swifts or the U.S. Government/military with the White House's Office for Information as well as the threat—real—of him going back to Federal Prison and the permanent closure of the newspaper should he not follow the rules.

Perkins even made a personal call to Damon and Tom telling them, "I am playing by the rules from now on. I do not know what the real story is but my source, and I know you are going to hound me until I tell you who that was, so I'll come clean now; it was a woman by the name of Claudia Winters. Anyway, what I got was that you had another of those missiles from your space friends that went haywire and it was only at the very last second Tom managed to get control of it and keep it from slamming into your buildings. Is that even close?"

Damon smiled at his son. "Dan. You know we cannot tell you anything or else you will be able to print it, so all I can say is that whatever it was we dodged it and there was only minor property damage. In spite of what your source told you it is all but fixed as of this morning. In a week nobody will be able to tell that it happened. With that I thank you for your cooperation, tell you I wish it had been like this over the years, and say good day."

With that and another smile at Tom, he hung up. The next thing he did was to call Harlan Ames about their "leak."

There been several deep sea submersibles capable of going down to the lowest point on Earth, the Mariana Trench close to the southern end of Guam.

Of the three manned missions, two made it down and back with a famous-in-his-day movie director being first, the second and third men were U.S. Navy submariners in a specialty submersible, and the third mission—a failure all the way around—had been a Chinese mission where fifteen men lost their lives and all within about a thousand feet of the surface of the Pacific Ocean. It had been a cock-up in just about every conceivable way.

An older nuclear submarine from their Navy had been retrofitted with special internal bracings meant to keep the hull from collapsing, an internal pod built in the control room for the men so outside of it the sub could be pumped full of compressed air to shove out as hard as the sea wanted to shove in.

It was a *theory* that might have worked.

What they failed to take into consideration was the pressurized air needed to be added only once the sub was under at least eight hundred feet of water. The unequal pressure damaged the hull integrity from the start.

The live video feed up a wire to the surface support ship showed everything going as planned until nine hundred-eighty-three feet at which point one entire wall of the control room was seen in three frames of video to have collapsed... followed by dead air.

It was sadly assumed the special pod also imploded with the enormous and immediate flooding with high-pressure water.

The video cable was severed and it was up for debate whether the Chinese on the surface did this or it broke. They dumped the reel of cable over the side before heading for port.

Now, Tom was telling his father he intended to take the *SeaKing* —his space sub model—across the Pacific giving it a good all-around test before heading to the bottom of the trench.

"And you are certain the ship can handle that depth?" Damon asked. "I wonder about it because you are wanting to take the largest open space vessel ever to hit the seas down to conditions nobody has attempted when you get to Neptune."

"I don't think we need to go to the very bottom for this test, Dad. From what I've seen of the data on Neptune, the deepest point will equate to about seven thousand meters of water pressure and the trench is nearly eleven thousand. I only want to test this to nine thousand meters. It'll be safe. Besides, I have to prove the design of the final and this one-fifteenth-size sub will give me all the data I need to complete the big design and build."

While the current submarine was really just a model, it was fully functional and had at least one unoccupied chamber under the control room that was designed to simulate what the final sub would have for wall thickness, internal pressure and a full set of sensors so nobody would need to be inside if anything were to go wrong.

Unlike the deadly Chinese sub disaster, Tom would keep a normal 15-psi atmosphere inside the model down to a few thousand feet. Pressure sensors calibrated to one hundredth of an atmosphere would constantly report on any increase in internal pressure that might indicate the hull was not withstanding the depth as it ought to. At half the intended dive depth, pressure would be released and inside the sub it would be held at just one psi.

When Arv called Tom to come take a look at the space sub model before he closed things up, the inventor asked if it might take place in an hour.

"Sure, skipper. I'm not in a great hurry and can use the extra time to do some cable bundling to neaten the insides. Right now there is a bit of a rat's nest of wires all over the place." He explained it was from the more than two hundred sensors all feeding into a quad of L'il Idiot computers.

Tom arrived at the appointed time and stood in the doorway amazed at the sight.

The space sub, even in this smaller form, was an incredible sight. It was sleek, futuristic, yet also reminiscent of World War II submarines, except for the fact it was a combination of white, light blue and a red stripe down each side. There was a third such stripe Tom had not spotted under the bottom and all marked the placement and length of the modified Jetmarine drives.

He approached it slowly, reached out his right hand and gave the hull a small stroke.

"She's absolutely beautiful, Arv. Everything I'd imagined and tried to put into that CAD program, but... gosh, this is so much more!"

The model maker beamed. He'd taken a few liberties with Tom's design in order to make the craft a little sleeker and more fancy and it was now paying off. At least, as far as praise from Tom went. Only time and the forthcoming trials would tell if his changes—almost entirely cosmetic on the outside—would have little or no impact.

Both men walked all around the ship as it sat in its low cradle in the middle of Arv's workroom. When they arrived at the opposite side, Linda Ming stepped from her office and stood, arms crossed, smiling at how they were "ooohing" and "ahhhing" over it like a pair of small boys looking at a race car.

Arv pointed at her and made a finger crook to tell her to come over.

"Linda here has done something you did not specifically ask for, Tom. She took Bud's idea for what we are calling the pre-heater and added them at the entry of each intake. Tell him about it." He looked at her and she nodded.

"Well," she said taking a deep breath, "even though this model runs on a power pod and we all know they do not create much heat, I've added a circulation pump with almost pure glycol/ethanol inside that heats up to the same temperatures a reactor will produce. That, in turn, is sent to the mesh of tubes—stainless steel by the way—that criss-cross just inside the intakes" She pointed to the closest one and Tom peeked inside.

"So, rather than just send the hot liquid from one to the next to the next, the pump system splits it into three circuits. Each one is controlled by a small computer board that checks the temperatures of the liquid coming in, again at the mid point and at the rear and adjusts up to six times a second to give the right amount of heat to maintain the desired internal pressure and temperature. The intent is to keep the slushy methane coming it at the right level so it can be heated and ejected to provide constant and reliable pressure and therefore speed.

"And, of course, we are using high pressure thermal pumps to simulate the intense heat to be used in the full-size drives."

Through her explanation, Tom had been nodding and looking over the top of the side hull at the maze of tubes, wires, and other systems inside.

"Did you get a chance to work with Gary over at the small pressure tank he built?" She nodded. "Great. No issues?"

"None we spotted in a fifteen hour test. He managed to get the tank down to minus three hundred-three degrees and under a pressure equal to five thousand feet under the Neptunian surface. As long as the intakes were on, things were fine—and we did a small test shutting them off and the whole thing, well, *froze* up. Literally."

Tom had to digest this a moment before he brightened. "But, yours is an electrically-driven system and relies on that power to also provide heat. In the real ship the very heat we are using will help keep circulation going even if we lose power to that pump system, so we'll have a few minutes before things get too cool." He seemed to be thinking about this a moment before stating, "I have to account for that in the real space submarine. Maybe an emergency power and pump system that can be switched to. Hmmm?"

A half hour later, happy with what he had seen, Tom headed back to the big office. As he was passing Trent, the secretary told him a phone call had just been placed on hold.

"It's from someone with a vaguely Asian accent and coming from Washington DC. He said you would take the call." He shrugged.

"Okay," and the inventor headed for his desk.

"Tom Swift. Who is calling, please?"

"Is this really Tom Swift, or is this someone else trying to intercept his calls?"

Tom counted to ten. "Unless you tell me who you are, this call will end in five seconds."

The man at the other end paused for three of those seconds before answering. "My name is Edgar Li, spelled L-I. It is actually Li Eg Gai, and I am the Vice Ambassador for the Glorious People's Nation of China. I repeat my question; are you Tom Swift."

"I am. What is the nature of your call, sir?" He had an idea what this was about and did not like it.

"It regards the forthcoming mission you are mounting for China and a few other nations to the planet of Neptune. We have been angry to find that you and your company is not responding to our almost daily demands for meetings and information. Your own government is forestalling our attempts at communications in a most unsatisfactory manner."

Damon came into the office and indicated Tom should put the call on the speaker; Trent had told him about it. He made a motion telling Tom to not mention his listening in.

"You do realize that Swift Enterprises' undertaking this project comes with the agreement that no nation may make demands of us or of the mission, don't you?"

"That is of no consequence to us. You are being paid to perform this mission and for the massive levels of funding we are supplying you will do what we demand."

After taking a cleansing breath, Tom responded. "No. We will not. If you do not agree to the pre-stated terms, then that must be brought up with the Vice President of this nation. The nation, by the way, providing a higher level of funding than China by a factor of nearly two times. Was there anything else?"

"Now you listen you young... well, just you listen, boy. We demand that you guarantee to bring us at least two metric tons of the diamonds you will find there. We—"

"We have performed tests on highly pressurized methane and created small diamond-like crystals that vaporized once returned to normal atmospheric conditions. It is highly likely anything we try to bring back will do the same thing."

The man's voice rose and became louder. "You do not have the same level of experts that we have in China. Our experts, obviously not young boys like you, tell us these diamonds will be of the purest quality and will remain pristine for centuries!"

"Then, your so-called experts are kidding themselves." He was about to say more but Damon's index finger came down on the phone cradle and cut the connection.

"Let them complain to the V.P. You and I will now call Pete Quintana and let him know of both this lack of respect for the project boundaries and his insults to you."

When the senator, a recently happy man facing no competition in the forthcoming election—for his fourth term—answered, he quickly grew angry over what he was being told.

"I'm calling the President right after this. He has to let the V.P. know that if this continues, or is repeated, and without him calling the Ambassador and his... *minion* on the carpet, that a very public statement regarding the attempts by the Chinese government to turn this into a personal money-making venture for them is going to be made known to the world."

Damon said he might like being in on that sort of public appearance, except that it might reflect badly on Swift Enterprises.

Peter agreed and added, "And the one thing the current Chinese leadership most certainly do not want is for something like this to come out! With nearly fifteen percent unemployment and another fifty percent earning less that subsistence wages, they do not want either the world or their own people to learn they want to pad their own accounts!"

"Are you telling us we did okay by hanging up?" Tom had to ask over the speakerphone.

"Better than okay as I'm guessing that your phone system and Security team have the entire thing recorded. Assuming this is so, send me that file as soon as possible. Thanks, and my apologies for you being subjected to that attempt at bullying. You don't have the levels of expertise, indeed! My aunt Mathilda's fanny you don't," he mumbled before adding, "Let me have an hour and I'll get back to you."

After the call ended, Damon looked at Tom. "Well, I started to feel I was letting my anger get the better of me and that might be a problem, but I think it was just what needed to happen."

While they waited for the senator's call, another one came in from Harlan.

"Just wanted to let you both know I've taken care of the Claudia Winters problem, to a point. She is, according to her own admission, a bit of a drinker and spouted off to a friend in a restaurant and just the next booth over from our favorite newspaperman, Daniel Perkins. She says he never approached her but she did notice a recorder sitting on his table when she got up to go to the ladies room. She swears she never directly told him anything. All I could tell her was that she might lose her job over this and told her to seek help via Doc with the drinking problem."

"When do we make the decision?" Damon asked.

"Well, you remember an old friend, Bernt Algren with the FBI down in DC?"

"Sure"

"I received a call from him ten minutes ago telling me they are taking this situation most seriously and will be taking the investigation over and will let me know what they believe needs to happen. That could include anything from placing it all back on us to hauling her off to jail. The problem with that way is that we never announced to the employees they had to keep mum about that little explosion we had."

After thinking it over and checking with Tom who shrugged, Damon asked, "Do we let her go if this was a combination honest mistake and snooping in a public place as we know Dan is known to do?"

Harlan said he had no answer for that. Other than to suggest that if she completed a voluntary program and kept her nose clean she might be given another chance. "She has an exemplary record during the fifteen months she's been here."

It was decided to table the conversation for a few days.

The two Swifts had no sooner hung up than Trent buzzed them with the news that Peter Quintana was back on the phone.

"Yes, Pete," Damon greeted the senator. "News?"

"You might say that. The President is personally calling the Chinese Ambassador into a mandatory meeting that will also be connected to the folks back home in China. Like you, he feels that a really good worldwide announcement of the greed of the Chinese and a demand to know just how that money—if it ever appears their precious methane diamonds stick around—will be spent to better their people."

Tom leaned slightly forward to the microphone. "Do you think that will keep them off our backs?"

Pete snorted. "Better than that. I'm pretty certain we are going to hear that it must have been a translator problem, and they never wanted tons of diamonds but only a handful."

Damon groaned. He'd heard all sort of excuses before.

"There is one good thing," Pete said. "A special committee has approved using Fearing Island to launch the replacement for that, um, *lost* Navy package. They should have it to you in three weeks."

With the space sub model now ready to go, Tom had one of the two remaining large cargo seacopters brought up to Enterprises and the model was loaded in the back.

Rather than take down a jetmarine, it was decided that the seacopter's hull could withstand at least down to five thousand feet in depth, and the model could be kept on a thin wire tether to control it and retrieve data.

As they passed over Hawaii on their way to an overnight on Guam, Tom gave the controls to Bud so he could grab a couple hours of sleep. He had, the night before, been up past three a.m. working to finalize the programming for the control systems.

"Go hit the sack, skipper," the flyer told him. "Zimby will keep me occupied and awake with his tales of his days as a test pilot for the Navy. Did you know he flew more jets that never saw the light of day than anyone else?"

As tired as he was, Tom grinned and shook his head. "Love to hear about it... later. You go ahead and regale the flyboy here, and be sure to tell him about the XB-49 you flew into near space!"

Bud did a double take having never heard about that plane before. He knew that planes and jets with the "X" designator were experimentals and frequently were used just to try out new control surfaces, propulsion devices, or even landing gear.

As Tom rounded the corner and stepped into the small bunkroom, he heard Zimby saying, "Yeah. It was a test bed for a self-arresting carrier jet that could come in at about ninety knots, and once over the deck it would go into heavy reverse and set down within fifty feet! It malfunctioned and I got shot straight up to an altitude of more than one-hundred-thousand feet before..."

It was, of course, a fabrication of Zimby's and he trooped it out for new pilots but had never been certain if Bud might not just go and try to look it up. The look Tom gave him said, "Now's the time!"

When he came to wake the inventor four hours later, the were just fifty minutes out from the joint Air Force and Navy base on the northern end of the island nation.

The base commander met them as they shut down the seacopter's systems and stepped outside.

"Welcome to Fantasy Island," he said jokingly. "Actually, I'm

Captain Max Goodwell, U.S. Navy and nominally in charge of all of this around us. You, I recognize from your pictures, are Tom Swift." They two shook hands and Tom introduced their host to the other three in the party, Bud, Zimby, and a submersibles technician, Stephen Boskwick, from Fearing Island.

"A pleasure gentlemen. Let me show you to your quarters for tonight and if I understand correctly, and assuming your tests tomorrow are successful, you will be back tomorrow evening and leave for the States the next morning."

They each had their own room, all officer's quarters, so they were moderately sparse but clean and neat.

Following a great night's sleep—even for Tom—they lifted off at seven the next morning heading for a spot about eighty miles to the south of the island.

Tom settled the seacopter on the water and a built-in hoist was used to lift and set the sub model into the water. Within minutes it was heading down, the seacopter was closed and ballast filled and the blades reversed to suck them under the waves.

Down and down they went, nearly a thousand feet every twenty minutes, until the seacopter reached its depth limits. The model, however, continued downward trailing its tether line that was sending back vast amounts of information about everything inside and the pressures being exerted outside the model.

By the time the model was four thousand feet above the near total darkness of the Mariana Trench bottom, Tom announced it was time to slowly begin to draw the air pressure from the inside.

"We are going to get it down from the normal fifteen psi to about one and that will give us the equivalent of an additional four thousand feet of depth. Depending on what we see from the sensors, we either call this a success, or go back home and try something else."

He hoped it was going to be a success.

The results of the pre-heater for the incoming seawater were encouraging. It showed that the water around the sub was a constant 14°F, eighteen degrees below freezing and yet still a liquid. Temperature along with the tremendous pressure made the water about as thick as pancake syrup, and the heating allowed it to come through the propulsion system at a rate sufficient to drive it forward at up to a speed of fifteen knots.

"Here goes," Tom announced. "We're shutting off the Barclay Slush Warmer System." He grinned when the flyer's head snapped around and Bud looked at him with amazement. "Oh," Tom said with an innocence that could only come from practice, "did I forget to mention that we are using your little suggestion? Golly. Sorry."

The sub slowed down to a crawl of only three knots and continued forward for another three minutes. Then, it slowed even more and finally came to a halt.

Tom's hands raced over the controls as his eyes scanned the sensor reports.

"I'm afraid we've frozen the sub in place. Give me a few seconds to get the BS system working and we should get back underway."

But, no matter what he tried, the submarine refused to budge.

CHAPTER 11 /
ADJUSTMENTS TO COVER PROBLEMS

AS BUD and the others looked on, Tom kept setting different controls and trying to move the sub. Nothing happened. Finally, Tom sat back and sighed.

"I might have just lost us the fine model Arv and Linda Ming built," he admitted. He turned to board over to Zimby. "Keep an eye on things. I have to get a cup of coffee and splash some water in my face," he said as he stood up, stretched, and headed for the small kitchenette.

Tom was gone all of eight seconds before he raced back into the control room. "Zim? Tell me what the temperature is of the circulating fluids, please?"

"Umm, Just about thirty-two at the intake and two hundred-nine at the pump. Why?"

Tom slapped his forehead. "Stupid me. Try resetting the pump breaker. I'll bet the pump stopped, well, pumping as soon as I shut it off, which is what I wanted, but it tripped its breaker when I started it back up. Or, rather failed to start it again."

The other pilot moved his right hand over the part of the control panel that handled the interior electrical circuits. In seconds, he let out a happy shout.

"Got it! That was it, skipper. Great call!"

But as he maneuvered the small submarine to aim it back into a rising position, fate played a dirty trick on them.

"Tom! Strong current is shoving us one way and the model is still sluggish. The cable is about to—" and they all more felt than heard it as the *snap!* sound reverberated throughout the seacopter.

For three minutes Bud fought the controls before gaining the upper hand and reversing the rotors to send them toward the surface, or at least less violent waters higher up.

Finally, when everything had settled down, Zimby looked morosely at his boss. "Sorry, Tom. I lost her."

Tom let out a rueful short chuckle as the technician took over the seacopter's controls. "No, Zim. I probably should not have reeled out everything we had on that tether. I never thought we'd get shoved one direction while the model went the other." He sighed, heavily. "Dad will be annoyed, but I'm going to tell him we're coming back to retrieve the model. Maybe not before our little Neptune mission, but soon. We will get that little sub back!"

Standing up and giving his friend a slap on the back, Bud stated, "That's the ticket, Tom. We will get back here. Besides, now you've proved you can overcome the depth thing, and we get home from Neptune, maybe we can use the new giant space sub to come back. Might even take a good look around and see what else is down here."

"Not likely to be much," Zimby commented.

Tom had to concur. There were a few reports of ships sinking nearby, and of course the Chinese submarine they might try to find out the truth about, but most known wrecks were a little farther north along the shelf just below Guam.

"Let's go back to the base and... no." Tom changed his mind. "Let's go back down as far as we can safely manage and see if the little sub is just sort of floating at the same depth. If it is we might be able to sneak down a little, very slowly, and get it back now."

Alas, it was not to be.

As they searched for the little craft in the midnight darkness of the deep water, a series of breakers inside the model shut everything off in response to loss of control signals. Dark and unpowered, the space submarine model sank lower and lower. It would hit the bottom, slow enough so it would likely sustain no damage, about an hour later.

Before that point Tom gave up and ordered the seacopter to the surface.

He made a radio call to his father bouncing his signal off one of the series of Swift communication satellites high overhead.

Damon was disappointed for his son, and only slightly bothered by the expense of the loss, but realized it was not Enterprises' money sinking in the South Pacific.

"You can go get it back someday, Son. For now, if you believe you proved the worth of your design and the ability to handle the pressures in the ocean depths of Neptune, I'd say you had a good day!"

It was an audio call only or Damon would have seen the deep sadness on his son's face as the younger man agreed everything had proven to be more than satisfactory.

"Then, get another good night's sleep at the Guam base and come home tomorrow. I expect you'll drop into the grounds sometime around midnight, so I'll wish you a good flight and see you when you come in *after lunch the next day*. Understand?"

"Yeah. I do. And, Dad? Thanks!"

By the time the younger Swift got back to the big office, it was nearly two in the afternoon after the return trip. He'd spent an hour telling Bashalli all about the trip and the heartbreak of the little sub's loss, but she told him the same thing his father had.

"If you succeeded and did not spend your company's money, then how can you be sad? Did you have great plans to use that sub thing over and over again?"

Sheepishly, he admitted he had no such plans.

"It's just that I hate losing something that beautiful and sleek. But," he had sighed as she reached over to turn off their lights, "we'll get started on the full-sized ship in a week or so. All I have to do is make certain the circuit breaker problem cannot occur in the big version. 'Night, Bash."

As Tom told his father about that conversation, he was philosophical. "I can't say that I was going to be able to do much more with the model, but Arv and Linda worked so hard on it. I guess I'll need to go tell them."

Damon shook his head. "Not unless you want to hear them tell you they already know all about it." On seeing Tom's reaction, he said, "Sorry if I stole your thunder but I needed to know if they could understand the circuit breaker issue and if it was just this miniature version. They both assure me it was almost certainly the small size of everything. And, they understand that it was the currents and the necessary thin cable that let you down, not their work. Also, it was *not* your design!"

The rework of the blown out runway section had been completed more than two weeks earlier but the FAA was a sticking point in that they did not assign an inspector to come out for the check and recertification. In fact, they could not say when such a thing might happen.

It was frustrating for Damon and for his Facilities manager as well as for the Control Tower manager as it meant sending—and remembering to—all east-west and west-east traffic out to the farthest, parallel runway.

It also meant the rush to get the work completed might just as well have been put off by a few weeks!

In his frustration, Damon called the Admiral to tell him that not only had the Navy's check for the work failed to arrive but the FAA was being reticent to come give permissions to use that damaged runway.

The Navy man took a deep breath. "Yes. Of course. The check is being held up because we can't tell the lower ups at the GAO exactly why we are paying for damage to a private concern. We're working on that via a small committee within the Senate. Give me another week, please. As for the FAA, I have, as you no doubt realize, zero input except in cases on U.S. Naval facilities."

Damon had an idea. "How about if you remind them that the Navy and indeed the Government use our facility and that if we can't offer them all our runways it could lead to a disastrous accident? You might mention the President uses our runways for Air Force One."

The Admiral laughed. "Well, I can certainly try that. Not too sure it'll carry any water, but what the heck. Why not?"

While this was going on, Tom was getting over his disappointment at losing the miniature space sub. To be brutally honest, he had gotten over its loss on the flight home but had still worried something he'd done or decided might have been to blame.

After hanging up Damon called to the Manager of Fearing Island to check on the status for the replacement launch of the Navy's destroyed satellite.

"We've got the rocket ready but the payload is going to be a day or three or ten late, and we have no exact word on when it will get here. Sorry to have no info, Damon, but we're being kept a bit in the dark on this."

"The wheels of government and the military grind exceptionally slowly," Damon said with a little sigh. "Well, I'll make a couple of calls and then get back to you."

His next call was back to the Admiral.

"Damon? Uhh, I don't have any more information if that's why you're calling."

The inventor explained about the tardy payload. "Our belief was it was coming from you folks by today and going up tomorrow. And, unless it arrives in the next hour that will not be possible. There just won't be enough time to mount, test and fuel the rocket."

The Admiral swore. "Okay, I had been told it was already on its way there last evening. Let me check. I'll get back ASAP."

While waiting, Damon wandered down the hall to see what Tom was up to. On his way out he asked Trent to page him back when the call came in using the auto-send box Tom had devised to help the secretary who absolutely hated the "voices in my head" aspect of using the TeleVoc other than as his security badge. So, with the press of one of six buttons, the box sent that message to either Tom or Damon's TeleVocs.

He knocked on the door and was only mildly surprised to find it was not fully closed. Pushing it open he stopped and watched his son who was taking notes. Evidently he had been taking a lot of notes as he was close to the end of the notebook and did not seem to be anywhere close to stopping.

As quietly as possible, he closed the door and walked on to the small kitchen where Chow prepared foods for the executive staff and invited guests.

"Wahl, hey thar, Mr. Swift," the old ranch cook called out from the large pot of something he was cooking, likely for lunch. "C'mon in. I'm just fixin' up some lamb stew fer one o' tomorrow's lunch offerin's. Need a coffee or a cookie or somethin'?"

Damon laughed. "No, Chow. It seems I have a little time on my hands and Tom is very busy, so I came by just to snoop. Uhh, lamb stew, you say?" the inventor asked hopefully.

Chow knew it was a particular favorite of his boss and nodded. "I'd be right pleased if'n you'd give it a taste and tell me if I need anythin' else in it," he said picking up a large soup spoon from a tray of them next to the stove.

The inventor grinned, came forward and dipped it into the brown and thick stew. He came up with a piece of meat and a small bit of carrot. As they went into his mouth he let out a delighted moan. "That's incredible, Chow," he stated around the food which he quickly chewed and swallowed. "Anne's a great cook but her lamb stew is missing something this one has. Care to share the secret?"

"I put a little dried rosemary an' some marjoram in my spice grinder an' then powder that. It mixes in with no little herby bits and give it that great taste. An' don't tell Bud that secret. I've got the boy convinced I put in powdered cactus!"

"Well, it is an amazing addition; I'll look forward to eating it tomorrow. I guess Tom and I will be eating in the office today, but I have no idea when he'll be acknowledging the rest of the world. I'll have Trent give you a call in a bit. And, thanks for the sample."

As he walked down the hall he was in time to see Tom open the lab door and walk swiftly toward the office.

"Going to see me about something?" he called out.

The younger man stopped and spun around, a grin on his face.

"Yes. I found out something about that multiple levels of currents down where we lost the model."

Damon pointed to the outer office and they went inside but not before Trent stated, "Nothing, yet."

Sitting in the conference area Tom picked up the remote control for the large screen monitor on the opposite wall. He soon had an undersea chart up and got up to go point at a few things.

"There is something the Navy dive team discovered and it has been born out by the dropping of several small probes into this area. It is a cyclical event with no fixed or at least plotted period over when it occurs. Something shoots icy water upward from the depths and that causes warm water at the top of the shelf to spill over and get much colder pretty quickly to replace the icy stuff, and that forces a lot of water down the face. It shoots off at several locations causing the swirling that shoved us in the opposite direction, but the one thing it does is bring down a lot of fish and other ocean life."

Damon had to think a moment, "Did you detect any of that when you were down there?"

"No, but when things hit we really weren't looking outside. Anyway, where it shoots off the cliff it causes currents that head one direction while the rest heading on down sort of suck surrounding water in and that causes an opposite current. Now, I'm more than determined to go back down once this Neptune trip is finished and see what there is down there that might cause this. I also have a good plot on the likely location of the model, assuming of course that it eventually sank to the very bottom."

He was about to say something else when Trent knocked and stuck his head inside. "It's Admiral Hopkins on two."

"Hello, Admiral. It's Damon and Tom. Did you find out anything about the payload for the first launch?" he said trying to bring Tom up to speed on the reason for the call.

There was a pause during which they both could hear the man's huffing breaths. "Right. And, yes I did. Some nitwit very junior Congressman from Alabama is on the oversight committee for these, uhh, special launches, and knowing how badly the first one went for us he has ordered a hold until we can prove our launch system is more reliable. He didn't read the memo about us now using your tried and proven rockets. How he ever managed to get things stopped is beyond me and beyond anyone above him being able to answer. As a consequence, things ground to a halt on the final build and test of the package. They are back at it but it means a two-day delay. Can you still help us?"

"Yes, sir, we can. We have one launch scheduled for the day after tomorrow, which will take place during a window from about seven in the morning until five minutes past nine. As I recall, for you insertion to go as you need it, your window for launch the day after that would be about a fifteen minute window somewhere between eleven-twenty and eleven-forty. Is that what your information shows?"

The Admiral confirmed it.

"Actually, and don't tell anyone I said this, but we can launch about any time but we need to hold off on firing the package's insertion rocket until the right time."

"That might be, but the orbit we will put it in only allows it to remain near that altitude for thirty minutes before gravity begins to exert a bit too much pull. I suppose you could stretch that out to a full orbit but I'd rather put things up on time and have you just hit the continue button then and there."

"Me as well, Damon. Me as well. I have to go but expect the package to arrive with a small honor guard around three the afternoon after tomorrow."

"Tell them to make it darned small and without the obvious weapons, please. That is part of our agreement. And, keep that junior fool out of my hair."

He placed another call to the Fearing Island manager letting him know of the delay and the new schedule.

"I knew my wife made a mistake when she voted for that idiot!" he stated after hearing who had caused the delay. "His bother is an idiot and his father was a moonshiner who struck it big when the State blew up his still and he got injured. They had to pay out a couple million dollars and he used that to buy respectability for his older son. Pretty certain he'd all but given up on the younger one by then. Anyway, enough of down home politics. We'll be waiting."

"Is there anything I can help you with," Damon asked Tom as they heard the approach of Chow and his rattling wheel lunch cart.

"Not right now, Dad, but thanks for the offer. I still have a lot of little things to check and fix or adapt or change in the designs before I'll be ready to send the plans through to Jake at the Construction Company."

"How long do you anticipate this taking to construct?"

"Honestly? With the vacuu-form beds they have over there and most of the insides being things we've made before or build today, about nine weeks. Then, the fun begins because we are going to take the various sections into orbit and put it together up there."

"Did you get the message the President is going to announce the project officially to the public tonight?"

Tom nodded. "Yes, his secretary called to let me know he was also naming me as the head of the team, and that he was going to state, without naming nations, that we have been bothered and possibly hindered in our efforts by at least one of the participants who were demanding we retrieve a wealth of riches they assume will be up there." Tom shrugged. "He also is supposed to refute the notion this is all going to be a glorious success because of his political party and their influence in making this happen."

"That's pretty much what I heard through Pete Quintana. I guess we tune in and watch and find out how much of that is true and also what else he might say."

That night Tom told Amanda he and Bashalli needed to watch the Presidential address and she was welcome to join them, but the kids needed to be closed into the playroom for the duration.

"I'm not much for politics, Mr. Swift, so I'll be in there with them. Thanks for the offer, though."

The address, which had been scheduled for the eight o'clock time slot on all the major networks, began a minute late. He started by thanking the networks for giving up their valuable time and assured the public this was not to announce anything bad.

"In fact, it is very good indeed," he said into the camera. "I know there have been rumors of a new manned mission into space going around for a few months, but with the election just a few days away, and all that I'll need to be involved in with the incoming President once elected, I thought it best to do this tonight.

"Man has been to the Moon, to Mars where they are today, and into the vast reaches of our solar system, and a bit beyond, mostly courtesy of men and women at the various national space agencies and courtesy of the Swift organization. And, it is my pleasure to announce that the Swifts are heading a brand new mission into space, and man's first ever visit to another ocean-covered world, the planet Neptune."

He paused to give the home audience a moment to digest this.

Next, he outlined the multination consortium behind the funding for the mission and got into some of the dynamics and issued behind working with so many countries and their differing opinions of what should be done, how it ought to work, and what they wanted from it. He specifically named Tom as the lead for the entire project and stated his confidence it its ultimate success as long as the inventor was not pestered by the other interests.

Tom took a deep breath waiting for the ax to drop on China. Instead, the President simply said that a few of the nations had what could be termed, "uneducated and unrealistic" expectations, but that the mission was purely one of information and samples gathering so we might all have a better understanding of the planet.

"Now, there are some within my own political party who have asked me to tell you all that we are responsible for this. That just isn't true. The fact is Damon and Tom Swift are the ones responsible for this and will be the ones to see it succeed when it finally takes off a few months from now."

He concluded by stating that it was the indomitable spirit of adventure and mankind that would see this through to the end.

Tom turned to Bashalli. "I guess with a promise like that I'd better get going with the build!"

CHAPTER 12 /
AN HOMAGE TO JAPANIMATION

OVER THE next week, Tom looked at every square inch of the design and each and every circuit. In the end he had to agree that it was the complexity of the miniature and possibly a faulty breaker that had doomed the small model.

He also looked more closely at the overall design and concluded that the basic idea was sound, but there was still resistance from the shape of the outer hull. So, he undertook a redesign before anything of the real space sub could be okayed for construction. Other than the drive units for under the surface.

For use getting down to the surface—and back up again—he still toyed with repelatrons but had the feeling they might have issues with the liquid surface. It was an offhand remark by Hank Sterling that sent his brain in a different direction.

"Plasma jets," he told his father at lunch. "We power the ship with plasma jets to get down to the surface, taking the fuels we need with us, but—and here's the great thing—we load up on the liquid methane and use that for the trip back up to orbit and to the retrieval point for the black hole."

Damon looked stunned for a minute before his eyes focused on his son and he smiled. "Sure! That makes a lot of sense. You can safely use that methane for power and not cause any overspill of fire because there isn't the oxygen to cause anything outside of your plasma field to combust. But," and he suddenly looked very serious, "will that provide enough energy to lift you off?"

"I believe so. I am going to build a small test rocket, heavily weighted, take it off shore down at Fearing, and see if I can get it to climb out of about five hundred feet of water and into the upper atmosphere."

Damon nodded before his eyes went wide. "Oh, gosh. That reminds me I have to make a call to Admiral Hopkins in—" he glanced at his watch, "three minutes." He quickly wiped his mouth on his napkin and set that down next to his half-finished plate. "Join me," he suggested before moving the plate out of range of the video pick-up. Then, he remembered this would just be an audio call and pulled it back, picked up his roast chicken sandwich and took another big bite.

He buzzed Trent and asked the man to make the connection down to Washington DC. In a moment the red light on the table phone blinked red then green and the older inventor reached over and hit the button.

"Admiral? It's Damon and Tom."

"Ah, good. Hello you two. Listen, this call is going to need to be fairly short, but I believe ultimately sweet for all of us. It concerns the recent... erm... problem and what we want to do to keep that from ever being repeated. I am sure you recall certain packages you delivered to low orbit way back when you were building your Fearing Island base and the one very recently?"

"I certainly do. We used the scale model of my old *CosmoSoar* rocket as a last minute emergency delivery vehicle for that initial one."

"Right. So, in speaking with a certain politician who was instrumental in getting permissions to transfer our newest package to your excellent care this week, no names please, he said you have been launching a small rocket, one of more traditional shape, you build and have used for at least five years to launch a series of satellites for NASA at—and I have troubles believing this—one-tenth the cost of their own suppliers. Is that true?"

Damon laughed. "Yes, Admiral, it is true. Originally it was capable of lifting three hundred-fifty pounds into low orbit of one hundred to one-twenty miles, or two hundred-fifty pounds up to about one hundred-sixty miles. But, that was then. The payload numbers have risen by about sixty pounds for both altitudes."

There was a relieved sigh at the other end. "Good. Very good, indeed. I realize you did not loft this using one of your repelatrons, but did use a more traditional rocket that I need to be able to tell some... well, less than knowledgeable individuals about. You see, there is a long series of our packages we will want to have launched at the rate of about one a week and they need to go to no higher that one hundred-ten miles before they lift themselves to their final placement. Those positions being top secret as are the packages. Uh, I hope this goes nowhere else, but we have a series of forty of them to go up in the next year starting in fifteen days. If I can get the Chief of Naval Operations to agree to prepayment of at least fifty percent, are you willing to take this on? Can you?"

The inventor described the basic rocket and capabilities to him.

They discussed what it would take including Damon asking that any transports coming to the island not be accompanied by armed fighters unless they peeled off and returned to the mainland rather than insisting on touching down on the island.

"That will be a tough one, but I believe I can get permissions. Oh, and that brings up another question or request. After our mishap, you said something about Tom creating a safer and more powerful monopropellant. Is that really true?"

Tom spoke up. "Yes, Admiral, it is. We used it when we refurbished the main body of the older GPS and global communications satellites. Safer, more stable until ignited, and about thirty percent more powerful so less needs to be stored. That brings me to a question I hope you are allowed to answer. Is that extra propellant for constant repositioning, or is it just for the insertion?"

"The latter, then it is only used a final time when it comes time to re-enter where everything burns up. Can't say more."

Damon had been doing computations during this part of the conversation and now spoke up giving the Admiral a breakdown on the per launch costs including use of Swift personnel.

"I see. Great price and easily a twelfth of what we've been quoted by NASA. Even our own little attempt ran four times that. So, you have yourself a deal by agreement and by contract in a couple days. We'll draft the document and let you and your legal folks fill in all the blanks. If I may, can I arrange for our next package to come down in thirteen days?"

"Yes, assuming we receive the first one when you say it will be here and adhere to a delivery schedule for the others. I'll see that the rest of the run is on the schedule."

Three minutes later, the call was over and Damon took the last bite of his sandwich and smiled.

Tom got up and went back to his desk for a minute before heading down the hall to the lab and his CAD computer. There, he began changing the outer design of what had looked like a more traditional submarine of the diesel variety into something with a prow, or nose, still along those lines, but the hull shape became a little less tall, considerably wider, and more tapered at the back end.

Next, he "peeled away" the outer skin and added a few refinements to the interior along with adding a representation of the plasma system he envisioned. This led to a revisit to the outside and placement of the necessary scoops to bring in some of the liquid methane and to store it in a pair of interior tanks.

He had to take an hour to compute the needed load of such fuel to get them back off the planet and into a high orbit where they would rendezvous with the black hole he intended to leave at a Lagrange point between the planet and its moon, Triton, the one moon orbiting retrograde to the rotation of the planet, but that would play in their favor as it was large enough to have the gravitation to hold the black hole steady and to not let Neptune influence it very much at all.

Tom believed the black hole would be safe there for up to five weeks even though he felt it would be about ten days at most.

Satisfied with the changes he walked over to have a chat with Arv about making a small model, just five feet long, to put into both the smaller wind tunnel as well as the water tank where they could simulate moving through liquids at up to five hundred miles per hour.

"Sure I can run that up. Anything inside other than possibly some fins to use for directional changes?"

"No fins, Arv. The actual vessel will use small plasma jets to swing the back end around and a few more in the nose for fine tuning of direction of travel."

It only took a few days for the model maker to come up with the model. He had decided to use highly compressed nitrogen in place of the plasma jets because it would work in both the wind and the water tests.

A central mounting point would allow it to be controlled and also would provide feedback from the fifteen sensors Tom requested.

The wind tunnel test came first with the two men standing outside the sealed chamber.

"Please bring it up to fifty knots," Tom requested, "and be ready to increment up about twenty knots at a time to the full speed of the tunnel."

"Got it, Tom," the woman on duty told him as she moved her hands across several of the controls.

A minute later the big counter-rotating fans at the right end began to roar to life and everyone watched the close-up camera shot of the model. If it were going to have troubles moving through a gaseous medium, small vibrations would show up at even the slower speeds.

It held rock steady all the way to the top speed of six hundred! Even using the nitrogen jets to move the nose around a bit made little difference to the aerodynamics of the model.

The same thing occurred in the water tank.

As the two men carried their model back to Arv's truck to be taken back to the workshop, Tom was all smiles.

"Tomorrow we start the real build," he declared.

When the young inventor arrived at the Construction Company the following morning at eight, his father was already there in conversation with the company manager, Jake Aturian. They waved Tom over.

"You ready to see the start of your dream... uhh, I guess the term Damon just mentioned, space sub is pretty good. So?"

"I sure am, Jake. And, I can't begin to tell you how much getting the start of all this going will mean to getting about nine other countries who have been doing anything from being steaming mad at not being let in here to point and demand things to jumping up and down as if they have to find a bathroom is going get them off everyone's backs. This ought to settle things down for a little. The ones who've kicked in the most money are anxious to see something. They sort of poo-poo'd the miniature. The Chinese called it a little trick to make their people think the project was well underway."

Jake laughed. "Perhaps they do not have a concept for a miniature test vehicle."

Tom nodded. "Yeah. Maybe so. Anyway, which shed is this all going to happen in?"

He referred to the three giant assembly buildings that filled about a third of the property at the company that had once been the primary Swift Company concern. While a lot of things had been moved to Enterprises, Tom knew that some of the individual part fabrication equipment still resided at this older facility.

"We'll be using number two. It has those two giant flatbed vacuu-form beds we can use to make a lot of the hull panels. Hank Sterling has figured out how to get the more curved parts ready for the ovens. I think it has to do with some of the wooden jigs he's built this week. Says he'll take the necessary panels out, partially curved, and lay them over the jigs before draping them with sandbags. Can you imagine?"

Tom could. Hank had already told him of his experiments doing just that and had stated, "It looks crazy and like it ought to not work, but it does! We just have to do it at the right pace so nothing gets stretched."

Tom looked at his father.

"I guess someone needs to press the figurative start button and let's get this underway."

A moment later then entered the large building and Tom could see where some things had been removed to make room for each of the five long sections to be built, one at a time. In their place was a cradle shaped, to his eye, exactly like the bottom of the space sub.

About fifty men and women stood ready to begin. Tom waived at them and in a loud and clear voice told them, "Okay. Build that space sub!"

A small cheer went up from the team and each of them turned to their equipment, materials or other positions.

The three men wandered over to the vacuu-form equipment in time to watch Hank as he lowered the upper cover over what must have been seven or eight layers already in the bed. From the shape of things Tom believed it was a hull bottom piece about fifty feet long and twenty feet wide.

Soon, the bed was flooded with a white solution he knew was a special polymer that would set with a slight gray-white tone. Pumps started to suck out all air including thousand of tiny bubbles from within the layers so that once that vacuum was released, the polymer would flood into all those spaces.

Hank turned and smiled.

"It's gonna take about an hour before this opens and we put it over the shaper, but you're welcomed to stand there or come back."

Tom responded, "I think we all know you've got this well in hand. We just wanted to watch as the first piece of wood was nailed down to build this house."

Every day Tom headed for the Construction Company to watch the different pieces become full sections of the hull. These were transported on a double-length flatbed trailer in the middle of the night to Enterprises and through a temporary hole in the wall made so the giant sections could actually fit inside. Neither of the regular gates had the clearance.

A second set of cradles was inside Hangar 9, a large enough structure to fit the entire space sub inside and keep it hidden from prying eyes.

Twice during the move of the first two sections, Security caught people with cameras and even night vision equipment trying to get pictures and videos of the sections.

Because the project was deemed to be Government Secret, Swift Security were allowed by law to take the equipment and all storage devices and clear them out before returning things to their owners a few days later.

A lot of shouting and threats were aimed at Phil Radnor and Gary Bradley and their teams, but those would be spies were given an official document and the choice of arrest and permanent confiscation of all their equipment, or simply forfeiting their images and being trespassed by the County Sheriffs.

As each section arrived and was stabilized, other teams swarmed over them installing all the equipment, electronics and the trio of Jetmarine-inspired drive units. A few additional bulkheads—walls— had to be built and installed once larger equipment had been moved into position.

Tom and Bud spent a lot of time inside the different sections as they arrived and were being worked on over the nine weeks of the build. The flyer was amazed at the spaciousness of the craft while the inventor was constantly looking worried as if he were forgetting something vital.

"Don't sweat is, Tom. Everyone has your back. Besides, this isn't any miniature and there will be no thin cable. Everything will be inside and within your or my or anyone else's reach."

Tom gave his brother-in-law a weak grin.

"Yeah, I know that but I just know there will be something we forget to do. Like when you pack for a trip and go over and over the list of things you need then get there and find out that you had whatever pulled out and set aside, but it never made if off the dresser and into the bag."

"Then, do what Sandy does. Go buy what you forgot!"

Tom knew Bud was being silly in order to take his mind off the situation. *Besides,* he thought, *if it isn't inside the ship when we leave, it won't be available once we get going!*

Tom stood before the mostly completed ship's central section, the one where the crew would eat, sleep and get some exercise. It was going to be the fifth and final piece lofted into space to meet up with the two forward pieces that held all the ship's computer and navigation systems in addition to the Attractatron that would hold firmly onto the black hole, and the control room.

In its cradle the hull bottom was a mere foot off the ground, but it was enormous in exactly the way any submarine is out of water.

Even his original, tiny Jetmarine, barely thirty feet long, looked huge when out and dry.

To the rear were to be the two parts with the drive and power reactor of the space sub. Both shells were complete with two teams working double shifts to install everything other than the reactor. That would be brought out from the Citadel a day or two before installation and lifting of that section. This was so the reactor did not need to be fully powered on before it was almost due to start powering systems inside the huge ship.

Damon came up to stand beside his son.

"Have you got a name for her, Tom?"

Tom took a deep breath and sighed it out. "Well, the more I look at her and the more I realize where my idea came from, the more I feel I have to give it a name to recognize what I've built. Do you remember that Japanese animated sci-fi show, *Battleship Yamato*?"

Damon nodded. "Not only remember it but I was young enough to see the original back in the seventies. The one you saw was a remake from about thirty years after the original. That aside, I think you have captured the spirit of that animated space submarine, so I agree to the homage."

"I've wanted something that is both clever or at least meaningful and possibly historical. Then, when christening time comes in a week or so, I'm going to call her the *Yamato II*."

His father smirked trying to figure what Bud might call it.

Tom caught his grin and nodded. "Yeah. I know that flyboy is going to have some strange name already in his mind. So, I am prepared for *Charlie the NepTuna*, *The Neptube*, and even The *Loch Nep Monster*."

Damon shook his head. "Have your sister either knock or kiss some sense into the man." He smiled knowing pretty much what Sandy could and would do to get a point across to her husband.

Still to come would be the two forward sections that included the large control room Tom believed to be reminiscent of several early twenty-first century television and movie spaceship control rooms.

This one would be about thirty feet front to back with a series of screens wrapping around the front, twenty-five feet wide with a pilot station between where Tom or whoever was the shift commander and the actual pilot of the ship sat, and the front of the room. And, like many of those fictional Captains, Tom chose to place the command chair about a full foot up from the deck so he or she would have full view of the room.

In front of that was to be the forward maneuvering section along with the samples collection equipment. There would be ample high-pressure tanks to draw in dozens of samples of the liquids they would encounter, a core drilling rig that could be swung down and then lowered onto anything solid they came across. That would be capable of self-emptying as many as two dozen thirty-foot cores—each about four inches wide—into holding bins that would seal the contents inside.

There were gas collection tanks and input ports plus a variety of sensors right up in the nose.

And, a few windows.

Tom believed people did not want to be fully enclosed and even with the one hundred-degree view in the control room he had also designed about two dozen windows into the living section and another four up in the nose. Anyone could avail themselves of these when they chose.

Of course, to save on air and recirculation equipment, Tom would keep the forward section under very low pressure. It would be like walking along the top of the tallest mountain in the world. Sure, there was technically some oxygen and air pressure, but it would make most people sick and unconscious in a minute without supplemental oxygen.

There was enough air in there to maintain a minimally heated space so all anyone going inside needed was an air tank and a mask.

And likely a heavy coat because Tom had no intention of wasting power keeping an unoccupied space at a comfortable temperature.

CHAPTER 13 /
ANOTHER BIG SPACE BUILD

THE BEST place Tom ever found to assemble things in space was in geosynchronous orbit around the planet. That meant things had to be lifted to about 22,300 miles, the same height as the old Outpost in Space. But, that was not an obstacle now he had the *Goliath*, his giant lifting ship with its wide, flat cargo disc and powerful repelatron.

That was the target of the ship as it lifted off from the grounds at Enterprises one night—taking place at night and in the wee small hours meant little chance of anyone looking in to see what was going on—heading upwards slowly enough to not cause much turbulence in the surrounding air until it was above thirty thousand feet.

On its cargo deck sat the first two sections of the *Yamato II*, the very aft propulsion section and the next one, the power and systems section.

The trip up took longer than normal because Tom wanted them to go slow and steady and take no chances. Especially as they approached the old Outpost. Now in mostly civilian hands, the new owners were a little overly cautious about anything approaching.

"Outpost One, this is Swift ship, *Goliath*. We are on final approach to your location with the first two pieces of the cargo we have already discussed. Our position will be five thousand feet off your trailing edge."

Tom meant they would technically be behind the station that was travelling at the exact speed the Earth below rotated. He did not want to be in front of the station as that might pose small safety issues; a lost tool could eventually find itself hitting the station behind. This way anything misplaced would drift farther away and eventually be drawn down by gravity.

"Roger, *Goliath*. Uhh, can we ask that you stand off by fifty miles, please. We have been warned the cargo you carry might be radioactive."

Flatly, Tom stated, "No. And because I have a suspicion who might have sent you that warning, I will tell you they are in violation of an international agreement regarding what this ship we intend to put together just off your station is about to accomplish. So, get the station commander on the line and prepare to receive us."

He turned to Bud and shrugged. "They have not kept up with their payments to us and by contract I could be a hard case and tell them we are reclaiming the station, but I really don't want it. I just want what we'd agreed to—"

The station commander appeared on Tom's monitor.

"What's this I hear about you throwing your weight around, Mr. Swift?" He sounded more curious than angry.

Tom relayed what the duty radioman had told him and also related the issues with the Chinese.

The commander considered things a moment before replying, "I see. Well, that radio call we received came from somewhere around Beijing so if what you say is true then I'll give my permissions to have you come in to the agreed position. Can you give me five minutes to check with Washington?"

Tom agreed.

When the commander came back he was red-faced and apologetic.

"I really hate being put in a position like that. Of course you can come in. That radio call we got was meant to poison our desire to receive you and did not come, from what I can see, from any legitimate source."

Tom thanked him and said they would come over to the station in an hour to say their hellos.

"So, are you going to bring those people a fortune in diamonds to reward them for being such jerks?"

"No, Bud. For all their troubles and troublemaking, they get half a pound at best while all the other nations involved get at least twice that."

While the five-man moving crew suited up and got ready to release the two giant space sub sections—to be tethered together and to the ship for safety the first few hours—Tom and Bud donned long-range maneuvering backpacks and headed for the station. They landed on the "top" of the station and headed inside the large cargo airlock.

Once the pressure was equalized, Bud reached over and pressed the OPEN button, and the two men stepped into the reception room.

A man waited patiently for them to remove their helmets and suit gauntlets before stepping forward.

"I am so sorry for the mix-up, Mr. Swift," he said extending a hand to shake.

Tom reached out and shook it, a flat-lipped grin on his face.

"I really do not enjoy being told about three hours after agreements had been made that things were changing. Please inform your owners that they are to insist your radio personnel be trained to immediately pass along any negative or changed permissions in the future." Tom took a deep breath. "And now that I've got that off my chest," he smiled, "I'd like to offer you a large tank of oxygen we brought up to supplement your atmosphere while I and my people occasionally come over for a rest."

The man smiled back at the inventor. "That's great. Our hydroponics system is a little under the weather right now and we're struggling to make enough for the current population. I don't suppose you have anyone who might look at the system and try to spot what might be wrong?"

Tom shook his head. "No, but I'll have the right man or woman on the next shipment of big parts in three days on the ship. They will be able to tell you if it is a small or large problem and perhaps send for things to remedy you troubles on our final shipment up in seven days."

After heading into a couple of the spokes to say hello to the five people then knew up here, Tom and Bud excused themselves and headed back to *Goliath*.

The crew already had both sections released and floating about one hundred meters off the side of the lifting ship, and they were taking a short break.

"We'll get them maneuvered together in the next two hours, Tom," Hank Sterling told him. Hank was not just the top all-around engineer at Enterprises and their chief pattern maker, he was one of the most reliable astronauts in the company and a man who naturally could accomplish things like building a giant space submarine in the microgravity of high orbit space.

An hour later the entire crew was outside and the process of connecting the two sections began in earnest.

For strength, each section overlapped the next one by six inches with one end slightly slimmer the other piece at the overlap point. These areas were first connected by special Durastress rivets and heat welded together using a plasma torch.

Once together they could not be taken apart unless cut apart.

It was a tried and proven method of putting things together in the airless void of space. All the large ships from *Goliath* to the *Sutter* to the giant *Space Queen* space station had been put together in this manner.

Once the two parts were tightly fitted together, and while the rest of the crew worked on the heat welding, Tom and Hank headed inside through a temporary airlock in the second section to begin connecting all of the cables and piping and such. It was a more difficult and demanding job than the outside work, but careful labeling and pre-testing of all connections meant things just slid together, snapped into place, or screwed tightly into each other.

The welding work took eleven hours—performed in three parts of a maximum of four hours—while Tom and Hank worked practically non-stop.

Fortunately for them, and because Tom had shipped up the sections sealed and with breathable atmosphere inside, they could work without their bulky spacesuits.

By the time they finished, the outside work was only fifteen minutes from completion.

Both men pulled out pre-moistened cleaning towels from the pockets of their suits and wiped themselves down. They had been sweating quite a bit and neither man had paused long enough for more than a small sip of water. Now, that was starting to tell as Tom felt his legs cramping.

"I might be in a bit of trouble, Hank. Dehydration is starting to set in and my legs are feeling the worst of it. How are you doing?"

The big man was sitting beside his boss. "Not a lot better, skipper. Too bad this isn't the living quarters or we'd have the first aid setup and those self-injecting saline bags Doc came up with."

Greg Simpson was a very good doctor and over the years he had asked Tom to build him a few things to make his job easier. But, about three months earlier he had come to the inventor with a design of his own for an arm cuff that sensed a viable vein or artery, positioned a small-bore needle in the right spot and stuck it in, setting the flow of the purified water according to three possibilities with buttons controlling them.

The saline bags were also of his design and fitted around the cuff where a pair of small arms gave the bag a constant squeeze and held it in place allowing the "patient" to move around.

Tom grinned and then grimaced as his left leg cramped up. Seeing this, and not feeling quite as bad, Hank positioned himself so he could lift and stretch Tom's leg up to relieve the cramp.

After a minute, Tom nodded. "That's much better. Thanks. Let's drink another pack of water and try to get out of here and back to *Goliath*."

Both men were feeling better ten minutes later when Bud called to tell them he and the others were heading back.

"Want me to come help you two?" he asked.

Tom told his friend about their predicament and asked if at least two of the crew could stand by at the airlock to give assistance should either he or Hank become unable to get themselves back.

"Sure, Tom. Uhh, do you want me to jet over and bring back a couple of Doc's magic sacks?"

Tom groaned. Leave it to Bud to come up with a pun name for something that might be a lifesaver someday.

After looking at Hank who shrugged and stood up, Tom replied, "No. We'll avail ourselves of those once we get back and can shuck these suits. Just be out there in three minutes when we open the door."

Everyone got back to *Goliath* safely with Tom and Hank heading for their small rooms, each with a couple saline bags and one of Doc's cuffs. Half an hour later, and now properly rehydrated, both men changed into clean, dry and un-smelly clothes and headed for the upper deck area where the others were having a meal.

"Take a seat, you two, and let chef Bud fix you something. Lasagna, beef stew, or chicken pot pie?"

All foods served in the micro gravity of the ship had to hold together so things featuring thick sauces were favored.

Tom had the lasagna while Hank opted for the stew. As they ate both teams exchanged ideas on what went well and what might need a little fine-tuning for the connections for the final three sections.

"It would help a lot it we had about eight or so hold down points where we could get lines connected on both sides and sort of pull things together, skipper," one of the techs suggested. "We really need that rather than all getting behind one section and pushing."

Hank took a note and said he would attend to that for the next sections. "I might need to come up and rig something on the existing power section so that will work."

"Go ahead and note that. I don't believe a special trip will be necessary, but we'll plan on spending several additional hours up here next go-around."

By the time they returned to Enterprises a day later, the build was officially a half day ahead of schedule. Adding the connecting points would eat up some of that margin on trip two, but Tom was confident they had ample time to do that and still take off on the

Friday a week after the next one.

Tom was happy to see the living and control sections were already at Enterprises and would be staged and lifted onto *Goliath's* deck the following evening.

Doc, who had been notified automatically when the saline injecting cuffs had been used, demanded to check Tom and Hank out.

"This is nothing to fool around with and if I do clear you for another flight any time soon, you have to take along, *and drink*, at least a half liter of water with some electrolytes every hour. That along with a mandatory five-minute rest period. Understand?"

They both nodded.

They also both passed his exam and he declared them able to make the flight the following day.

"One thing. I'd like to ask you both to get at least eight hours of sleep tonight. Toward that I am sending you both home with a little pinkish pill that is a powerful decongestant that also acts as a sleep inducing aid. Take it a half hour before bedtime and then give into its request you close your eyes and relax. There will be no lasting effects so you will rise and shine in about the prescribed eight. Oh, and please remember the water thing?"

Both Tom and Hank grinned at Doc and said they would take his advice. Neither man had enjoyed the cramping and both had promised themselves to drink more.

This time, as *Goliath* approached the Outpost, there was no refusal to allow them to come in as close as they needed to be. Tom and his hydroponics expert, Mallorie Dunlap, the woman who had designed much of the most recent equipment for the Martian colony, came over and were taken to the upper level gardens.

The tanks were moving slowly past a series of windows and solid ceiling pieces to give bursts of light and semi-light to the plants. They did not have a lot of room and so there was only a two-tier system where they were exposed to this light for about four hours and then four hours underneath that level and what would be like an hour before sundown.

She suggested it was going to take an hour or more to do her measurements so her look told Tom he was not needed or especially desired to be hanging around. Ditto the station commander.

The two men left her and headed for the central mess area of the station where they had coffee and discussed the previous attempt by the Chinese to influence the station into refusing to let Tom come anywhere close.

"I can't begin to think why they believe that might have stopped or even slowed us," the inventor told his host. "I mean, we could do this anywhere along the geostationary orbit, it is just that we wanted to be close to the station for the larger living space it offers." He shrugged.

"The person, or someone our radioman says sounded a lot like the first one, called again an hour before you got here today and made another warning. Something along the lines of, 'If you allow Tom Swift and his deadly space platform to come close, your station will be destroyed. If not by him, then our glorious peoples shall do the job to keep you from bringing contamination back to infest the Earth.' I guess that is more an outright threat than a warning, huh?"

Tom nodded. "Let me have a copy of that transmission, please, and access to your radio room. There is a certain someone back in Washington who needs to have that."

Twenty minutes later Tom's call to Peter Quintana finished with the senator swearing that the President was going to hit the ceiling.

The construction went better than the first time up and a lot of that was due to the addition of the special hold-down spots allowing a small winch system Tom had also brought along, to do most of the heavy moving work.

Inside, Bud worked with Tom and Hank to attach everything. He had set his smart watch with a reminder for every fifty-five minutes and was not shy about letting the others know when it was time to stop, sit and drink.

They did and there was no repeat of the cramping.

Plus, with the additional set of hands, even the short breaks were more than made up for and their work was finished three hours faster than in the first instance.

The final load consisted of the front section and two tanks. One contained the methane to be used in the plasma jets fore and aft, and the other one was almost pure oxygen to be used to replenish the air inside the ship over the entire duration of the voyage.

Mallorie Dunlap had remained in the outpost and had been tending to the hydroponics line where she made great strides in getting things back on track.

"They had over-fertilized the water for a start," she reported to Tom as they sat in *Goliath* an hour before heading home. "Then, and to try to overcome the problem, they had put straight station water into the tanks and that brought with it a few bacteria that should not be in the tanks. Fortunately I was able to control that and get the water balanced so they are now back to about ninety-three percent of their needed capacity and it will improve over the next week to one hundred percent!"

Tom told her that was very good news and asked if she had left them with explicit instructions.

"Well, sort of. They are going to pay for me to come up next month for a recheck. Between now and then I will design a small fertilizer-infusing device they can use to automatically check and replenish what is needed. Some of that will likely just be bubbling a little extra nitrogen into the water while some might be a de-bacterialized organic compound." Seeing his forthcoming question, she added, "Purified, non-stinky and liquidized cow manure."

The ship was taking its final form now. Tom spent a full day over inside both walking around checking connections, but also performing small tests on subsystems. The larger tests would come three days later when *Goliath* returned to collect the two empty tanks and bring up a skeleton crew of six to assist him.

For now, everything was working. He even tried tripping entire sets of breakers only to watch as they performed immediate checks and reset themselves in just seconds.

He discovered several things he did not recognize but figured they were necessary to the running of the ship. A few were electrical circuits and then there were six small valves in the aft section attached to one-inch stainless steel pipes that just disappeared into the walls behind a panel.

Tom told himself to ask about them but an hour later he had lost that thought and was deep into checking the control panel for the pilot's position. It was, like most newer Swift craft, a curved one-piece monitor panel where all the instruments and controls could be moved into the position each pilot thought best for them. The surface was smoked glass so until it was energized, it looked like a dark brown and very shiny surface. The thing was, once powered up, the surface became anything but glossy and would not reflect any light so the pilot was never presented with any glare.

He sat in the "captain's" seat and nodded to himself. This was a beautifully designed and constructed craft. The interior design was thanks in large part to Arv and his sense of aesthetics. It was also due in no small part to what Hollywood had made almost synonymous with spaceship design.

But, it was the outside he was quite proud of. With its wider than tall shape and vertically pointed bow it was a combination of that traditional submarine look, one that would aid in traversing the slushy ocean of Neptune, along with the broad and stable stance of a surface ship. All tests in the computers back at Enterprises, plus Arv's two-foot miniature runs in both the fast water tank and the deep chill methane tanks had proven it to be the best combination for the job ahead.

He could find no fault in the ship. Even the bunks in the individual rooms were comfortable and a little wider and longer than any he'd used in his previous spaceships or submersibles.

The sixteen men in the crew would work in three shifts of five with him retaining overall command. That way, no shift needed to work longer than six hours before they had twelve off to rest, eat and even be entertained.

He felt mostly comfortable as he suited up and left the *Yamato II*, but deep in the back of his mind, something lurked spoiling his complete relaxation.

Tom knew he would need to figure out what it was or else he would have troubles sleeping until the mission was well underway.

There was a bit of a bother the next day when the FAA inspector who had "finally found time" to come out to certify the repaired runway took a look and walked away stating he was not about to play games.

Damon was called and intercepted the man at the gate where Security was holding him as he had departed his escort and driven back on his own.

"I'm Damon Swift and I'd like to know just why you are refusing to certify, or even to closely inspect, our repairs."

The man was angry but he answered, "Because you called me out for nothing. There isn't any sign of a repair as far as I could see so I assume this is some sort of joke."

A thought came to the inventor. "Do you mean you could not detect the repaired area? Doesn't that tell you it is an expert job? Besides, if you have never heard of it, we operate repair vehicles that work on asphalt or concrete and make such invisible repairs."

He described the process and as he went on, the man's attitude changed.

"Okay. Take me back out, please, and show me the exact spot where the old ends and the new begins."

Damon and the Facilities Manager did, and the inspector was flabbergasted at what he could only now detect.

He looked at Damon and apologized. "My predecessor told me you folks do the impossible. I thought this was some sort of preplanned test. A big joke on me. I am sorry for the confusion and my misplaced anger. You hereby are re-certified to use this runway for anything it was previously set to handle."

CHAPTER 14 /
HEADING TO NEPTUNE, AS YOU DO, ON A THURSDAY...

THE *Yamato II* was built, tested and ready to go a full day early, and Tom could not come up with an adequate reason for not starting the trip as soon as possible.

Even Bashalli, generally reticent to have him leave, told him it was fine, "But I am holding you to a promise you made five months ago. You must be back here for our child's birth! No excuses, Tom." She paused as tears came to her eyes. "Please?" she nearly pleaded.

Tom took her into his arms and hugged her for five minutes before he said, "I promise, Bash. This is a six day out and ten days there and six days back mission. That's a day over three weeks and you are not due for another six weeks. I'll be back in plenty of time. You'll see."

They had spent most of the previous four days together other than the three hours a day she went into work at the Shopton Advertising Agency and he headed into work. But they had their lunches and afternoons and evenings together.

Amanda, their nanny, realized they needed time just to themselves and so she kept Bart and Mary very busy in the afternoons. This changed at dinnertime when the family, and Amanda, all dined together and chatted and laughed.

When that Thursday morning came and Tom kissed Bashalli and Bart and Mary and told them all to be good, it was just five days before Valentine's Day and almost exactly six weeks before the baby was due.

"You will be very carful," Bashalli told him. It was not even close to a question.

Tom smiled at her and kissed the tip of her nose. "I will be so careful, Bash, that I might even come home a day early."

She gave out a small snort. She knew better. She also knew that given her near tantrum and temporarily leaving their home when Tom went to Venus on a mission to rescue a fallen and very costly probe, she needed to be brave and supportive.

He asked, for the fifth time, whether she wanted to come out to Fearing for the takeoff, but she refused. He and his fifteen man crew would head up in the *Challenger*, transfer over to the *Yamato II* where it sat off the old Outpost, and then rendezvous with the *TranSpace Dart* that had already gone out to retrieve the small black hole that would drag the *Yamato II* out to Neptune and back.

If everything went on schedule, from initial take-off until the time *Yamato* would pass the Moon should be five hours.

After a tearful goodbye where even the usually stoic Bart nearly refused to release his father's neck, Tom drove to Enterprises where he met up with Bud and five of the others who would be coming along. They included Red Jones and Slim Davis who would be pilots along with Bud, Mike Jayston their communications man, the technician from the miniature test dive, Stephen Boskwick, and Chow with his obligatory last minute ice chest of food. Accompanying them to the ship but the man who would bring *Challenger* back to Fearing was Zimby Cox.

Sixteen other crates of foods and cooking and eating utensils had already been installed into the living quarters section before it went up.

Tom's Toad stood ready for them next to the Barn, fully fueled and checked out by Bud.

Standing with the men were Arv and Linda. While he shook their hands and asked for someone to bring him back just one tiny Neptune gem, Linda had a small talk with Tom.

"All along the process Arv and Hank and I made tiny changes to the real ship up there," she told him. "If you come across anything that just doesn't seem right, radio me. Have the duty operator call and wake me up if it is after hours or even in the middle of the night. Okay?"

She looked pensive and so Tom smiled at her and nodded. "Of course. Nothing I like better than to wake a sleeping woman at three in the morning. We will be just fine, but if there is anything out of whack, I'll be calling. Be certain to not sleep with the ringer turned off."

Linda gave him a little hug and then walked over to Bud. Seeing her coming and having also seen the hug she'd given Tom, he stepped back involuntarily.

"Come over here, Bud, and take a friendly hug from a friend!"

Sheepishly, he obeyed and even hugged her back.

Tom and Bud climbed into the front of the Toad, closed the canopy, and started the two turbines. As they came up to speed, Bud radioed for taxi and take-off clearance.

"*Roger. Use runway two-seven. Winds are just about on the nose at five, surface temperature is one degree colder than the air at fifty feet and is sitting at fifty-one degrees. Barometer is three-*

zero-point one and steady. You are clear to taxi but hold for take-off. Shopton morning commuter to Albany is one minute from their take-off and will be traversing the area. Your hold should only be three minutes."

"Roger, tower. Taxi and hold at two-seven. Call when we can release and roll."

That call came within two minutes of them stopping at the end of the runway. They had watched as the older 27-seat commuter turboprop passed by Enterprises. It would settle in at just ten thousand feet before dropping down to Albany while Tom and company would head quickly to twenty-nine thousand feet and cruise down the Atlantic coast.

"Rolling now," Bud announced to the tower.

They advised him to switch to the upper tower's frequency when they passed one thousand feet.

He did that a moment later and the taller, hill-situated tower passed him on to the FAA controllers one level up.

"Swift Two, you are cleared on your flight plan direct to Glousester and from there south to Fearing Island. Be advised to remain above two-eight thousand feet at all times until Fearing Approach clears you for descent."

"Roger. Understand and out."

Bud looked over at Tom. "I guess that means they don't want to have to see us in the sky, huh?"

Tom shook his head. "No, Bud. It means that the President is taking off for his last tour of the nation starting in about a half hour and they want all traffic out of the area or too high to be a bother. Peter Quintana told dad about it yesterday and he called me last night. So, up we go," and he pulled back on the joystick pointing the nose of the jet about twenty degrees up.

All too soon, or not soon enough for some, Tom radioed the Fearing Island tower asking for approach information. He was immediately cleared to descend to five thousand feet and to slow to three hundred knots.

"You'll be on runway Left coming straight in. Uhh, when you get to five thousand, call and we'll give you more. Be advised, you may need to stand off five miles. We have a private launch taking place in nineteen to twenty minutes and that will be about when you get here."

"What's that about?" Slim asked from the seat behind Bud.

"Dad has agreed to make a couple dozen launches for the Navy this year. I forgot today is one of them. Unfortunately for us, we likely will have to circle as their payloads are very time critical. As in I hear this window is just four minutes long."

"That's pretty tight," Red piped up.

"Why's the big hurry, Tom?" Chow asked.

"Well, we don't know and for security reasons can't be told what is going up, but for a few of them positioning is the most important thing. Dad and I believe, privately so no blabbing this, a few of them are meant to sit very close to Russian, Chinese and even Indian spy satellites to see what it is they are getting shots of."

That left them all thinking the matter over in silence until the Fearing Tower came back on.

"Skipper. Sorry about this and we all know you're eager to get up, but we have to send you once around. Standard five-mile clearance. Ought to give you a good view. We'll call out the final ten seconds. Over."

"Understood. Thanks. Tom out."

The view was spectacular as the small rocket headed quickly into the sky. Built in three sections, the initial booster was a solid stage just five feet tall. It burned for only thirty-seconds before dropping away from the main, liquid-fuel stage that had it passing twenty thousand feet just a few seconds later.

A utility van met them as they stepped from the Toad and whisked them to the waiting *Challenger*. After settling in, they took off heading for their first rendezvous to take place about fifty minutes later.

None of them other than Bud, Hank and Tom had seen the *Yamato II* fully assembled. It hung in the nothingness of space all whites, grays and a series of reds that were where the outside view ports were in the living, power and very back of the control room sections. As they neared the vessel, several more red windows could be seen in the nose section.

"What are those things that look a little like turrets on top, skipper?" Slim inquired.

"Well, the forward one is the three-sixty camera system to give us all the views we'll see on the screens at the front of the control room. The back one is a backup for that plus a seat and viewport for anyone wanting to take a direct look out the front. Those side windows are only that; side views of what we are passing.

"And, if you can see it, there is what looks like another observation bump behind that second turret. That is one of the main intakes for gas samples."

He gave them an all around tour pointing out the two main drive intakes of both sides forward of the control room section and their exit points far back in the ship, almost half way back on the final aft section.

"There is one more like those underneath," he added.

He had been scooting around the space sub keeping the big windows in the control room facing *Yamato II* to give them all the very best view possible. After five minutes the inventor decided that they could sit out here for hours, but they had a mission to get to, so he asked them to all take their seats for the maneuver over to the airlock.

"We did not put any sort of docking mechanism over there, so it will be closed suits and careful drifting over," he warned them. Everyone readied themselves and he slipped the *Challenger* over the final nine hundred feet until it sat just thirty feet off.

Tom traded places with Zimby telling him to wait for a radio call before leaving.

Suited up and having checked each other the rest of the team met Tom in the large hangar. They would depressurize it and use it like an airlock so they could all exit at the same time.

Red and Bud went over first with the flyer taking a cable over to be used to bring Chow's cooler. Once that line was attached, Tom helped the cook get the ice chest attached and it was quickly over and stowed inside the air lock.

Tom was the last man over and he joined the others in the 6-man airlock on the side of the ship. It took three minutes to get the air pressure inside up to that of the rest of the ship, and the door pulled in an inch and slid to the side.

Everyone stopped and just stared at the beautiful surroundings. Individual rooms were set along both walls with Tom informing them this was just the upper level with about three-quarters of the rooms. "The others plus our exercise area and the entertainment area are down those spiral stairs," he said pointing at the somewhat wide set of steps heading down.

He suggested everybody take ten minutes to explore and then he wanted them prepared to run through a few practice sessions for receiving the *TranSpace Dart* and her cargo of their black hole. That would come in about six hours.

"Before that we will use the plasma engines to get us about a thousand miles from the Outpost so they can't gripe about any potential danger."

Bud was the first to notice that each room had already been assigned and one man's name sitting in a small holder to the right of that door. He grinned seeing his was next to Tom's.

Tom took them as a group back to the power room and explained many of the controls.

"Some of you will be working back here almost exclusively and have had a few days in a simulator to get ready for what you will be doing. Ditto that for everyone else working in the control room. Only Chow could be absolutely trusted to understand his job without the need for any training," he said with a grin.

Everyone chuckled and agreed that Chow needed no training in how to be a great cook.

"We will be working in our gravity onesies until we get to Neptune, and then we will rely on the gravity of the planet. That, by the way, is about ten percent over that we're all used to so I, at one-eighty, will seem to weigh one ninety-eight."

"Guess we'll all feel like we need to go on a diet, huh?" Hank said coming into the power room behind them.

"Some more than others," Bud quipped but when he looked to Chow he was reminded that the cook was now a full twenty pounds lighter than when they'd first met him. "Just not Chow so much," he added trying to not get in trouble with the man who would be feeding them.

"Yer durned tootin', but say Tom... if we're all gonna be a mite heavier, why the exercise set-up?"

"Easy, Chow. That's for the trip out and back, but mostly for the trip out. I want everyone to have a good hour a day to tone muscles, so I've set up the emitters in the ceiling in that area to one-point-one gravities or what we'll experience when we get to our destination."

Ten minutes later the crew were standing and sitting at their stations, with each position manned by the person who would be there for the first shift and the other two standing behind them watching and going over the duties in their minds.

Because the *Yamato II* was not significantly different in how it was flown from most other ships—and especially the *Sutter*, which had the only other plasma drive set-up in the Swift fleet—there were no real hiccups in the first run through. All three of the pilots were well versed in *Sutter's* drive system so it was only a matter of deciding where they wanted the different instruments.

As each would key in at the start of their shift, those instruments would rearrange as needed to suit them, and all in about two seconds.

"Those first three runs went great," Tom congratulated the men in the control room directly and over the intercom to the ones in the power section.

"I believe we are ready to get that black hole delivery and then head out. So, helm, take us out one thousand miles from geosynchronous orbit and hold position. Communications—and I'm sorry we couldn't bring two more like you, Mike, but there won't be a constant need for manning that position—call the *TranSpace Dart* and tell her to rendezvous in one hour. Bud'll feed you that exact position."

As powerful as the plasma drive was, it took a few minutes to overcome the large ship's inertia and to noticeably move away from the old station. Soon, however, it was scooting along so much Tom leaned forward and had a quick and quiet conversation with Bud to make certain he did not go too fast and overshoot their planned stopping point.

"Thanks, skipper. I guess my enthusiasm was getting the better or me. I'll slow her down starting in five minutes."

The rendezvous with *TranSpace Dart* was going to be something they had never attempted. Normally Tom might have just had the *Yamato II* head out to the handy Lagrange Point where the small black hole—probably something that had been thrown out of a much larger black hole at some time in the distant past and that had been captured within the asteroid belt between Mars and Jupiter—and pick it up there.

But, that would have added as much as a half day of travel as Tom was under strict orders to not exceed a certain speed inside the Moon's orbit other than with his ship, the *Challenger*.

By having the *TranSpace Dart* bring it in it meant they could connect to their main drive mechanism before even leaving the Earth's orbit. And, once in the clear they could accelerate so quickly and up to about .7 of light speed before they needed to swing around and use the same forces to slow them, it would cut a lot of slow and actually difficult travel out.

"The *Dart* is hailing us, Tom," Mike called over from the communications station.

Tom picked up a small earbud sitting in a tray on his chair arm and inserted it into his ear. Not only would it provide for a private conversation, if desired, it also could simply act as a replacement for a microphone mounted on a traditional headset.

"Tom here. We're well on our way."

"Skipper? It's Dwayne Dimmock acting as comms for the *TranSpace Dart*. We are nearly in position and will be waiting for you. The Captain sends his regards and asks if you could hurry. Our little black friend seems to be a bit, umm, squirrelly today."

Tom could picture Dwayne, a man of color himself, grinning at the "little black friend" comment.

"Okay," he said slowly. "Define squirrelly please."

"Well, it is as if it really does not want to play today. It seems to not want to stay directly in front of us and that makes the nose of the *Dart* swing a few degrees to one side or the other. We think it might be our problem, but would appreciate it if you could get here and see what you believe."

"We'll be there in one hour. Tell your captain to keep a good hold on our *friend*. Tom out."

As they neared the other ship, Tom could see how the *Dart* was slowly spinning in a counter-clockwise direction. He estimated it might be a full rotation every three minutes if it was not checked, and the Captain of the ship was doing what he could every fifteen or twenty seconds to arrest and reverse the movement.

After indicating to Mike to open the radio frequency, Tom said, "*Yamato* to *Dart*. We are here and can see your predicament. Can you put Captain Bodack on the line, please."

"You've got him, Tom," came the slightly strained voice of the man Tom had first met via Bud when they were trying to get a handle on a tectonic plate shift problem. "I believe we've pinned this thing down to a faulty mount for our Attractatron and I have everyone other than me trying to wrestle it into position... hang on one," and the transmission cut. A moment later Deke was back.

"Wow. Talk about an unexpected two hours of fun... not! I just got the word we really need to give you the potato and then, and I guess only then, can my crew get that mount tied down."

"We'll ease up and try to match any movement you have, Deke, but this might be a little tricky. No matter what, make certain that ship gets more than the once over back at Fearing. I'm having Bud attempt to lock onto your computer data and then get us swinging with you. Give us a few minutes."

Four minutes later his pilot informed him the other ship was just turning faster than the large space sub could match.

"I know this isn't standard, but could they sort of let it go and we move in and grab it?"

"Uhh, leaving it to do whatever it wants to do in the meantime?"

Tom asked, both cautious and with some level of hope.

"Pretty certain if we time this right between them dropping the ball and me scooting in and grabbing it, it'll only be on its own about two seconds."

While he thought this over, Tom contacted Deke Bodack to see what he thought.

"Well, you know I trust Bud with my life, Tom. And, I think if I get the guys to jam something in the wobbling mount to freeze it for at least a minute I can stop the rotation as we get back around to the point Bud can grab the hole. I'm willing if you are."

Decision made, Tom agreed and they discussed how long it would take to get back around. It was thought to be about two more minutes and Deke had, while Tom was considering things, told his team to jam the mount in the least acute position possible.

It required two tries but the black hole was now released by the *TranSpace Dart* and being held by the *Yamato's* Attractatron.

Deke radioed his best wishes and said they were, "...heading for dirt." Tom thanked him for his work and to tell the crew they had an extra day off once they landed.

With the black hole firmly in the grasp of the forward mounted Attractatron system, Tom ordered the ship to be pointed toward their destination.

"Let's bring the ship up to full acceleration just after we pass the Moon," he told the crew. "We might be a day early overall, but this delay put us a couple hours behind."

The voyage—a first for any manned mission—to Neptune had officially begun.

CHAPTER 15 /
AN EVEN BIGGER, BLUE MARBLE

IF TOM and the crew thought the Earth was a beautiful and blue marble in the solar system, the sight of Neptune as they came to within a million miles was a shock.

It was, as they knew, larger and almost entirely blue and even in the soft and faded light of the distant sun, it hung like a colorful beach ball in the monitor at the front of the control room. In fact, in Tom's mind the comparison of Earth to Neptune was like marble and a... well, it was *not* a beach ball. That would be too large to represent what they were seeing in the forward monitor. More like a golf ball next to a softball someone had painted in a gentle blue with a few wispy white streaks.

And, there was even a hint of a gleam from the distant sun reflecting from the surface. This was enhanced by the computer that handled all the video inputs and brought the brightness up so everything looked more like it might if the planet had as much sunlight as the Earth.

They had been in slow down mode for nearly fifty hours and would go into orbit in another seven.

"Have I ever used the exclamation, Jetz before?" came a near whispered question from the inventor's left where Bud stood, mouth agape.

"You have. Many times."

"Well then, forget all the other times, and I say *Jetz!* with all my being. This is as beautiful as Sandy and Bash together, and they're gorgeous!"

Next to Bud and slightly behind him stood Hank.

"So, Mr. Barclay," he intoned in a voice that would have done a prosecuting attorney proud, "are you saying you would trade that planet for your beautiful wife?"

Bud turned red and then blanched white as the meaning of this hit him.

"Oh, gee! Heck no, Hank. I just meant that... well... ummm— I meant that as girls and ladies go I think Sandy is a knockout and so is Bashalli, but as planets go, this blows my mind."

The engineer had to agree but did not want to let the flyer off that easily.

"Well, when we get back you'd best not let on to Sandy that you've found another love."

"Come on, Hank, Give me a little break, okay?"

Hank tried to look like he was giving things a good consideration but soon broke out in laughter. "No worries, Bud. And, confidentially I agree. As planets go this even beats the good old Earth!"

The flyer nodded. He had never really been worried about being tattled on with his jealous wife.

Not really...

During the previous nearly six days the ship had been cruising along at top speed for just a few hours over half the trip, and had been slowing down the rest of the time. They were currently flying tail first toward the planet but Tom had the aft camera view up on the screen so they could all watch the approach.

And, for much of the time the crew had been going though drills on everything they would need to do once they arrived. From the orbital insertion to the dropping of two probes and even all necessary steps to slow the ship down to bring it into the atmosphere had been practiced. About the only thing they had not tried—at least in the computers—was dropping off their black hole.

That wasn't to say Tom had not computed and recomputed the position they must be in so the hole did not become attracted to either the planet or the moon, Triton. In fact, he had checked his figures based on at least fifteen positions around the planet as the moon orbited.

He was happy to find there was no real difference and that meant something else to him.

Neptune, under all the methane ocean, was almost certainly to be a ball with no greatly raised areas. If there had been any that would have subtly thrown off the position of their parking place. Now, he felt there were no worries as long as they could come back to reclaim it within eight to ten days.

Even at their greatly reduced travel speed it was obvious to all they were coming closer and closer.

At the three-hour mark Tom asked that all stations be fully manned and that a final check of their drive system be made. This entailed giving an additional short burst of the plasma drive, which had the effect of slowing them slightly, but he had accounted for this by having their speed slightly above that desired.

"All systems and stations reporting manned, ready and fully

functional," Mike Jayston at the communications panel reported.

"And, all helm controls show nothing but green," Bud added.

Chow, who had been keeping the crew fed during the trip came forward and stood slightly behind Tom. "Want anything like drinks or snacks before we head in?" he asked quietly.

Tom turned his head and looked at the chef. "You know Chow, that sounds great. I'd just make it a single choice on the food, something light so nobody gets sleepy, and then something with a little caffeine to keep us all alert. Thanks."

Three minutes later, an attesting to Chow's having prepared something "just in case," he came back with containers of chocolate pudding and some coffee and tea. Knowing what each man favored, he was only surprised when Bud asked for a tea rather than his normal coffee.

When everybody had theirs, Chow headed back to this small kitchen and made certain everything was put away and all doors closed tightly.

He'd been caught short once in *Challenger* when a maneuver to avoid a collision had sent him falling backwards, breaking his arm in the process, and dropping about thirty containers and some silverware down on him.

Never agin', he'd told himself at the time.

He'd been so embarrassed by the incident he had asked Tom to outfit all major vessels that had kitchens with a small switch that flashed a green light at the command station to notify whoever was captaining that Chow was ready.

Seeing the "Chow" light, Tom smiled to himself. He'd promised the cook to never tell Bud about that special signal unless it was absolutely necessary.

"Okay, everybody, let's get this ship into orbit. I want to do two full orbits before we start our descent and even then it'll be a little tricky. Since we are going to back down to the planet surface, we need to be very aware of any winds that might toss us around. At the first sign of troubles, Bud will hit full power and get us back out. We have enough spare fuel onboard for up to three tries, Then, we'll need to head home if we haven't been able to set down and refuel."

Not part of the piloting crew, Mike turned in his seat and asked how they would go about refueling.

Bud spoke up. "That's an easy one, Mike. That whole ocean below us is just about nothing but fuel for this ship. Almost pure methane and already in liquid form so we just suck in a good load and it stays just the way the skipper want it. Ready to go!"

"Gee. That's pretty handy, isn't it?"

Now, with a smile, Tom replied, "The whole mission relies on it, Mike. In fact, even though Bud is generally correct, we have to slightly heat that liquid methane up while it is in storage and bleed off the small amount of hydrogen in it. Otherwise, it is a little dangerous. But, don't worry. We put that all to a test back home and it works out even better. That slight elevation in the temperature means the methane will turn into plasma with slightly less energy needed."

At the inventor's command, Bud applied a little more thrust to the plasma engines and the ship began to slow down enough to go into a very wide orbit. This was going to be a delicate maneuver as the end result was to get them within a few miles of the point where the black hole was to be dropped off.

When his three pilots had questioned why they were not using the black hole for this final maneuver before they had left the Earth, Tom's response had been they just didn't have finite enough control over the pulling power of the hole.

"I would really hate to lose control and grip on it by letting it out too far. Otherwise, it would just keep tugging us along. So, this appears to give us the best maneuvering and control. We will just use the repelatron for the last bit to keep the hole away from us until it settles into the Lagrange point."

It took longer than he'd planned to get everything into position, but they still had ample time for everything in the mission. In fact, he had purposely planned for an additional three days to make up for such delays. It was only prudent as this had never been attempted so there were more unknowns than actual knowns.

"Stand by for a tiny bit of shove and then we use the nose jets to back away. On three, one... two... and three."

Red, who was at the Attractatron controls, gave the black hole a slight push—more a little tap—as Bud energized the forward plasma jets. The effect was what Tom wanted and they soon stood a full mile away, out of the influence of the hole.

"It still amazes me, Tom," Red said as he shut down the station, "that we can harness a thing as powerful as a phenomenon that is capable of drawing in entire solar systems."

"Ah, but that is in the full size model. While we just don't know where this one came from, it has never proved to be anything but mild by comparison." This came from Bud who was staring intently at his controls with only the occasional glance up at the monitor.

With a nod, Tom concurred. "We can't get close enough to not potentially have problems with the detachment process, so for now we take what we get from our little friend. Okay," he said.

Bud used the forward plasma jets to back them farther away before swinging the ship around so they would orbit backwards. This way he knew they could slow even more and enter the atmosphere without significant further maneuvering.

As the ship orbited Neptune, Tom asked for a high sample to be taken to see if there was an indication of methane or even of the lighter gases like hydrogen and helium. The former one would generally remain mixed but helium, at least on Earth, had the habit of freeing itself and heading into space where it was lost for all time.

That was the main reason why the helium wells operated by the Swifts for the benefit of all mankind were so important. The other natural source was a well offering a natural decay of hydrogen—a deep cave in Kansas—and through a process involved in the purification of natural gas, typically done at a refinery in Texas.

However, those sources had begun to drop in volume over the decade before the deep cavern discovery in the Atlantic.

Ten minutes later the analysis of what had come into the capture vessel showed about ten parts hydrogen per only a minute trace of helium and a fractional amount of ammonia. But, that was so scarce Tom had to believe it was more from escaping the gravity that an actual outer atmosphere.

"We've got some pretty nasty storms going on down there," Red said, now manning the station with the many sensors the ship carried. "Something like five hundred-eight miles per hour in the one I'm watching. That is about a thousand miles north of what would be the equator. In fact, I'm seeing a lot of clouds in a three thousand mile wide band all around the planet."

"That might point to an approach a bit higher up. Perhaps not near the top or bottom, but above that storm zone," Tom told the three others currently in the control room.

They orbited the huge planet twice more in the next twenty hours. Each of the teams on duty made many and careful observations. Tom had requested they look specifically for areas where the storms seemed to be at a lull and for more than an hour at a time.

When he came back on duty, it was to hear the report: "Well, that great blue spot they have—sort of like Jupiter's red one—isn't really a spot after all. It's more like a clearing of the clouds made possible by a constant storm swirl at nearly seven hundred miles per hour. Oh, and the edges seemed to have a lot of ice chunks in all that wind. I'd hate to have to go down through that!"

"Me, too," Tom told him and the others.

The other reports were not favorable. Certainly there were areas where the winds were low—under one hundred miles per hour—but nowhere other than at the two polar regions, where there was little of no wind for great periods of time

"Anything else to report?" he asked.

"Only that I'm seeing a lot of what I thought were darker areas down there, but now I think they are shadows from some of the thicker and higher clouds. It's kind of eerie, because I can't actually see though the clouds themselves, but off at an angle and with the reduced sunlight not getting through, they are almost a solid blockade and the shadows are much deeper and darker than on Earth."

It was something the astronomical experts at the Swift Observatory had told Tom during a briefing the week before they took off.

He'd also been warned about the ice chunks in the "air."

"They likely have the solidity of a well-packed snowball, but repeated collisions should be avoided, Tom," he'd been told.

Tom decided to orbit one more time to give everyone more opportunities to observe what they might be getting into. He also asked that the SuperSight they carried onboard be turned to look at the thin pair of rings they could see, vaguely, plus the third ring that was more of a ghostly image to their eyes.

When the report came in, it was partially astonishing.

"Those two main rings are not like the ones around other planets, skipper. They're uneven as all heck. Some parts must be twenty miles thick and filled with stuff while you go another quarter around the arc and it is only maybe a mile thick and has almost nothing. Same for both of the main ones."

"Okay. How about that thin one a bit farther out?"

"That one is a couple hundred feet thick, just about three times as wide, and from what we've seen, nothing much larger than a golf ball on any piece. Here's the odd one. Unlike the two larger rings with their jagged pieces, ring three is made of mostly rounded globules. Like," Stephen told him, "something melted and broke apart or was smashed apart and the hot little bits all got flung out and reshaped before they cooled. Weird!"

After three full orbits plus about a quarter of the next one Tom made the decision.

"Listen everybody. We are going to start our braking maneuvers only after we reposition ourselves into more of a polar insertion orbit. I'd rather go down through a lack of storms and flying icicles than through the worst this planet seems willing to offer. We're commencing our orbit change in three minutes. Probably best we all strap in. And to those off duty who might have taken a nap, sorry to do this but for the next five hours I'd like us all to be awake and ready to assist. Thanks."

He thought a moment and then went back to make another ship wide address. "Once we get to the surface I plan on us all taking about twelve hours to sleep, eat and get ready for what is to come."

With Bud back at the helm, it only took one more orbit before he had them running pole to pole and with the same basic tilt as the planet.

"We're over the right spot with this one, skipper," he reported.

"Good. I figure it is going to take us about two thousand miles to get down, so let's start the descent after we pass the equator by at least five thousand miles. That should get us to a point about ten degrees from the pole at the same time we are absolutely tail downward."

He looked at his tablet computer to verify his distances and nodded.

"Red, Stephen? What do those probes we dropped have to say?"

Red spoke first. "Well, to confirm what observations showed, probe number one, the one that was on a parachute for slow entry, got hit by a lot of ice chunks. Nothing that knocked it out, but they did collapse the chute before it got to within five miles of the surface. It hit, I'm guessing it went under, and finally bobbed back up, but it was so cold it only sent information for eleven seconds. Verified the liquid temp at minus 298°F."

"I see," Tom said a little disappointed. He took a breath and asked for the report on the other probe.

Stephen stated, "Like Red's, it encountered a lot of ice blasts but it checked the atmosphere all the way down, did not hit too hard, and popped the antenna, uhh, raft out and then sank to about the full three hundred feel before it went off line. Same temp reading down that far as on the surface. The one sample it managed to get inside before I think that entry froze showed slightly more hydrogen than the folks back home figured. Maybe a tenth of a percent more. Other than that..." and he shrugged.

Because their greatest direction of thrust, needed to slow and head down gently enough to avoid damage, was at the back, this entailed turning the craft with its nose pointing back into space so it would, in effect, back into the upper atmosphere.

"We've practiced this in the simulator," he told his pilot, Bud, "and everything went smoothly. I've no doubt we'll duplicate that here. I want everyone in their suits—helmets at the ready—strapped in and ready to go in five minutes. I'm ready to go so you take a quick break, flyboy, and do the same."

Bud relinquished the controls to Tom and headed to the living quarters. After six days of not being encumbered with a suit, he actually was not looking forward to the next half hour.

Tom gave then all five minutes to suit up. He had come on duty three hours earlier with his on and the helmet tipped back, ready at a split second's notice to flip forward and close automatically.

When Bud came back he tapped Tom on the shoulder. "I've got it from here, skipper," he said and Tom slipped out the right side of the seat as Bud came in from the left. Tom had not rearranged the controls so all Bud needed to do was place his fingers close to the slider controls for the thrust.

Tom tapped the intercom.

"I want everyone strapped down and tight. We will be standing on our tail until we get to the surface and then will tip over, hopefully upright, in just four seconds. I do not want anyone getting up until I give the clear. That means for the next half hour you are to stay put. Here we go."

Bud knew that was his cue so he brought the plasma jets on line and started to increase their thrust. *Yamato II* began to slow and it was evident to all that their pilot was maneuvering them into a more nose up position. They even felt the tug of gravity, real and not machine created, for the first time in more than a week.

It both felt good and a little strong.

The more the ship entered the atmosphere, the more the small buffetings became stronger.

Each man had been given a small packet of fast-acting motion sickness tablets. About half of then pulled theirs out and crunched down on a liquid-filed capsule.

The effects came on in about a minute but during that time at least one man, off duty and in his assigned seat, lost the small lunch Chow had fixed for them all three hours earlier.

Up front Tom clenched his teeth and the ship lurched to their right and bumped up and down.

A moment later and things settled down.

And as suddenly as things went quiet, the ship was tossed to one side and was no longer tail down. It was about parallel to the surface.

"Bud! Get us righted and out of here! Now!" he commanded.

He needn't have order the action because Bud's trained pilot mind already told him they were in trouble and it was not time to see if he could set down somewhere safe.

The *Yamato II* shot forward and he eased the nose back up into space.

Ten minutes later he reported they were back in orbit, but no longer in their polar orbit.

It was going to take them another orbit or two to get back in position to make another attempt at landing on Neptune.

CHAPTER 16 /
DIVING INTO THE ATMOSPHERE OCEAN

TOM ORDERED the *Yamato II* to be readied for the descent into the Neptunian atmosphere nineteen hours later. It was try number two and with the additional maneuvering to get into the polar orbits, both times, Tom feared it would be their last, safe try.

He knew the plan was to settle down onto the surface of the liquid and float there for several hours before heading under the surface. Tom had already announced they would go back to shirtsleeves for the remainder of the voyage, once down, so everyone got back into their spacesuits for this maneuver with minimal grumbling.

Except for Bud. And then, only to himself.

I don't like them, besides, he thought grimly, *if we do crash then these suits are going to protect us from the freezing condition for less than fifteen seconds!*

As he sealed the front of his suit he shook that thought off, checked his air supply mini canister readout on his arm display, and went back to his piloting station.

The rest of the crew was either still in the living area getting strapped into the seats back there or were already in the control room. Most, recalling the shaking they'd taken before, had already taken their motion sickness capsules and were ready.

"Okay, skipper. I hereby relieve you and take control."

"Great, Bud. Thanks." Tom next activated the ship-wide communication system. "Tom to crew of the *Yamato II*. I realize this getting suited up is a bit of overkill, but we just don't know what sort of stresses the ship is about to be put under. Obviously the strapping in is just good practice given what we encountered the last time. This one ought to be different since Red has spotted a pretty clear path for us to take down without a lot of wind. We're still in for a little bumpiness. Anyway, we are going to hit the retros in two minutes. Check in if anyone is having difficulties or if you see anything out of order. Tom out."

Nothing was reported so, on time, Bud started the sequence that would see them on the surface twenty-six minutes later unless they had another difficult time.

Twice, as the ship took a broadside gust, Tom nearly ordered them to head back out, but something made him stop. Some of it might have been Bud shaking his head as if emphatically saying "not this time!" so the inventor and Captain of the ship held his tongue.

Twenty seconds to go and all outside air motion ceased. He leaned forward against his restraining straps and watched as the rear-facing cameras showed the surface coming up to meet them.

"Hover for a second and then set her over," he said to his pilot. On the ship wide system he announced, "We're about to tip over and set down. Brace."

The tail of *Yamato II* dipped into the liquid, and the space sub sank nearly its entire length before the nose jets pushed them over and they bobbed to the surface, level and upright.

It was no worse than a rough landing in a large commercial jet and in a moment, all drive systems had been shut down and the dull roar that had vibrated throughout the ship stopped.

It was quiet in *Yamato II*.

"Tom to crew. Well, we are here in case you didn't realize it." From around him and from the room behind came a cheer from the men of the ship.

Tom leaned forward and whispered, "That's for you, Bud. You got us down. Thanks! Remind me to tell you how close I came to ordering us back out."

Bud snorted. "Remind me to tell *you* how close my finger came to stabbing down on that button... but missed."

After requesting a full systems check, Tom released the crew to get into comfortable clothes and to have the following half day to relax.

"And, what will you be doing to relax, skipper?" Slim asked with a knowing grin.

"After I talk to the folks back home," and he glanced at his watch which had been set into 24-hour mode, he sighed, "except that it is three in the morning back there... but I was going to say I want a good four-hour nap, something warm and filling from Chow, and then I need to run a test of the Jetmarine drives. Oh, and refuel us so we don't have to take on much in the way of ballast."

"And, now?"

"Nap, food, talk and then test."

Tom's nap extended to about six hours, but he felt much better for it and headed for the special radio that allowed to split second communications with Enterprises rather than old-fashioned speed-of-light radio that would take upward of four hours at their current distance from Earth.

But thanks to a gift from their Space Friends, Tom now had six of the transmitter/receivers at his disposal. And, he had all but cracked the technology himself when he opened—with extreme caution and an understanding that he could be killing one of the precious pieces of electronics—and found that there was only one component that could not be duplicated with current Earth technology.

Unfortunately, he believed that was the secret of the faster-than-light transmissions and must work in another dimension.

He nearly fainted when he put it all back together and gave it a try.

It worked!

And, now he had taken detailed notes and even worked up a schematic, all he had to do was to find a way to either duplicate that inter-dimensional piece, or get the beings that had deserted the solar system more than a year earlier to send him a few more.

The one in *Yamato II* made contact with Enterprises and he was soon transferred to his father's desk.

"Hello, Son. Are you still battling those winds or did you get down? Or, give up?"

"We are down and floating on the surface near what would be the North Pole. It was about the only place where the winds allowed a landing."

He gave his father a brief accounting of the difficulties and asked the older inventor to pass along the entire crew's thanks to Doc Simpson for the anti-nausea drugs. When asked about the probes he had to report they had been mostly a lost cause.

"If we or anyone comes back, any probes will have to be so well insulated and with a near fire-temperature interior, they might as well not set anything down. At least, nothing they want to work for more than a few seconds. As it is, the ship, without the triple hull and Hank's incredible honeycomb insulation barrier, we would be running the reactor at full steam just to keep ourselves warm."

He also said he was sending a data-only transmission in about an hour with all of the observational information on the gaseous atmosphere and Neptune's Great Blue Spot.

"I'm certain the people up at the observatory will be most pleased with that, and will also get it broadcast out to the scientific community. Uhh, I hate to ask," Damon said, "but what about the consortium of nations funding this little jaunt?"

"They get it in fifteen minutes, right after I talk to Bash. Uhh, I plan on coming to the surface at least once a day to call, probably about this time of day, for the first three days as we travel no deeper that about two thousand feet. I hope to have a lot more to tell you tomorrow. For now, can you have the call sent to my house?"

He knew Bashalli was now taking all but her Fridays off to take care of herself and the coming baby, but this was Monday."

When her voice answered, it was filled with excitement.

"Tom!" she practically screamed. As they had spoken three times during the trip he wondered if she was trying to get her voice to carry all the way out without need for the radio.

"Hey, Bash," he responded in a calmer and slightly less loud voice. "How is my absolutely favorite girl?"

"I don't know about this mystery woman, but I am fine," she replied with a hint of mischief in her voice. "What is happening? Did you get there and are you coming home soon? And just to me?"

He told her about the aborted landing and the successful one and that they were just now starting the clock on their time on the planet. "I may be a day or two or three late on the original schedule, but I'll be there for the important event. Promise."

They spoke for another two minutes before he said he had to start sending all the data but would call back the next day.

"I promise we will not go anywhere until you call," she told him. She then told him she loved him, three times, and promised to not tell Sandy about the call until Bud had the chance to call home in about an hour.

The next order of business was to transmit the approximately fifty gigabytes of information to Enterprises, which would be simulcast to all the supporting nations. Even at the tremendous speed of transmission, it took nearly a half hour to complete. He then had to retransmit it without the special encoding that had been mandated by those nations so it could not be deciphered by anyone not so authorized. And, that included Enterprises.

So, he resent everything, unencoded, to his father.

Then, he turned over the radio to the men who wanted to talk to their wives or other loved ones back home. As with his own conversation, each had to limit their time to just five minutes so everyone could have an opportunity before they got back to work.

Most of the crew had remained awake for the first eight hours of the rest period and so they all turned in for the final four to get some sleep. The fortunate ones on third shift would be able to continue to sleep if they wanted or needed to.

Tom had a word with Chow, who he could see was nearly exhausted, and ordered him to go to bed, "...for at least eight hours. You deserve it."

"Wahl, I cain't say I'm not gettin' pretty tired, but I also cain't let nobody go hungry."

"And, they won't. I've watched you put leftovers away and anyone who gets up and want to eat, can have those. Okay?"

The old Texan nodded and placed a hand on Tom's shoulder. "It's a deal. G'night, youngin'."

As the cook headed for the spiral stair to go up to where his room was, Tom smiled. Chow was the oldest man on the crew and had been working almost non-stop since they left home. With three shifts to cook for, he was about to run himself into the ground. So, Tom made a decision that there would just be two sittings for their main lunch and dinner meals. He'd ask Chow to make enough for the other shift and they, in rotation, could do the leftovers thing.

He wandered to the rear of the living section, opened the hatch between that and the power section, and went over to talk to the two men working back there who were checking the system every hour to make certain the icy cold did nothing bad.

"We're all refueled, skipper," one of them announced. "Hope you don't mind, but we got to testing the intake systems and just figured we might as well finish the job. Hope that's okay."

The inventor shook his head. "Nope. Just fine. I came back here to see if you might do that a bit early so we can leave in a hurry if we run into troubles. Thanks!"

So he would not wake anyone trying to sleep, Tom personally told the seven men still awake he was about to give the under surface drive a brief test. Several offered to help, but he said it could be done by one person, and it might as well be him.

In the control room he sat at the pilot's station and activated the instruments. With a little rueful chuckle Tom had to spend a few minute looking all around to see where Bud had moved the ones he wanted. Then, he realized those had likely been put into standby to give the flight instruments and controls priority. He found the necessary switch and soon had what he wanted sitting right in front of him.

He energized the intake pre-heating system's operation board and saw that the reactor coolant had been running at a reduced level through there for some time. The temperature of the liquid inside the front 10% of the tunnel was up to a "steamy" minus 210°F.

Using the slider control first for the drive under the *Yamato*, Tom gave it a little goose and the sub moved forward about one hundred feet. He repeated this with the two side-mounted drives and was rewarded by moving *Yamato II* nearly one hundred-fifty-seven feet.

With a smile mostly to himself, he turned the drive controls off and headed out to tell Bud about his system being a winner—something that was mandatory now or else the mission would need to be shortened and the ship taken back off and heading for home.

When the flyer heard Tom's report, he giggled as quietly as he could so as to not wake anyone, but he was exceptionally pleased. He even pumped his fist in the air three times to celebrate.

"I know you tell me I sometimes say things that make you think in a different direction, but this is sort of the first time I've come up with a solid idea that has worked out without a major overhaul. Right?"

Tom nodded and shook his friend's hand. "Yep. One of many more to come, no doubt, Bud."

Bud's big grin turned into a sort or grimace. "Yeah… we'll see, and I'm not holding my breath, or telling Sandy this might be my one and only!"

Tom gently slapped his best friend on the back. "Believe me, flyboy, it truly is not your first nor will it be your last. And, thanks!"

When Tom returned to the control room he was surprised to find five of the men up there, most working on testing the various systems and cleaning the displays so they were gleaming and showed no fingerprints.

"Wow," was all he could say not believing the room had actually been cluttered with old cups, some papers and even a scuff mark on the pilot's station where someone had scraped something along, leaving a three-inch dark mark. That, too, was gone.

"I guess I'd better get to doing captain-y things," he said to Slim who was just turning from the sensor monitoring board with a tablet computer in his right hand.

"You're doing all those sort of things even in your sleep, skipper," he responded. "So, if you really want something to do right this minute, could you go plug in my tablet and get it recharged for me?" he looked hopefully at the inventor and tentatively held the device out.

Tom took it with a smile. "Of course, Mr. Davis. Whatever you ask for, Mr. Davis. Did you want that to be the red electricity or the green sort?"

They both laughed and were joined by Bud who had just stepped into the room.

"Sounds like grunt work to me," he quipped. "Just the sort of thing I'm designed for." Taking the tablet from Tom's hand he turned and walked back out of the room. Returning thirty seconds later, he sat in Tom's seat and sighed. "Well, that's tuckered me out for the next five minutes!"

With less than a half hour to go before Tom intended to take the *Yamato* under the surface, he called—or rather Bud circulated and made certain everyone who was supposed to be on duty was and those who were asleep had strapped themselves in—for the duty team to man their stations.

It was mostly a useless exercise as everybody from both that shift and the one to follow were ready for the call to action.

Chow came into the control room to see if anyone wanted anything to eat or drink. He'd taken full advantage of Tom's almost demand he get some sleep and was feeling, "Rarin' ta go!"

"Okay. It seems like we all are ready to head down a little early. I suppose since we took a couple of extra orbits, or five, to get down here we might just as well make up a little time. So, can I have half ballast set and then let's move forward at three knots. I want to see how the drives and steering act just a few feet under the surface."

Everyone felt the ship begin moving forward, and it felt as smooth and as effortless as if the ship had been in one of Earth's oceans.

"Ballast set and we are now cruising along with just the very tippy top poking up and out of this thick mush," Bud reported.

"What's the relative difference in needed thrust versus back home?"

The pilot looked at his board and pressed a button. "Nearly three-point-two times the necessary thrust, skipper."

"Okay. That is well within what I anticipated. Thank you everyone. Now," Tom told them—including a link just back to the power and drives sections—"stand by to submerge. We are going to one hundred feet at first and then I want a full report on our drive systems. Let's do it."

Yamato II, almost as if it were laughing off any differences, easily headed to the requested depth and leveled out. It was only then Tom and the others appreciated that just like an Earth submarine, the ship did go about five degrees nose down to make the dive.

Every system was checked and double-checked. All was in perfect working order, so Tom asked for another dive to five hundred feet.

Like the first one, this was finished in quick order and all stations reported they were still showing nothing but green indicators.

"How's the viscosity of the slush?" Tom asked and Red turned to smile.

"About one percent thicker at five hundred than on the surface, but my downward thermal sensors are showing a trace of higher temperatures under us. I'm guessing that's another couple thousand feet deeper, but it sure looks as if the scientists who say this planet has a hot enough core to not freeze means it ought to be smoother sailing for us deeper down."

"Great! Just what dad and I also believed before we came out here. So, let's cruise at this depth and get a few samples and study outside for the next hour before we go down again. This time we go deeper."

"How far do you want do go this shift?" Bud asked. "Not that I have anywhere else to go, just curious."

"We will go to five thousand in the next two hours then we'll head back up to give a thorough look at what all our sensors have been picking up. I also want to do a small spectra-analysis on our liquid samples. Speaking of which, let's be sure to get one every time we level out."

Things went so smoothly that when they resurfaced just four hours after heading down, Tom decided to let Hank take the command seat and get them down to twenty thousand feet while he went back and took a sleep break.

With everything he'd felt he ought to do during the previous break period, the one thing the inventor had failed to do was take a nap. And, he really needed one.

Before he did head for his cabin, he made certain the data transmissions to the consortium and then to Enterprises were set to send. Along with the Enterprise data stream, he added a private message to Bashalli assuring her all was well and they had begun their test dives, which also were exactly as they should be.

Tom awoke seven hours later, still very tired but knowing he had to get up or he might wallow in his bunk for another several hours. He needed... no, that was not right. He *wanted* coffee and something solid in his stomach. He *needed* to check with Hank or whoever was manning the command seat to see what they'd done and what there were heading to do.

Chow noticed Tom coming across the living space from his kitchen and hailed the younger man.

"What kin I fix ya, Tom? Got some omelets ready to be nuked to fluffy goodness, or maybe a san'wich? Coffee's in the machine and I'll get ya a cup in two shakes."

Even with his desire to see what had been happening, his head was foggy and he knew he needed to have that coffee and maybe a small sandwich.

He gratefully accepted the sippy cup of hot beverage and asked if it might be possible to have one of the cook's breakfast sandwiches.

"Shore. Ham or turkey along with yer cheese and egg?"

Tom selected the ham. He had a feeling that he might be a little dehydrated from the recycled air. The first several sips of coffee helped a little and his fog started to clear.

When Chow handed him the sandwich, he noted with a smile the cook had wrapped it in some absorbent paper so he might take it with him as he headed forward.

The door opened and Tom stepped inside. He spotted that Slim had relieved Hank and that Hank was sitting at the pilot's station intently watching the forward screen.

"Is everybody doing double duty when I go off for a little nap?" Tom asked, his voice telling everyone he was joking.

"Well," Slim replied turning to face the inventor, "someone has to stay up late to make sure the kids get home before curfew."

Tom smiled and asked for a status report.

All systems were still running smoothly and, as Red had anticipated, at a greater depth the liquid around them had heated up by a whole two degrees.

It meant very little as it was now thicker due to the pressure of everything above them, but the trio of drives was maintaining their speed.

"Which is, and how deep are we now?" he asked.

He was astounded to learn they were only at three-quarters throttle and traveling at nineteen knots and at a depth of *twenty thousand feet!*

CHAPTER 17 /

TOUCHDOWN

BECAUSE HANK had floated a transmission buoy to send an emergency signal should they encounter difficulties before he took them back under the surface, and it was now having its own difficulties being pulled through the thick slush at the speed the *Yamato* was traveling—and still remaining on the surface—Tom opted to cut it loose before the cable broke. This way, it would transmit a locator signal so they could, if desired, circle around and come back to retrieve it any time during the next forty-eight hours.

Tom was pretty certain he would just write it off as the cold would eventually shut things down, and it would remain on Neptune forever. Besides, they had several more in their inventory.

Before they had departed Fearing Island, one of the technicians working on the probe and the several others like it had asked Tom about sterilizing everything so they did not take bacteria to the pristine planet.

"Well, Harold, with the immense cold up there, close to absolute zero, there is nothing on this planet that can do more than go into terminal hibernation. Most things, like bacteria, will perish in about two seconds, so we are safe not dousing everything in disinfectant and vacuum-wrapping it. But, it is a good thought and one we need to do any time we go someplace more hospitable."

Slim, who had just come over to ask the inventor something added, "Anything with even a minute trace of liquid will immediately super freeze and explode. And, anything that does not explode will die. So, the skipper's right." Harold had thanked them both and left.

Now, Tom was taking mental stock of their supplies of things like buoys. They had brought four and had expended two. He wanted to keep one on hand for any last minute emergency, so he knew they had to be careful.

He had them brought up closer to the surface and asked for a test of ninety percent throttle.

Yamato II was traveling at a depth of about twelve thousand feet below the surface two hours later and making a brisk twenty-six knots now they were not trying to take care of the released buoy, and were taking measurements of their surrounding liquid as they moved along.

"I'm seeing slight variations, almost striations and apparently vertical ones where the levels of hydrogen seem to have come out of suspension and are in pretty high concentrations, skipper," Slim reported an hour later. "Some as high as three-point-two percent of the mix."

With a nod, Tom said, "Keep tracking that and marking our locations. You can never tell when I might change my mind and want to take on some hydrogen to try instead of the methane in the drives. Might make for some additional thrust to the plasma engines."

A day later and with Tom, Bud, Stephen and one other tech in the control room, the ship headed down farther than they had been before. By the time Tom called a halt to their descent, *Yamato II* was nearly thirty thousand feet down and coming close to the solid mantle of the planet. At least, within this range their SONAR was picking up something solid beneath them.

"Let's slow down to five knots and cruise at this depth for a bit," the inventor ordered.

As the ship slowed, the report came forward from the propulsion section they needed to perform some minor maintenance on the lower, third, Jetmarine drive.

"We picked up some small chunks of ice at the forward intake and need to back flush things. It'll only take a minute, skipper, but it'll mean slowing us way down. Can we do it?"

"Yes, but let me slow the ship to about two knots. How long, and I mean in actual seconds, do you think you need to run it to clear things?"

"Between twenty and thirty seconds. We won't know precisely until the sensors tell us things are clear. Sorry to not have better info, Tom."

Tom let out a rueful chuckle, "Nothing to sweat over, Jimmy. I see Bud has already got us slower, so give me a countdown of twenty before you actually reverse things. Thanks."

He made a quick announcement to the rest of the crew warning them the ride might become a little bumpy for the half minute.

When the time came, there was very little indication anything was happening other than Bud reporting the nose of the ship wanted to come up from the back pressure underneath them.

"Nothing I can't handle, Tom, but it is surprising the amount of power those drives have, even in reverse."

A call came up from Propulsion.

"We're seeing about a seventy percent clearing, skipper but a couple pieces are wedged in really tight. Can we stop until the heating tubes melt those enough to blow them out?"

Tom agreed to come to a stop, "But, only for one minutes. I really don't want to pause here too much. Give me a report at the one-minute mark. Oh, and Bud is slowing us down, so we will be at a stop in about five seconds."

The back flush of the Jetmarine system, or at least that one drive unit, took a little over thirty-seconds and was only about 90% successful. The drive would, hopefully, clear as they sped up, but the fact it did start to freeze shut like that worried Tom a little. He really wanted to get to the very bottom of the ocean and get core samples to take home for study and not have to pause periodically and repeat this process.

What Tom wanted to do was get home as he had promised Bashalli, and the two-day—Earth days—delay they had dealt with so far was eating up their extra time.

"Take us down to within two hundred feet of the bottom at about five knots," he requested.

Bud soon had them moving forward and down. It was slow going. As thick as the slush outside was, they managed to only drop downward by about thirty feet a minute, and the sub was a mile or more from the lowest point they would need to travel.

Nine hours later, Tom was awakened by Stephen while taking his sleep break.

"Skipper? Sorry to do this but Red says you'll want to come forward. We've spotted the bottom!"

Tom rolled out of his bunk and pulled on his shirt and the sandals he'd taken to wearing for their ease of slipping into and out of.

In a minute he was stepping into the control room.

"Oh, wow," was about all he could say seeing the nearly featureless floor of the ocean.

"Yes, Tom. Looks like we made it. We've been traveling along here at just two knots and getting all sorts of video of that well, that *nothingness*. I saw the videos from the bottom of the Mariana Trench that movie guy brought back. That is like a veritable playground of things compared to this."

Tom nodded. "You're right, Red. I'm not certain what I expected to see, but this is what the experts back home theorized would be here."

Red snorted. "So, not much growing in a nearly all frozen methane ocean? Who'd have thought that?"

Tom watched as they moved forward. There was little change and for some time he wondered if they were actually moving. The only things they could see on the big screens were occasional small crystals poking out of the surface, and in one spot—where they stopped to get a sample—bubbles were issuing from a small fracture.

"Must go down to the core and that gas is coming up and out. What do the test results say?" Tom asked.

Stephen was back at the panel with that information. "It looks like almost pure hydrogen, skipper. And, I took a quick look at the upward camera. It is getting absorbed into the surrounding ocean before it is three hundred feet up."

Tom asked Red to get them moving again. "We'll go another kilometer, see if we can crank up a little more heat to the tubes in the drives, and take a good core sample or two."

When the time came to set the ship down on the solid surface, Tom asked all hands to brace.

"Just like how some people thought the moon might be so brittle and the surface really thin, we have to be ready for almost anything."

"Other than giant squid," quipped Bud who had come into the room to take over at the pilot's station.

"And," Tom continued over the PA system, "as our own Bud Barclay reminds me, we can expect to see no giant squid down here. If we do, then we all have to buy him a beer. That's all."

The *Yamato II* settled onto the surface with Bud's hands poised to hit the ballast dump button and get them back up if it became necessary.

It wasn't.

It also wasn't as solid as Tom might have liked.

"Take a core sample and let's see what we're sitting on."

They all felt as the coring probe lowered down beneath the sub and began it's rotational drilling into what was below them. In three minutes, and with only four feet of the drill inside the surface of Neptune, a cry went out from their man on the drill.

"We're in a pocket!"

His words were punctuated by the appearance of a great deal of bubbles streaming out of the hole and up both sides of the sub.

"Bud? Raise us as soon as the drill is back onboard."

Fifty seconds later Bud touched his controls and they lifted to twenty feet above the surface. The downward facing camera caught a great deal of bubbles from whatever they'd drilled into rising and running up both sides of the sub.

As they watched, fascinated, the slushy ocean began to freeze up around the hole stopping the bubbles within a minute.

"Well," Tom said to the men in the control room. I'm hoping the rest of the planet isn't just a surface crust over air or whatever that was."

"More hydrogen, skipper," came the report from Stephen. "I sucked in a sample as we rose."

"Good man," the inventor complimented him.

They soon began moving forward at about three knots.

A kilometer later they all had to laugh as the ground below them dropped away.

"Looks like we were on some sort of mountain. Very flat, but my guess is the real solid surface is down there." Tom pointed toward the deck of the room. "Okay. Let's head out another kilometer and then go down. Call out when we have a SONAR reading of the next low surface."

There was trouble to be had in the next hour.

"Skipper? SONAR isn't really giving us much. Like, it sees something false about two hundred feet below us, but it is dropping at the same rate we are. Want me to shut it off?"

"No, keep a watch out in case we come over anything that might pose a danger.

Another half hour went by with nothing solid spotted. Then…

"Even with the SONAR not working very well down here, I'm seeing a flat surface, Tom. I think we're almost at the bottom."

A cheer rang out from the other men in the control room.

"Slow us to just one knot," Tom commanded. Twenty seconds later Red stated they were at one knot. Jerry Van, manning the sensors at the moment, added they were now one hundred-ninety-five feet above the new flat area. "And, from what I can see on the scope, it seems to go on at least another kilometer. Not sure after that until we get farther along."

"Do we keep going?" came from Jerry.

Tom made a decision. "Nope. All stop. We're setting down here and taking another core sample." He got on the intercom. "I want the sampling team members to clean out the intakes and get the core drills ready to extend fore and aft. Unless we hit something too solid, I want the full thirty feet of core brought into the ship and stored. Or we hit another gas pocket, I want that team to notify me immediately and stand by to withdraw their drill. If both drills hit the same pocket, we may have to break off and leave them behind. I don't want us to get into any trouble this deep. Thank you."

As he was finishing, two men walked briskly through the control room and over to the hatch to the forward section. They grabbed heavy coats and breathing masks from a locker next to the door and got them on, stepping through the hatch. In seconds it was closed again.

"Aft team ready," came the first report followed by, "Forward team also ready, skipper."

"We are coming to a halt. We'll be stopped in about five seconds. Start your gear in ten seconds, please."

While they waited to see if the drills remained in solid ground, Tom had a thought. He called for Hank to come forward.

"So, what's up," the big engineer asked taking the last bite of the grilled cheese sandwich he'd been eating.

"I have a question for you and possibly a request. I believe we have a couple very small cameras in the stores. Could you rig one up to a drill head so we can get a good look down inside anything we might come across? By that I mean a gas pocket."

Hand scratched his right cheek while he thought about it. "Yes..." he stated cautiously, "but it couldn't be outside the drill tube unless we build a special housing that would sort of shove things to the side. It can't be inside because of the same reasons. Then again, it would clog up pretty fast unless I build a sort of shutter system that only opens once the drill head is inside such a cavern or bubble. Give me an hour to look into this and see if I can come up with a design."

He stood, looking at Tom. The inventor smiled at his friend and nodded. "Go on. I'm anxious to find out if we have the ability. Uhh, are we going to have trouble with the extreme cold?"

"The solid state nature of our electronics ought to mean we have good use of the cameras. I can't speak for the lens frosting over, though, and I doubt we can rig a heater sufficient and still small enough. Again, give me an hour." With that, he turned and left the room.

Fifty minutes later both drills reported they had finished their downward coring and were being retracted so those samples could be stored.

The aft crew reported they had hit a brief pocket of gas but were through it in seconds. "It was probably about five inches high, skipper. The drill head bit into solid ground before we could register it up here."

Now, Tom wondered if he had sent Hank on a wild goose chase. The only place nearby where such a camera setup might be useful could be back up on the plateau behind them. He would have to proceed with more corings to see. Of course, that would mean their storage capacity for such samples would be quickly filled. He decided to perform three more drillings using just the aft unit over the next ten hours, moving forward by several miles each time. Then, the sub would head out for up to a thousand miles before they would try again.

Hank had come back earlier to tell Tom it was going to be next to impossible, but he'd give it a try if the inventor said to.

"Well, unless we turn back to that mountain, which is the only place we encountered a gas pocket of any size, I'd guess it'll be an exercise in futility. But, don't erase any design you've made because if we do find another pocket, I'll want to stay in that area and have you build that magic picture box for us."

Hank stood up straight and saluted Tom, "Ready and in stand by, Captain!" he stated, and then grinned and relaxed. "Boy, I need to do more stretching. That actually felt good. Pardon me while I go back to the workout area."

Tom finally asked Hank to do his magic a day later when they came to a rise on the floor of some two hundred feet. They circled the area of approximately one-quarter mile diameter for half an hour before Tom decided to rest on the top and do a core drill.

Within nineteen feet they hit another gas pocket. While Tom decided they could just expel a little ballast and lighten the ship's downward pressure, he also knew that each time they paused for more than an hour the intakes for their drives tended to start to clog with frozen pieces. So, and hoping this pinprick also healed up so whatever gases were down there did not all escape, he ordered the drill retracted and the ship to perform a one-mile circle of the area until Hank was ready.

That required three hours of the Engineer's undivided attention. Even at that, he asked that Tom lend a hand at soldering one of the very small circuit boards he required.

During that time the hole did seal for the most part, but bubbles of about one-inch diameter slowly leaked up and headed toward the surface. As before, they did not make it more than a few hundred feet before they were absorbed by the surrounding slush.

Hank reported he had a camera working and had tried it in their small super cold chamber.

"It works at least down to minus two-seventy-three, Tom. I have every faith. Now, tell me which of our drills I need to put this on; by the way it will be outside so we may need to drill slightly off to one side of the existing hole to give it a better chance of not getting scraped off during the downward stroke."

"Uhh, you do realize the entire outer case of the drill rotates, right?"

Hank did not answer for a moment. "I do now. Well, I guess I need to be extra certain it stays attached. Give me another hour to get another bead of cold-proof epoxy around the edges and also to fashion a good, strong strap."

Back in the small workshop, located in the drive section because it contained only enough equipment to fill 70% of the space, Hank sat down on his stool and pulled over the camera and its housing. Using a small, pressurized container of the fast-setting epoxy, he laid a bead down along one side before setting the container to the side and using a gloved finger, smoothed out the bead.

"It is just like using silicon caulk," he told Bud who wandered back in time to watch him do the third side. "The only thing is you can't wipe or wash the stuff off because it sticks with the tenacity of a bulldog chomping onto a steak. So, I have to put down just a bit less than I might normally."

"How long do you have to work it," the flyer asked.

"Seventy-five seconds before it stiffens. Another three minutes and it is almost as hard as rock. Five minutes and it is completely set."

"Jetz! I guess you don't want to keep your finger in that stuff for too long."

Hank chucked. "The first time I used some of this back home, I had to get Arv to come over and chisel me out. Good thing I was wearing a rubber glove then as well. The only thing is this epoxy slightly grows, so I was stuck because the finger was squeezed tight." He finished his work and moved the housing unit to one side before cleaning up.

Ten minutes later they took the camera and its housing forward to show Tom.

"Great looking work. So," he asked thinking he already knew the answer, "how does it send in the videos?"

"As you probably suspect, it is all bluetooth connectivity. And, the great thing is as cold as the surrounding area is, that signal will travel about ten times farther than back on Earth."

"Let's go, then."

Hank and Bud, who offered his assistance, headed forward into the nose section, but not before donning the air masks and heavy jackets... and leather work gloves.

When they returned to the control room seventeen minutes later, both men started to rub their arms and legs.

"Skipper?" Bud asked, his face scrunched up in question. "Can we spare a little power to heat that space up from what must be about ten degrees below zero? And, I mean that as in Fahrenheit, so it's more than a bit cold up there."

Hank nodded his agreement.

"Oh. I guess I haven't been keeping a look at that space. Sure. Jeff?" he turned to the man on the ship's systems board, "bring that space back up to the forty degrees I originally meant it to be. Thanks."

Hank said the drill was now outfitted and the camera also had a safety cable attached so in the case it was scraped off, they could still retrieve in up into the drill's storage space.

"We're ready to go," he told everyone.

Fifteen minutes later the drill re-pierced the gas chamber. Tom had the special light system turned on, and they all gasped. The chamber they sat atop of was massive. As in, even the special lights that back on Earth could show things through water five miles away barely could detect the sides and certainly could not see the bottom.

A truly good sample of the gas, or gases, was drawn up with most of it going into a storage container while a small sample went to the spectrograph.

It turned out to be almost pure helium.

"Well," Tom told them all, "since we know helium is created by a nuclear decay reaction with hydrogen, my guess is there is some sort of natural nuclear source way down there and a source of hydrogen. This is going to set the scientific community a bit on its ear. Nobody I spoke with said there should be any indication of radioactivity out here."

After taking some more video, Tom asked that the drill and camera be brought back.

"We need to get a move on, and travel a lot more miles before we head home. Who knows what else we might find."

CHAPTER 18 /
THE VERY ODD FIND BEFORE...

THE FLOOR of the methane ocean, the real solid surface of Neptune, continued to be more desolate than any part of any ocean back home Tom or the crew had ever encountered. Not just bleak and flat, there was zero detritus such as plant life, bones, parts of ships or even the smallest sign of life of any sort.

In other words, *it did not look real.*

It looked like an artist's rendition of the bleakest thing he or she could imagine and paint before a computer took out any tiny hint of brush strokes or other painting features. And, it stretched everywhere they could look and see. The only "feature" they had encountered was the mountain plateau they had first thought might be the ocean floor. Other than that...

With the *Yamato* gliding just fifty feet above the almost featureless surface, and unnaturally lit by the ship's undersea lights —which Tom had noted early on only extended out about six hundred feet—it was always surreal.

Overall, the ship had traveled under the liquid three thousand four hundred and fifty miles since it had first plunged down from the surface. The solid core never varied much from the depth at which they traveled—other than that first mountain top plateau. And, the never changing surface below them was getting to be so incredibly boring that Tom asked the crew to change to a four hours on and eight hours off schedule. Nobody had an issue with that as it still meant they only had two work shifts per Earth day and two shifts to get sleep, eat and continue their exercises.

The effects on the men in the control room were seen almost immediately. Now, shifts ended with them all still happy and attentive instead of bleary-eyed and somewhat mentally weary.

Tom smiled to himself as he thought about what Doc Simpson might say about this change. Likely, it would be, "Just what this doctor would have ordered!"

Twice Tom stopped the sub briefly while the small articulated arms in the nose were used to gather some of the smaller crystals their spectrograph told him were actually a form of diamonds, although not at all pure carbon. They were absolutely perfect with no discernible imperfections other than a high level of trapped hydrogen and a little helium, but that was so well integrated with the carbon from the methane it took almost the full power of Tom's microscope adaptation of his SuperSight camera to detect the nanoscopic bubbles.

On Earth, he believed, no jeweler's basic microscope, and certainly their loupes, would see them.

"How much of the Chinese request for a couple tons of those will we really be bringing home, Tom?" Bud asked as they sat eating on the ninth day of the Neptunian visit.

"Unless we come across a whole giant field of them, and even then our limited storage will keep that amount pretty low, I think we'll have thirty pounds or so of them to share. Maybe up to forty, but we'll need to see how many can be packed into our available space. The one thing I do not want to do is have them sitting out inside the general areas of the ship. We'll just have to let someone else decide who gets how many of them. I don't want to be in the middle of that battle."

Bud looked sheepishly at his friend. "Do you think we mere crew members might avail ourselves of small ones? I'll bet Sandy and Bash would love to be the first in town to sport something truly out of this world!"

Tom told him he'd have to think about it and probably would need to bring Damon into the decision.

Continuing on, the ship encountered more of the same as the other 99.9% of what they had seen, meaning they saw nothing.

Or, they spotted nothing until the following afternoon when Hank, spelling Red at the pilot's station for a few minutes, called out, "We've coming up on something really strange out there. Look!"

As he touched one control and zoomed in the view on the big monitor up front, they all could see what looked like a flattened sphere. As they neared the location it was obvious it was only about three feet across, or had been at one time, if it had actually been a sphere at all.

"Call Tom," the big engineer said to his communications man, Mike.

The inventor came forward three minutes later having just got out of bed and was in the process of dressing. He stepped in barefoot and just pulling his shirt over his head.

"What have we got... oh, my!" he exclaimed as he saw what they were hovering near to. "That... well, that looks like a *constructed* object. Sort of like it may have been some type of a tank at one time. Can we grab it?"

"Looks just a little too large to bring inside. I could get it with the hands if you like. But, we can zoom in a little more for a good look."

"Do it."

As the camera got them closer, the flattened sphere now seemed to be exactly that. There even had been some sort of label on it at one point, but that had frozen off leaving a ghostly image of what had been there. None of them could discern what it might have said or even what language—if it were a product of Earth—it had been written in.

"Whatever that was must have hit the surface pretty hard," Hank opined. "Some sort of small probe?"

"I have a notion about that, or at least what it was," Tom told them, "but I don't think I want to make a wild guess and be wrong. So, let's take a good series of pictures and I'm hoping we are recording the video and can take a local liquid sample to see if there is anything hanging around that might have been inside that..." he checked with Mike who nodded and smiled, "...then in a couple minutes we'll travel on. Let's be on the lookout for anything more out of the ordinary."

Four minutes later, Red had returned and retaken the command seat. He stared at the anomaly for a minute before telling the helm to get them moving again.

Half an hour later he reported to Tom they were encountering a strong current. It was the first time since they ducked under the surface.

"It's heading about our general direction, skipper, and at nearly twenty-eight knots. Our over-the-surface speed is up to sixty-one knots. Do you want me to slow us down or steer out of it or just go with the flow?"

Tom had come forward again leaving a lengthy written message from his father sitting on a table in the mess area.

"Let's dial down our speed about twenty-five percent and let the current shove us, but if it starts to deviate from the course we've been on, or we start coming within sight of anything other than the endless flat out there, try to steer us to get us out of the current even of that means heading up a few thousand feet. We've got a lot of ocean over our heads. Might as well use it."

Returning to the message, Tom had to smile at this new occurrence. It was one of the things he'd been asked to see if it existed. About half the chief scientists from the consortium nations said there absolutely had to be currents in the Neptunian ocean and the other half stated that the ocean was far too thick to support that notion.

The Germans called it a "silly notion from clueless would-be experts!"

Some people are going to be smug and others are going to be disappointed, he thought.

Damon's message, which had come in before their latest dive, was mostly about what was going on back home. Bashalli was being, in his father's words, "stoic," about her husband now being more than four days behind his promised return. It made Tom realize the ship had to complete as much of the circumnavigation as possible in the coming four days and then head for home.

> Even your mother is a little anxious about your delay, Son. Sandy is beside herself over missing "her Bud," and asks me at least three times a day if he is okay and to tell you to get the heck out of there, but we all know that is status quo for her. I wonder, sometimes, how your mother and I raised two kids a little more than a year apart who turned out so different. Imagine me sighing heavily at this point.
>
> The new President has contacted me with assurances he believes in what Enterprises is doing for this nation, so he is an ally. So, by the way, is his V.P., a man who I had met maybe ten years ago and took an immediate liking to. And, Pete Quintana likes him as well. Win-win? I hope so.
>
> Tell Bud he is in for an interesting reunion with his wife, but do not tell your mother I said so. She still believes her little daughter is innocent of any of that sort of thoughts.
>
> As soon as you surface, please send the data from your now eight days under the surface and then get a call through to your

wife, followed by one to me.

Love, Dad

Over the following day they came across nothing else of visual interest other than a few rises in the floor Tom now believed were indications of trapped gases, and likely to be mostly hydrogen and helium. He decided to stop at one of the larger ones, once they found one, for another drill and core sample.

Other than these rises, nothing else was spotted to differentiate one patch of the surface from another.

Around what would be midnight, something changed.

Tom was in the command seat at the time having spelled Hank.

"Will you take a look at that?" Slim exclaimed from the pilot's station. He was looking up at the monitor and at an incredible sight illuminated by their underwater lights.

Outside and perhaps two hundred feet below them were veritable pinnacles of what looked to be ice. Sharp like stalagmites, they glistened in the special underwater lights of the *Yamato*. They must have been really, really tall.

Could those be giant Neptune diamonds? Tom asked himself.

"As beautiful as those are, I don't want us to run into a tall one, so take us up another three hundred feet, please and proceed slowly," Tom requested.

Knowing the floor of the ocean was currently two thousand feet farther down gave Tom a shudder as he realized these monsters were very tall and as thin as they appeared, they were either very stable or exceptionally strong... or both.

"Think those might be very large examples of the methane diamonds the Chinese were going on about back home?" Hank asked as he came into the room. "If they see the video, they will ask why we didn't strap a couple on the upper deck before coming home."

Tom thought about that possibility. "You know, Hank, I was thinking the same thing. I mean about them being diamonds, not the 'bring us one' thing. I guess we need to find one we can maneuver down and around and try to break off a chunk to see what they really are."

Slim maneuvered them until the nose of *Yamato II* was within fifteen feet of the top of one of the taller spires.

Using the articulated arms from his station. Stephen reached out only to discover they were short by about six feet.

Carefully, and at almost no momentum, the ship inched forward until Stephen called out he could now touch and grasp the tip.

"See if you can tug on it and not pull us any closer," Tom requested.

That proved difficult to do. The spire was as solid as a, well, as a diamond and also seemed to be heavily anchored to the surface far below. It didn't budge but *Yamato* inched forward, and Tom asked for a little back up.

An attempt to twist the mechanical hands to break off the tip was unsuccessful, so Tom said to let things go and bring the arms back into the ship.

"If we want part of one of those I think we need to find a very small one. We've seen the starts of some of those before; perhaps there are some of the tiny ones down on the surface. Slim? Back us away until we are clear of the field and take us down for a look."

Try as they might, the ship's crew and sensors could detect nothing of a size they might try to pull inside. They continued to find a few patches of smaller gems, ones in the one-inch range, and Tom began to wonder about them. Were these the "seeds" of the taller spires? If someone came back in a hundred or a thousand years, would these be hundreds of feet tall?

Perhaps someday he might send an unmanned probe up with a transmitter buoy to float and a camera component to sink to near one of these fields to take a daily shot of some of the gems to see if they did grow over time.

Some day.

The ship was closing in on the three-quarters mark in their circling of the planet when they detected another rather tall rise. It was much like the first mountain they'd come down on top of, being about a kilometer above the rest of the surface. However, it was not nearly as steep.

Tom asked they be slowed and ballast blown to get them above the top.

Like the first one, this had a nearly flat top, likely worn down over millennia by the currents. It was more than four kilometers across.

"Okay. Let's set down and drill into that with the camera-equipped coring unit. If this is like others we've investigated, we ought to hit a gas pocket. On the other hand, this one could have a very thick, uhh, skin and we might just hit nothing but solids."

The ship came to a halt some fifteen hundred feet in from one edge and lowered the drill. It came back out with just about exactly what they already had enough of in their existing core samples but hit no pockets or bubbles of gas.

Tom had them moved another five hundred feet closer to the center of the plateau and another sample taken.

Nothing different came up.

Before giving up he wanted to try at the exact center of this plateau. He had not gone straight there because he believed that if there was a gas pocket out there, it would be close enough to the surface to make for a fragile crust, and he did not want to get the ship into any trouble.

The core drill went down and down and was within a foot of its maximum when it broke through into a gas pocket.

A small cheer went up in the control room and throughout the ship when Tom announced success.

The underwater light in the camera pod was turned on and everyone looked at the scene beneath them. The bottom was only a few hundred feet farther down and was jagged, bumpy, and even had areas that appeared to have folded over on themselves at some time in the distant past.

"I'm guessing that indicates some sort of volcanic activity down there. Hot magma causing the surface to undulate and roll and make for those features. Let's get a full three-sixty slow rotation and video."

Next, the inventor suggested they try to get down at enough of an angle to get the wide-angle camera pointing to get a view of the roof of the bubble.

This time they remained over a core site some fifty feet away for more than two hours. They had hit three small gas bubbles on the way down the first rime, and he hoped they might make it back into the large gas cavern. The drill ended up barely poking through and so Tom had them set down with a bit of a jarring collision to see if the drill might be forced a foot or so father inside.

It appeared to work but to everyone's consternation, now they could see to the side but still not up to the roof of the bubble.

After a third coring Tom called a halt and had the equipment drawn out of the latest hole and replaced in its standby position.

"Let's get ready to move out," he told the control room crew. "I want us to get going on the last third of our circumnavigation, even if we are just ten degrees below the pole. At least we can say we made it around Neptune before we head home."

He made the announcement to the rest of the crew. Even if he could not hear their comments, he knew they were behind his decision. They wanted to complete the mission as much as they wanted to get on the way home.

With Slim at the pilot's position, Tom asked that they rise about a hundred feet and proceed forward at fifteen knots. But, after three minutes Slim turned in his seat, his face a mask of hidden emotions.

"Uhh, Tom, we are not moving forward. Not even at a snail's pace. In fact, my board says we have nothing coming out the back end of our drives!"

"How were things before we stopped? I thought we were doing fine."

"Well, not really. We had a lot of slush piling up in front of the pre-heat tubes. There may have been only enough for our small series of moves. Bud's system is great most of the time, but I think we haven't had the reactor running at a high enough level to make enough hot coolant for the drives as well as the pre-heaters. What do you want to do?"

"We turn everything on high, even the heat in the ship, and try to get the reactor hotter."

Everyone turned on everything they could find. Even Chow turned on his oven, the microwave oven, and his small dishwasher. For three hours they used as much power as possible, even to the extent they had the heat on full and the air conditioning on equally as high including the forward section.

No matter what they did, they could only get a small amount of the slush to become liquidy enough get into the drive and it, unfortunately, seemed to stop inside and not come out the back.

Tom was beginning to regret suggesting they stop for as long as they had. It appeared the slushy ocean of Neptune had just been waiting for an excuse to strand them *more than nine miles below the surface!*

CHAPTER 19 /
THE CIRCUMNAVIGATION

ANOTHER COMMUNICATIONS buoy was readied. This time there would be no strain on the cable so Tom had every faith they would be able to send and receive a message.

It might, however, take the buoy more than fifteen hours to make its way up to the surface.

During that period, additional power would be fed up and into it allowing it to maintain a high enough outside temperature to melt the slush enough so it could float to the top. By the time it broke the top of the ocean, the planet was about a quarter turn too early for a signal to be able to pass directly to the Earth, so Tom decided to wait.

Halfway into that time Tom composed the message he truly hoped he'd never have to send, but their predicament was very serious. They would not run out of power or even air before Chow's carefully packed for food supplies dwindled to nothing. That was still three weeks away, but he really did not have the luxury of time at the moment.

The message was loaded into the memory of the buoy management system and sent up to the ascending sphere. Once it broke the surface it would automatically send the distress call.

For now, all they could do was wait.

"Can we get any of that slush to move through? We've been heating up the reactor for hours," Tom asked Red who was now piloting them. Tom had asked that the ship maintain whatever forward motion they might be able to make. He also asked that the ship make whatever speed they could in a slow circle of about five thousand feet so the cable to the buoy was not unduly strained.

"I'm getting a little ooze moving along inside the three drives, but nothing to give us more than a quarter knot at best, Tom. Sorry. I'll keep trying."

"Actually, that speed will help keep the buoy attached to us. Don't try to go much over that, please."

Tom got up and headed to the rear of the sub. As he crossed the open area Chow poked his head out of the kitchen. Seeing this, Tom held up his right hand. "Sorry, Chow. Problems. Not now."

The cook shrugged and went back to stir the thick sauce he was making for a chicken and dumplings stew they would have that evening.

The inventor opened the hatch and stepped inside, and could immediately see the five men back there were busy trying to get their drive system to work back to any sort of efficiency. Even if they could manage to get one of the three drives back in action, they could give Tom some movement and that could allow them to go back to the surface.

He stood there, watching as they turned valves, rerouted things he was fairly certain had hot coolant, and made adjustments to their electronic control boards.

With a small inward sigh, he backed out. *They have everything as much under control as they can and me leaning over them will do no good,* he thought as he made his way back forward. He looked over at Chow who had his back to the open area.

Tom walked over and gave a light knock on the door frame. "Sorry about the haste and probably my being rude, oldtimer. We are sort of in a pickle and I was concentrating on something so hard I shut you out. Did you have a question or something?"

Chow had turned around and he was shaking his head. "Nope. Just wanted ta know if there's anythin' I might do other'n slingin' hash right now. I know I don't got a lot o' the skills the rest of you have, but I'm willin' ta watch anythin' or fetch anythin'." He looked hopefully at his boss.

Tom smiled and reached over to shake the man's hand. "Well, wherever you go you bring good will and great food. I guess having you walk around and telling everyone that no matter what, you've got their interest at heart and it means a lot."

They did their slow circle for more than fourteen hours before the buoy announced it had arrived at the surface.

The message stating the problems and requesting that all of the teams responsible for design and build of the ship be brought together to see if they had any idea the crew just did not know about.

They received an acknowledgement from Damon Swift eleven minutes later. In part it read:

> "Son, sorry for the delay. I won't say where I was but I could not just jump up and come to the phone. Anyway, I have the call out and everyone involved ought to assemble in the cafeteria in fifteen minutes. Let me know if you have any injuries or totally

lost systems, please.

Dad"

Tom sent back they had no injuries and were comfortable, just stuck.

At Enterprises, Damon got right to the point telling his team members the *Yamato II* had bogged down in the deep methane. It was not that it had frozen into place, but rather the thickness of the liquid at that depth meant it was nearly gelatin dessert consistency.

"Also, the slush inside the drive tubes appears to have almost solidified. Ideas?"

While the others went into small huddles, Arv and Linda had a small conversation. When she raised her hand—at Arv's prodding—Damon came over for a talk so the did not disturb the thought processes of the rest of the assembled people.

"I think I did something when I finalized the Jetmarine drive conversion," she told him. Rather than looking miserable as if she now felt responsible for the problems, she had a smile threatening to break out on her face. "It might make a difference."

"I see. But, of course I don't see so please tell me, Linda."

"Okay. Knowing that the reheat system suggested by Bud was going to be good for keeping the intakes clear and able to allow in the looser liquid, and let it keep moving through as long as they were under some fair amount of speed, I also did some computations on methane, liquid methane, under additional pressure. Like the pressure inside the drives down where they are."

When she paused to organize her thoughts Damon nodded and gave her a moment.

"The upshot of it all is I added something to the drives. It just seemed to me at some point that compressed methane was going to seize up under the compression of the Jetmarine system and that would hamper movement. I was worried that if they had some liquid inside and stopped, it could seize up. I see that has happened. So, my additions *should* be able to free them."

"Okay, but I am now getting anxious to hear what that is, so please tell me exactly what you did," he requested.

"I added additional hot coolant tubes inside the middle sixty percent of the drive tubes. All Tom and his crew need to do is to open a panel that is normally closed and then open the six valves inside."

"Six?"

"Sure. Three to send the coolant out and three to let it back into the closed loop for the reactor."

Damon was so happy he leaned down, took her face in his hands and gave her a big kiss.

"Goodness!" she said but had a smile in her face.

As soon as Linda's message was read out to the crew, a collective sigh of relief went up followed by a cheer as Tom said the process should take only about two hours before the circuits would report things were liquid enough to be used to get them moving along.

"We will make certain we have full mobility and then head on our circumnavigation of the planet. At our depth, that will take us just another four days. I want to remind each of you that I know we are supposed to have been two days from getting home by now and this run around the planet is going to put our three week trip out to greater than four." He paused making certain he really wanted to say this next thing.

"And so, I want to take a secret vote of the entire crew. Do we go on or do we go home? There is no right or wrong answer. I am going to catch all sorts of grief if we can't get back in time for my baby's birth, but I will take that chance in order to do what we all set out to do. If everyone would make certain your counterparts are awake, and you all grab a piece of paper from the pad hanging on the message board outside Chow's kitchen, just write a Y or an N stating yes, you want to continue or no, you want to go home. No names. I'll collect what is left in a box I'm having placed on one of the tables in half an hour. Thanks."

If Tom had any thought his crew would vote to skedaddle, he was wrong. It was an unanimous vote of sixteen to zero. Tom chuckled when he realized one person voted twice.

Before he announced the results, he said to the crew, "Okay. We have a vote and even though I abstained from this, there seems to be a sixteenth vote. I'm not going to point any fingers, Bud, but I think an unnamed crew member, Bud, may have tried to pad out the ballot, Bud. So, with that said, and I randomly removed one vote slip, Bud, and here is the tally."

He glanced at Bud who was studiously looking at his fingernails.

"By unanimous vote, we keep going!"

The cheer even back in the power and drive sections could be heard throughout the ship.

Just about when everyone thought they'd be able to move the

ship, Red, still at the pilot's station even after eighteen hours, reported they had liquid methane flowing and he could likely get them top speed if it were needed.

"Wait while I send one more message back to Enterprises and then we go topside for a rest period. We've all deserved it."

Tom's message, a live voice one, was just to say they were back in business and to tell Linda Ming she was due for an all-expenses-paid vacation.

The acknowledgement was a simple, "Bon voyage!"

Tom decided they could not afford to lose the current buoy so he told Red to get out of the control room, "…and don't come back until you've had a good meal, a sleep, and a wash!" before telling Bud, who took over, to spiral them upward and to have the cable pulled back in as they rose.

"Okay. Estimated time to surface is eleven hours, fifteen minutes."

"Then, let's do it.

Tom had asked that they get underway on their circle of the globe while he was resting.

"I don't want us to sit and wait just so I can nap. Make best speed and head down very low so we can get around in the anticipated four days we should be able to make this far to the north of the equator."

He had long ago decided that the approximately fifty days it would take to circle at the widest point on the equator was far too much for man, machine or Bashalli and so he and Damon decided to curtail the underwater cruise to only about five thousand miles.

By the time he came back, refreshed, Slim was in command and Red was on the pilot's board.

"We stopped about twenty minutes to get another core sample, Tom, and Stephen managed to get the manual arms out there to pluck up the start of one of those crystal shards. Its about three feet tall and was only lightly anchored." When he stopped, Tom looked as if he wanted more information.

"Oh, and the supposition was correct. That is a diamond. Not, by any long shot, a pure one, like everything else we've tested. There is far too much of the methane that is not carbon to make for that, but it seems to be holding together for now in a vacuum container."

Knowing that the surrounding liquid held four times as much hydrogen as it did carbon, this did not come as a surprise.

What did was that a diamond crystal could actually be formed in the first place, much less last out there in the deep pressure of its creation.

"Perhaps we might be able to bring back some precious gems after all," he stated to the men in the room. "I suppose we ought to be on the lookout for more of the smaller crystals."

Over the following day they stopped twice, once for a single two-foot-long crystal that eventually weighed in at thirteen and a tenth pounds, and the next time to gather more than fifteen smaller, three-to-five pound examples. All were placed under vacuum for the rest of the trip.

They also found something they would never have imagined.

"Is that... uhh, is that what it looks like?" Slim asked Tom as they halted near a mangled structure.

"I think it is, Slim. I believe the former Soviet Union actually got a probe out here and that is what is left of it. Crash landed, obviously from that level of damage, but that is what I would call of Earthly origin."

It was likely to have been about six feet across when "alive" and—according to the readout of the downward-facing Damonscope—had contained a radioactive "decaying-type" battery. The residual radiation had been dampened by the extreme cold of the methane ocean, but it was still measurable.

"An idea who sent that and when?" Bud's voice came from behind Tom as he entered the room.

"No, but I believe there were rumors in about nineteen-seventy-seven of a planned and likely launched probe to try to beat the two Voyagers out of the solar system by the Soviets. They were pretty secretive about anything that was not a total success and so my guess is they either lost contact with it or had so many other things going wrong in the eighties when it would have arrived here around eighty-nine they sort of lost interest in it. Anyway, Voyager made it here that August."

"Jetz! It looks terrible. And, if I may editorialize, like a cheap piece of junk. Did they ever put much money into what they built?"

Looking at the crumpled probe, Tom could see what Bud was suggesting. Where the United States, and the Swifts, would have built the probe around a sturdy frame, this one appeared to have been built inside of a thin-walled metal box with very little holding it together or in its intended shape. He now wondered if the flattened sphere they had previously found had once been part of this that had broken free during its death plunge.

Tom documented the find from several angles before they made an estimate of its position to send to Russia in case they were interested.

The vast amount of information they were gathering was going to provide scientists from the sponsoring nations, and indeed the world, with things to study for a decade or more to come.

But, rather than cut things short Tom decided to push for the full five thousand mile trip. He had the submarine's nose pointed slightly up and they were heading upwards as they continued forward.

The time flew past as they got to within three thousand feet of the surface, and everyone was excited about seeing some real sunlight, even as dim as it was out this far. So, once they parked and systems were placed in standby, everyone crowded to the ports on the left side of the ship so they could look out and see it as they neared the surface.

Tom called a mandatory rest period and was not shocked, nor did he argue, when Hank loomed over him and said, "And, that goes for the Captain as well, right?"

With a small chuckle, Tom replied, "Yeah, Hank. Little Tommy is a tired boy and promises to be good and crawl into bed once he visits the little boy's room. Hey, in seriousness, thanks for all the support these past days. You've made it possible for me to not pass out from exhaustion.

When he came back into the control room six and a half hours later, Tom noticed the men up there seemed more relaxed than they had during the entire circumnavigation. He had to admit it had been a tense eleven days and what with now being nearly two weeks behind their original schedule he knew they all wanted to get home.

But, this new attitude was a bit of a surprise. When he announced his presence, they all snapped into sitting attention.

"Okay, knock it off. Someone tell me what has you all, well, relaxed."

Bud turned in his seat at the pilot's station. "If you cannot see, then you need to go back to bed for another couple hours, Tom."

The inventor looked askance at his friend and brother-in-law for five seconds before it registered on his brain.

"We're on the surface?" he asked mouth agape at the sight on the big screen at the front of the room.

"Someone go get the skipper a cup of coffee and an eyedropper," Bud said to nobody in particular.

As if either by magic or by having been surreptitiously

summoned by Slim at the communications panel, the door opened and Chow came in with a big cup of coffee and a blueberry Danish pastry he'd been keeping back for Tom.

"Coffee an' a nibble," he announced handing Tom the cup. "Drink up, son. T'ain't all that hot 'cause we all figgered you'd need ta get it in ya right quick."

Tom sat in his command seat and did take a good sip of the beverage. It was exactly the right temperature so he drank about half of it as he looked at the screen, seeing the undulating surface of Neptune's ocean in front of them.

Finally, he set the cup in the holder on the seat arm. "All right. When, exactly, did we get up here and when, in round terms, do we head back up and go home?"

Red Jones, who had been standing to one side of the room, came over and tapped Bud on the shoulder. As the flyer got up, he took that seat.

Bud came over to stand next to Tom.

"As for number one question, about an hour and..." he looked a the ship's chronometer, "eleven and quarter minutes ago. Now, as for your second inquiry, I think that all depends on your decision. You are, after all, our lord and master and chief commander of the expedition."

"Ha-ha, Bud. Well, I suppose we need to do a complete systems check and—" He saw the grin on Bud's face out the side of his eyes. "Oh. Done?"

"Yep!"

"Fuel all checked and topped off in case we had to bleed off any pressure?"

"Of course. What do you take us for, after all? Amateurs?"

"No, of course not, Bud. Have I missed anything else on the check off list?"

"Just that a couple of us really ought to go to the little boys room before we start out because I do not personally believe I can last the four or five hours it will take until we are connected up and this chariot heads for home. So, may I be excused?"

Tom made a "Go" gesture and Bud disappeared out the back door. Once he returned, this time with a piping hot cup of coffee for Tom, he retook his seat relieving Red. This rotation of personnel went on until the shift had all had their chance at the bathroom.

Tom got on the intercom. "To all hands. It appears we are ready to go home. So, if you all would kindly strap in we are going to have to do a little skip across the surface until we get up enough speed to aim the nose up. Then, it is full power until we get to orbit. I might suggest those anti-motion-sickness capsules, just in case this gets a little rough. Ten minutes to go."

Yamato II achieved takeoff and escape velocity only after about 50% of their methane fuel load had been burned through It meant they were flying closer and closer to the stormy areas of the planet by the time Bud announced they were gaining altitude.

"About time," Red stated. "I was about to suggest Bud get out and give us a push. If nothing l figured without his dead weight…"

Bud grinned but said nothing. He was used to both giving as well as receiving good natured ribbing.

As they rose up into the upper atmosphere he checked his navigation instruments and searched for the moon, Triton.

"Got Triton, skipper," he announced thirty-seconds later. "It's a teeny bit retrograde to us but that's because of our extra-long takeoff. I'm making an adjustment, but I think we'll need to take another swing around the planet to get orientated correctly."

"Do what you can without jerking us around in a circle. This is not the place or the time to do a holding pattern circuit."

When they passed under Triton in its approximately two hundred thousand mile orbit, Bud let out a groan.

"What a bone head I am. I forgot it orbits in the opposite direction. Now, I have to maneuver us around over the next two or three orbits to get going the right direction!"

Tom slowly shook his head. "Nope. We'll do a flip and back around and go into orbit around the moon until we catch up with the black hole. Remember, we left it in a Lagrange point so it won't be orbiting. We just need to snag it as we pass close by. And, Triton always presents the same face to the planet like our own moon. We can do this."

Tom crossed his fingers that it would be that easy.

As it was, the *Yamato II* was very late for getting home. Still, not too late for the birth, but more than thirteen days past what they anticipated.

CHAPTER 20 /
COMING HOME NEVER FELT THIS GOOD!

WHAT TOM did not know was that the "forthcoming baby #3" was scheming to come into the world early. At least a full week early! And, it wasn't even telling its mother.

The maneuvering in orbit around Triton took longer than they hoped with six capture and pass tries taking place before Tom asked Red to run a computer simulation on what it might take to come to a near pause until the black hole might be in the grasp of the ship's Attractatron.

"How much spare fuel do we have?" was his only question. A thought had occurred to him and he believed it would be their answer.

Slim, now spelling Bud who had been at the controls eleven hours, looked at his instruments. "Thirty-four percent of full load. That does *not* include the reserves for getting underway and for repositioning the ship once we get home. It took a lot to get up off the planet what with several extra tons of samples. Will that do us?"

Red paused several minutes while he did calculation after calculation.

Finally, he looked at Tom. "Yes. We can do the tail stand maneuver, hold that for up to fifty-one seconds against Neptune's gravity pull, while we grab hold. Anything longer than that and we're in a bit of a catch twenty-two. Not enough to get back to the surface for a refuel, and barely enough left in the tanks to head for home at anything approximating a speed to get us there in a year if we can't use the hole."

"Then," Tom told them all, "we'd better be good and quick!"

He radioed his father to tell everyone they were on their way, but said the tricky maneuvering was taking a bit long.

What he did not say was that there could be trouble brewing.

Damon, not a man who failed to pay attention to unspoken subtext, caught on immediately and asked Tom, point blank, about what might not be said.

With a sigh, Tom told him about the fuel situation, Or rather, the *potential* situation.

"You do realize I can have the *Challenger* drag out another fuel cell for you and get there in a few weeks. So, don't believe for a moment you are going to be stuck on the proverbial slow boat. To our *friends* in China or anywhere else!"

It made Tom chuckle. He had begun to worry about those "friends" as he was keeping an eye on their diamond cache. So far, it was holding and nothing had begun shrinking or dissolving, but he had a grand total of just under forty-six pounds of the Neptunian gems to be shared among the consortium. He would leave it to the diplomats and also the new U.S. President to make the decision on how that split would go.

The last thing Tom wanted was to be involved in an international incident over who believed they deserved what. He was anxious to get the whole Chinese demand behind them all.

"Okay, Dad. I'll let you know how we fare. In the meantime, can you please tell Bash that I wanted to speak to her but can't spare the time for at least another few hours? Even then we might be in the shadow of Neptune at that time so the transmission strength will be weakened."

"I will do that, Son. You go ahead and take care of grabbing that black hole and getting on your way. I'll check up on the timing for an, ahem, little top up. Bye."

Tom gave a mental shrug. It was something that had crossed his mind although he had not been prepared to request it. In fact, Tom had his mind set on exactly two things: getting that black hole, and; getting home!

He shook off his feelings of both sadness and helplessness and cleared his throat.

"I guess if we are in position, we go for it, Red. What is our ETA?"

"Eleven minutes to optimum position, Tom. Then, if I have this figured right, three minutes to slow down to match the hole's speed and then our small window for the capture. If you're ready, I am."

Tom nodded and took a deep breath. "Yes. I'm ready." He got on the ship wide communications. "Tom to crew. We are about to do something this ship was not meant to do, but I have every confidence in both ship and crew, so if you are not on duty, it's another of those strap yourself in times. We start our final maneuvers to capture the black hole in nine minutes."

He knew he did not have to explain the maneuver to anyone; they all knew what was going on and what was at stake. He also regretted stating this was to be their *final* maneuver. He hoped those words would not come back to haunt them all.

When the time came, Red tilted *Yamato II* on end and sideslipped over to a position just five hundred feet away.

"Hey!" he exclaimed. "I completely forgot we're in a Lagrange area so we aren't actually expending a lot of fuel right now. Nifty! I'm going in for capture. Slim? Ready?"

"Absolutely!"

Tom smiled to himself having figured the situation minutes earlier but had chosen to say nothing.

The ship moved and in seconds Slim reported he had a tentative lock on their ticket home.

"Get me thirty feet closer, please," he requested.

Red complied and as soon as the green lights noting acquisition came on, Slim let out a big, "Yipee!"

Tom and the others found they had been holding their breaths and there was a loud *whoosh* as they now let them out in unison and took a few gasping breaths in.

"Let's swing around and get headed for home!" Tom commanded.

As the ship maneuvered into position to fire its plasma engines and get underway, Tom sat back and inwardly sighed. It had been a long mission and he realized just how mentally exhausted he was.

Because it would be a real test of the speed capabilities of the *Yamato II* as it crossed through the orbit of Saturn, Tom knew it would be a close call.

If Bashalli delivered early he was going to be in a world of trouble.

He'd been in contact with her several times a day since they managed to escape Neptune, and he could tell she was relieved as well as still frightened. As sure as he was she would be okay, he knew she needed him to be there to assure her he was safe.

"Things are starting to happen inside, Tom," she told him describing a few pains she had been experiencing. They were just as with their other children, only earlier than planned by them.

"Is it labor pains?" he asked.

"Not really, just a lot more kicking than before as if our baby is trying to get into a comfortable position for the final event. I'll try to hold out by not being too active. Just come home to us as quickly as your ship can manage." It was both a request and a question.

"Hold on, Bash. We're hitting the power at the upper stops but it is going to take another three days to get there. Just hold on!"

She laughed. "As long as the baby is willing, I am. I love you, Tom Swift."

"And, I love you, Bashalli Swift. And, baby. Be home soon."

Harlan radioed Tom when the *Yamato II* was halfway between the asteroid belt and Mars and getting prepared for the slow down phase of the trip.

"I just wanted to let you know the Chinese government has officially, and publicly, apologized for, as they put it, quote, 'The unauthorized actions and words of others who were not acting in the best interests of this historic project or of our ruling party,' end quote. According to Wes Norris down in DC who got word to us via a rather cryptic email, several scientists in Beijing and also an unnamed diplomat here in the U.S., along with at least one fairly senior Party official back there, had already set things in motion to take anything in the way of riches you bring back and disappear with them. To the point they were willing to shoot you down and recover things from the ocean floor!"

Tom felt himself gulping. "Uhh, and that has all been stopped?"

He relaxed when he heard his Security chief laugh. "Oh, it has most certainly been put an end to," he said but would not elaborate on that statement other than to add, "There were missiles and even a submarine confiscated."

"And, I don't want to know any more, do I?"

"Nope. Ignorance, especially in this case, is bliss. You just concentrate on getting back. Oh, there is one other piece of news. You remember your old teacher, Angela DeCorsay?"

"Of course I do."

"Well, after her trial last month where she was sentenced to about thirty years for the one murder we all knew about—plus the industrial espionage charges—it transpired she was accused of two more murders early this week, both when she was a teenager of seventeen. With no statute of limitations on murder, she is heading to a pair of trials next month. If she loses even one of those, she will never see the outside world again."

"If she loses both?"

"She'll be one hundred thirty-nine years old before she's eligible even for parole. Have a good rest of your trip."

The last dash was made even more desperate by a radio call from Damon Swift telling Tom his wife had just gone into labor.

"But, that's eight days early!" he gasped. "We're still five or six hours out! Not to mention the time to get back to solid ground."

Damon laughed in spite of the situation.

"Tell it to your baby once you get here. But, I'll tell *you* a secret. They do not listen to what you want. They arrive when *they* want to and rarely when it is convenient for either mother or father, which is why so many women go into labor at between one and three in the morning. Your mother did with you. Don't worry. Bashalli said it felt like false labor so she might be back home tonight. Oh, and that nanny of yours? Incredible young woman. Bashalli woke her at two in the morning. Amanda had the kids in their seats and Bashalli in the car in under four minutes and on their way to the hospital. Now, she has Bart and Mary home and from what I hear is trying to explain to Bart, in general terms of course, why mommy is going to come home with less of a tummy and another brother or sister for him and Mary."

Before responding Tom looked at Slim who stated in a low voice, "Another five hours and seven minutes to the halt spot and drop off of the hole."

Tom turned back to the radio. "Dad? I have a thought. Can you get the *TranSpace Dart* up to take the hole from us and also have *Challenger* to come along and take me off while the rest of this marvelous crew park the ship? Or, maybe I transfer to the *Challenger* first and let Bud and the others take charge of things?"

Damon laughed over the radio. "Who do you think you're talking to, Son? Some rank amateur? Both ships are waiting at the Lagrange point right now, and as you are just a few hours away, I'd suggest you stop talking to me and get yourself ready for a quick transfer. Oh, and do not tell your sister you are leaving Bud behind. She'd skin me alive if... no, change that. She *will* skin me alive when she hears about it."

Bud, sitting now at the sensors station snorted.

"I won't tell her, skipper. But, I'll bet she's right in that delivery room with Bash at this very second and when you walk through the door and I don't, well..." and he shrugged, leaving the rest unsaid.

When the time approached for his transfer over to the *Challenger*, Tom stood in the airlock of *Yamato II* suited and sealed in his suit, the air sucked out of the space and his hand hovering around the **OPEN** button.

When the call came back from Slim, he was ready.

"We're about thirty feet off *Challenger's* outer rail on the hangar and airlock side, skipper. You may push off when ready. They've got their airlock open and waiting for you. Good luck, and give the missus a kiss from all of us."

Tom stepped out into the airless void and used his legs to move away. In a few seconds he reached out, grabbed the safety railing around the "porch" of the other ship and used his momentum to swing his legs over it and into the airlock.

He radioed, "Whoever is in charge, I am closing the airlock now. Let's get going and I'll be up in three minutes!"

He felt the ship start up and noted they were at least three hundred miles from the rendezvous point by the time he got to the control room.

Tom Swift stood at the door of his wife's room. She was lying on her back, their new baby sleeping on her chest after she'd fed the baby for the second time in its young life.

Father was tired and mother was exhausted, but at least the other two, Bart and Mary, were being taken care of so neither parent had to worry about them.

Bashalli, suddenly realizing Tom was there turned her head and gave him a smile.

"Isn't she beautiful?" she asked. Tom nodded and grinned at her.

"Yes, but I'm looking more at his mother who is the most beautiful woman in my world. And, hers." He stepped closer and stood at the side of her bed. Leaning over he kissed her on the lips before gently pulling her hand up and squeezing it.

"And, you promised to come back in time," she said with a tired smile, "and you did just that, even though she decided to come see us early." Bashalli paused and closed her eyes a moment making Tom believe she might have fallen asleep. But, a moment later she opened her eyes. "She has your nose and ears. And, he doctor tells me she will have my darker shin tone once she stops being all pink. I hope that is okay with you."

"Bash. I really don't care if she is lily white or dark skinned as long as she is ours, healthy, and does not grow up to be completely like my sister."

Bashalli gently laughed for a few seconds. She paused looking at the man she loved. "Thank you, Tom, for being here with me when I needed you. When we get home I want to hear all about your trip and why you cut things so close."

He smiled back down at her and reached over to pull the one visitor chair over so he could sit down and be at he same level as her face.

"I might have cut this one a bit close," he admitted, "but I never had a doubt I'd be here on time, or that you and our new daughter would wait a few minutes for me. We will need to give her a name, don't you think? Something from your side of the family this time?"

Bashalli shook her head. "I love my family and my heritage, but I want our child to be one hundred percent a Swift, so can we find a good name for her? Something like Anne in honor of your mother? We already did Mary for your great, great grandmother."

Tom chuckled. "Just as long as it isn't Sandy. I don't think any of us could stand the smugness coming off my sister if we did that!"

As she closed her eyes and drifted back to sleep, Tom stood and blew her a kiss. "That is the most remarkable woman I've ever known," he whispered so only he could hear it. As he turned to leave Tom Swift thought he might never wish to go away from her and their three children ever again. Certainly not into the depths of space.

And, he was going to be able to hold to that for at least his next adventure when he would once again dive into the depths of the Pacific Ocean in a search for his lost miniature space sub, only this deep diving adventure would hold a shocking surprise for him.

This has been book 26 in the *New TOM SWIFT Invention Series*. Read them all, and look forward to the next books, also listed here:

{1} TOM SWIFT and His EvirOzone Revivicator
{2} TOM SWIFT and His QuieTurbine SkyLiner
{3} TOM SWIFT and the Transcontinental BulleTrain
{4} TOM SWIFT and His Oceanic SubLiminator
{5} TOM SWIFT and His Cyclonic Eradicator
{6} TOM SWIFT: Galactic Ambassador
{7} TOM SWIFT and the Paradox Planet
{8} TOM SWIFT and the Galaxy Ghosts
{9} TOM SWIFT and His Martian TerraVironment
{10} TOM SWIFT and His Tectonic Interrupter
{11} TOM SWIFT and the AntiInferno Suppressor
{12} TOM SWIFT and the High Space L-Evator
{13} TOM SWIFT and the IntraEarth Invaders
{14} TOM SWIFT and the Coupe of Invisibility
{15} TOM SWIFT and the Yesterday Machine
{16} TOM SWIFT and the Reconstructed Planet
{17} TOM SWIFT and His NanoSurgery Brigade
{18} TOM SWIFT and His ThermoIon Jetpack
{19} TOM SWIFT and the Atlantean HydroWay
{20} TOM SWIFT and the Electricity Vampires
{21} TOM SWIFT and the Solar Chaser
{22} TOM SWIFT and His SeaSpace HydroFarm
{23} TOM SWIFT and the Martian Moon Re-placement
{24} TOM SWIFT and the Venusian InvulnoSuit
{25} TOM SWIFT and the HoverCity
{26} TOM SWIFT and the SubNeptunian Circumnavigation
{27} TOM SWIFT and the Marianas AquaNoids (mid-2019)
{28} TOM SWIFT and the Starless Planet (possible title-late 2019)
{29} TOM SWIFT and His HyperSonic SpacePlane (possible title-2020)
{30} TOM SWIFT and His Space Friends Return (possible title-2020)

And, he has co-written a quartet of novels staring Tom Swift as he takes on the rescue of a secret slave colony on the Moon. Called the Tom Swift Lunar Saga, it includes:
- *Tom Swift and His Space Battering Ram*
- *Tom Swift and the Cometary Reclamation*
- *Tom Swift and the Lunar Volcano*
- *Tom Swift and the Killing Moon*

Collections of novellas, many dealing with some of the individual characters in the novels and/or the lesser known inventions coming from the mind of Tom Swift may be found in:
- *Enterprising Characters*
- *Swift-ly With Style*
- *The Spirit of Enterprises*
- *Enterprises Extras*
- *Tom Swift's Pocket Book of Inventions*
- *Tom Swift's Another Pocket — More Inventions*
- *A Newer Pocketbook of Swift Inventions*
- *Tom Swift's A Fourth Pocket of Inventions*
- *Tom's 5th Symphony of Swift Inventions*
- *Ten Tom's: A Collection of Invention Shorts*
- *The Operator's Guide to the Fat Man Diving Suit*

In addition to the teen/adult Tom Swift stories he also has a book of stories about young pre-teen Tom as he starts to find his way into the world of inventions:
- *The Young Tom Swift Stories*

Tom's father, Damon, stars in his own series of novellas and several novels. The collections include:
- *The Wonderful Damon in Oz*
- *Damon Swift Invents…*
- *The Duly Deputized Rhino and Other Stories*
- *Yes… It's Another Damon Book!*
- *A Pair of Rather Long Short Stories*
- *Damon Swift in Flight*

And, the Damon novels that tell the early tales of Damon Swift and his rather impressive empire:
- Damon Swift and the CosmoSoar
- Damon Swift and the Citadel
- Damon Swift's Greatest Enterprises

plus, a long-*ish* novella of how Tom Swift met Bud Barclay and Chow:
- Damon Swift and the Citadel 2: a Bud and Chow Story

Tom's mother, Anne Swift, stars in her own series of medical mysteries, The *Anne Swift: Microbial Detective* series contain novellas about her secret FBI work. There are three collections in this series plus a biographical novel about how it all began for her:
- Anne Swift: Making the Molecular Biological Detective

…Check out and download this little freebie, a short story—600 words—written for a contest back in 2011:
- *Tom Swift and the Frictionless Elf*

Find it at:
http://tomswiftfanfiction.thehudsons.com/TS-Yahoo/TS-Elf.pdf

Mr. Hudson has also written a couple of strange novellas that are available as Kindle ebooks. None are serious and were only written to amuse the author. Even so, he decided to share them. **Do not** expect life-changing literature for $.99 (US) each:

- *The Fiendish Bucket List of Dr. Fu Manchu*
- *Drew Nance: Up On The Housetop, Click, Click, Bang!*
- *Drew Nance: The Massive Mart Murder Mystery*

The Fu Manchu story is included in a trio of short stories staring Fu, Sandy Swift and Tom and Bud (and Sandy and Bashalli and a bad guy named "Mousie") all for just 40¢ more than the one story:
- *A Trio of Shorts: Three Short Stories in One Medium-Length Book*

And a collection of odds and ends (also a 99¢ Kindle book):
- *Don't Write Fan Fiction Until You Grow Up, and other short stories too short to sell individually*

Working along with Chow Winkler, Mr. Hudson has written several cookbooks. The first and second shorter ones are part of two of the short character collections. Numbers three and four are standalone books:

- *Chow Winkler's Three-Wheel Chuck Wagon*
- *Chow Winkler's Wide Open Range*

You might enjoy Thomas Hudson's first foray into the world of Romance novels. He wrote this as part of a bet with a fellow author that they both could not complete a romance story even if given ninety days. He did it in nineteen:

- *The Love of Skunk*

Finally (for now) on a dare, he wrote a strange story about a young girl with both a physical and emotional difference to 99.99999% of people out there. It is an <u>adult</u> autobiography/biography and features her life story starting when she was a young teen.

This is NOT a Tom Swift story in any way, shape or form!

- *The Life of BI: Complete*

Everything above may be found on Amazon.com in paperbound as well as Kindle editions, and many of this author's works can be purchased as Nook books from BarnesAndNoble.com